The Confessions of Jonathan Pratt

Being An Account of His Travels

Through the

State of New York

in

1848

and of the

Wickedness Which He Found There.

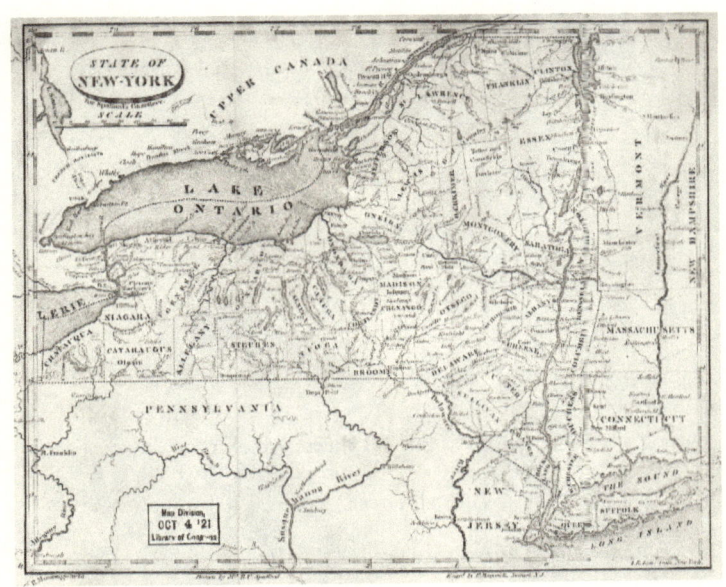

By Robert Wilhelm

CONTENTS

Chapter 1   1
A Reluctant Confession; Innocence Interrupted; Hard Lessons; A Fall from Grace.

Chapter 2   9
The Gospel According to Travis; The Fruit of Deception; A Hasty Retreat.

Chapter 3   15
A Floating Hotel; The Canalers' One Rule; Peace Disrupted; God's Will Revealed.

Chapter 4   24
Labor, Guilt, and Cider; In Vino Veritas; A Metamorphosis Unforeseen.

Chapter 5   30
Driven from the Garden; Descent into hell; Miraculous ascension.

Chapter 6   36
Another Change of Habit; Entering Watervliet; The Partnership Torn Asunder.

Chapter 7   44
A Midnight Search; A Hand from the Dark; Fit to be Tied.

Chapter 8   49
The Legend of the Canal Pirates; Judgment Day; Waiting for the End of the World; A Burden Transferred.

Chapter 9   56
Return of the Canal Pirates; Yet Another Transformation; Toil and Trouble, Sound and Fury.

Chapter 10   64
No Ladies at the Bar; An Elusive Queen; An Unscheduled Stop; Rancor and Reflection.

Chapter 11   72
The Hole-in-the-Wall; Shanghaied; A Long Lost Relation.

Chapter 12   80
A Glorious Proposition; Moses' Law; An Unwelcome Guest; Thy Will Ee Done.

Chapter 13   87
The Five Points Gangster; In The Tombs; A Lesson in Civics; And One in Theology.

Chapter 14   93
Students of Thievery; In Flagrante Delicto; The Badger Game.

Chapter 15   101
New Accommodations; The Wall Street Speculator; Pipe Dreams; A Battle, Biblical.

Chapter 16   109
A View of all Creation; The Farmer's Daughter; The Celebration of Pinkster.

Chapter 17   116
The Saugerties Bard; A Theft of Identity; The Poughkeepsie Seer; An Unexpected Excursion.

Chapter 18   123
Saratoga Waters; A Camp Meeting; Reunions.

Chapter 19   131
Hurry and Wait; Women's Rights; A Long Walk; A Short Voyage.

Chapter 20   139
A Devil's bargain; Perfectionism; Driven Again from Eden.

Chapter 21   147
A Cruel Awakening; A Solemn Oath; Target Practice; A Mighty Storm.

Chapter 22   155
Welcome Hospitality; Lingering Fear; Secrets Revealed; Communicating with the Dead.

Chapter 23   162
The Healing Tabernacle; Deadly Betrayal; Trials and Tribulations.

Chapter 24   169
Amen.

Chapter Notes   174

The Confessions of Jonathan Pratt

CHAPTER 1

A Reluctant Confession; Innocence Interrupted;
Hard Lessons; A Fall from Grace.

On the eve of my execution, they hound me, man after man, to confess to the crime of murder, the crime of which I have been convicted by a jury of my peers and sentenced to hang by a judge of the great state of New York; the crime which I did not commit. Men of the cloth, worried for my everlasting soul— and I believe I have been ministered by every sect—bring me books and tracts, read me sermons and platitudes. I must tell the truth, they say, to earn God's forgiveness. God will not tolerate a liar, they tell me, I must confess my sins, unburden my soul in order to enter the Kingdom; and I try to comprehend a theology where a murder is forgiven, but a lie is not. Clearly, it is not my soul but their own souls that worry them. Like the constables and magistrates of Monroe County, who, tomorrow morning, will take my life; as sure as they are of my guilt, they are still fearful of hanging an innocent man.

And the newspaper men who propagate like maggots around a hanging, they want me to confess to this and other crimes, not for the sake of anyone's soul, but for the sake of their journals, spewing venom today and wrapping garbage tomorrow. From as far away as Manhattan they come, confronting me with rumors and half-truths, demanding answers to their foolish questions. Why did I commit this murder? What about the others for which

1

I have been charged by the court of innuendo? How had I gone so far to the bad at such a tender age? What forces led me to this wretched life of crime? They demand a statement, any statement, anything to drive their story beyond the usual gallows clichés, and in this they are relentless.

So to please all, and to get some much-needed rest in my final hours, I have agreed to confess, in my own words, and in writing. The county has provided me with pen and paper, and all will leave me alone until the morning when the pageant in full begins. As I sit here ready to begin the task, I can't help but heave a sigh of relief — at last some peace. From the time I was arrested, through the trial, and until this moment, the din and confusion have been overwhelming. So yes, in the silence of the cell, by the light of this thin candle they have allowed me, I will write my confession.

I, Jonathan Pratt, confess to violating countless laws of the State of New York, and all of God's Commandments save the one for which I shall hang. There are those I have met in my travels, righteous men, for whom breaking nine of Ten Commandments would be sufficient for the gallows, but by the laws of New York, I did not commit a capital crime and should not pay the penalty of my life. You may say that all condemned men profess innocence, and you would be right; and in admitting to breaking nine Commandments, have I not also identified myself as a liar? Yes again, but that is the very reason I undertook to write this confession. For only a full account of the incidents which led to this cruel fate will explain my situation and I beg you, dear reader, to withhold judgment until you have read it all.

I was born in 1832 in Essex County, Massachusetts. The mother I never knew died during that delivery, and, looking back, perhaps that is why I never knew my father either. All of the mothering I received came from my two sisters, Sarah, older by four years, and Naomi, older by three. My brother Jacob, eight years my senior, had, to my mind, always been an adult.

We had a farm outside of Salem where I would work all day in the summer months, and in the winter months, do chores after school. I loved working on the farm, tending to the fields, taking care of the animals—feeding chickens, milking cows. Everything had its needs and its time, and I knew the schedule. It seemed to me less like work, as I was later to understand the word, than play. It was my role in the natural order of things.

The girls loved farm life less than I; they would tell me their plans for leaving it when they were old enough. We had a place we would meet, a tall oak tree on the south field—Papa and Jacob wished it gone, but had deferred its removal until more ground was needed. Under the oak, I would listen to the plans and dreams of my sisters. Naomi wished to marry a rich and handsome Salem man and spend her days shopping and her nights at fine dinner parties. Not Sarah; she wished to travel the world, to see the capitals of Europe, and then visit China and maybe Africa. When I told them I had no plans, and just wished to stay on the farm forever, they laughed at me, said I was just a child and would soon want to be off the farm as much as they did. I thought they were wrong; I could not imagine a life off the farm.

But things began to change. My sisters would ask Papa for money to buy some trifle, and he would refuse, saying times were hard, we must be frugal. Christmas and birthdays were smaller and less festive—more hard times. Then, true to their plans, my sisters began to leave. First Sarah said she was leaving to work in the cotton mills in Lowell. It made sense; she wanted to travel the world. Lowell was just the start. But in the back of my mind, I wondered if the hard times hadn't driven her away. Then Naomi agreed to marry Mr. Avery of Ipswich. Marriage had been her desire, but Mr. Avery was twenty years older than she, bald, fat and far from handsome, and though his farm was larger than ours, I would not call him rich. I could not second guess her judgment, but maybe it was hard times again.

Easter Sunday 1848, not long after my sixteenth birthday, I rode to church with my father for the first time without my sisters. Jacob rode on ahead, saying he had something to do in town after the service. It was just my father and me in the wagon, and we spoke not a word.

We belonged to the Congregational Church in Salem but seldom attended Sunday services anymore. We went for weddings and funerals, and of course, we still went for Easter. In former days we had owned a pew in the front of the church, but my father gave it up after Naomi was married. Now it seemed strange sitting in the back of the church among people I did not recognize as if we were guests in our own church.

My father did not speak as we left the churchyard that Easter Sunday, but on the road home, he broke the silence.

"Jonathan, I have been thinking of your future. I want to do what is best for you and for the family."

I nodded.

"I will get straight to the point, Jonathan, I will not be on this earth forever, and I must do what is best for all before I die. I am giving the farm to Jacob. I cannot divide it. Neither piece would survive without the other. Thus, I have arranged for your indenture to Mr. Pembroke the cooper, in Salem. You will work for him and learn his trade. When you have mastered it, your fortune will be in your own hands."

I was aghast, caught completely unprepared for this. I would be leaving the farm as my sisters had.

"I don't want to leave home, Papa. Can't I stay on the farm and help Jacob?"

"No, Jonathan. Without ownership, you will be nothing more than a farm hand. That is no life for a man. Times are too hard; the farm cannot support you both. You shall become a cooper; you shall leave tomorrow."

We sat in silence again, and I tried to imagine life away from the farm. I did not want to leave. It was all I could do to stifle tears. My father spoke to me in a soothing tone.

"You know, Jonathan before my own father died he divided his farm between my brother and me."

"You and Uncle Asa."

"Yes, but what I have never told you is that I had another brother, Samuel. My father knew the farm could not be split three ways so when Samuel was no older than you, he was indentured to a merchant ship out of Salem, and we never saw him again. I tell you this, Jonathan, to show you that, though you may think me cold to turn you out this way, I could have been much colder. Samuel, if he even survived his first voyage, was destined to a life at sea, the hardest life a man can endure. But I have arranged for you to learn a trade and prosper from your own skill and enterprise. You will save the farm from hard times as Samuel had, but what Samuel sacrificed is more than I could ever ask of you.

I sat quietly for a time, still trying to understand what was happening. I felt sad for Samuel, but how did his trouble make mine less? I said, "Papa, where did the hard times come from?"

He looked up at me, "What son?"

"Our lives were once so good," I said, "we work just as hard now, where did the hard times come from?"

"I curse the bankers," he said, "and New York speculators." It was a curse I had heard before, and I knew if he said any more it would only make him angry, and I would not understand any of it.

Next morning, after breakfast, my brother Jacob said his good-byes—shook my hand and gave me a gold dollar. We hitched the wagon, and my father drove me into Salem. I was off to become a cooper, and at that time I did not even know what a cooper was.

*

A cooper makes barrels; I saw that right away as we turned into the yard of Mr. Pembroke's workshop. Barrels stood in front of the shop, all along one side of the building, and behind it, down a long pier where men were busy rolling them onto a sailing ship. We had barrels on the farm—one by the side of the house to catch the rain, one in the barn to hold feed—they had always been there as if grown from the ground like tree stumps. It never occurred to me that someone had to make them, or that the world needed so many. I tried to reconcile myself to the idea that I would soon be making them.

Mr. Pembroke came out of the shop to meet us. He was lean and sinewy and wore a gray chin beard; he looked to me very much like a billy goat. He carried a cane that he did not seem to need for walking, and he never smiled. My father and Mr. Pembroke spoke quietly for some minutes then brought me into the conversation. After introductions and a few words of greeting, Mr. Pembroke read the contract. It was very formal and somewhat hard to follow, but I think I understood most of it. I would be indentured to Mr. Pembroke for seven years. During that time, I would be his servant, and in return, he would teach me the art and mysteries of cooperage. He would provide a bed and a suit of work clothes, an evening meal and a lunch of bread and cheese. I was forbidden to drink distilled spirits, ale or cider while in his service and I was not to frequent taverns, alehouses, or any locations where hard drink was served. I was not to marry, associate with lewd women, or visit bawdy houses. Work hours were sunup to sundown, Monday through Saturday. Sunday was a day of rest during which I would attend a Christian service; the denomination would be of my own choosing though he frowned upon Universalism.

The rules and duties seemed reasonable to me; I was accustomed to long days and hard work. I had no inclination toward hard drink and lewd women—at that time, I could not imagine either in my life. We stood outside the door to the workshop, and I could see men inside cutting wood and assembling barrels. The aroma of the sawdust was fresh and appealing. Maybe life at the cooperage would not be so bad.

As we spoke, a boy about my own age came through the door several times to fetch some long planks from a woodpile. I tried to catch his eye, but each time he only scowled back. On one trip he made a sharp turn and knocked my elbow with a wooden plank. Mr. Pembroke saw it and gave the boy a shove with the tip of his cane, so hard that the boy fell to the ground, the wood tumbling over him.

"Watch where you are going, you ignorant lout." Mr. Pembroke shouted.

The boy shouted back from the ground, "Keep the fools out of my way then."

Mr. Pembroke was livid, started beating the boy's head and shoulders with his cane. "You'll not sass me, boy, you'll not sass me. The boy you hit is from civilized stock; if you pay attention, you may learn some manners from him."

As the boy scrambled to get up from the wood and away from Mr. Pembroke's cane he gave me a look that chilled me to the bone.

"Oh, I believe it's he who'll do the learning," He said, rushing through the door ahead of another blow.

The boy's name was Stricker—they called him Pip, I never did learn his true given name. He too was indentured to Mr. Pembroke, and he was not happy about sharing that job, such as it was, with another boy. I tried my best to make friends with Pip, but he would have nothing to do with me. In fact, he took every opportunity to make my life miserable. He would belittle me to Mr. Pembroke, tripping me up when I was carrying wood and drawing the master's attention to my clumsiness. He would hide my boots, steal my food, put sawdust in my bed—I lived in constant vigilance, but still he would catch me off guard.

My job at the cooperage consisted of little more than carrying wood into the workroom and rolling the finished barrels outside. I would stack barrels, count barrels, and load barrels into wagons and ships. After I week on the job I had become quite familiar with barrels, but I had learned nothing of their manufacture. Sometimes I would stand and watch as the men worked the wood and metal, but Mr. Pembroke was never far away and would poke me with his cane to keep me moving. When I asked him about learning the cooper's trade, he told me I wasn't ready. I wondered how many barrels I would need to roll out the door to be ready.

Sometimes when the men were beveling the staves or hammering the rings—my estimation of what was being done, I wasn't there long enough to learn a proper cooper's vocabulary—the workmen would need an extra hand, and they would call for Pip. He would run to their aid and follow their direction and help them accomplish the task. Sometimes they would even let him use their tools, and as he worked in these brief moments, I could see he was learning their craft. This was the only way I would ever learn the trade of cooperage and Pip would never allow me that opportunity.

One afternoon in my second week there, I was sweeping the floor in the workroom, and two of the workmen, Will Stevens and Bill Johnson were assembling a barrel. One of them (I couldn't tell Bill from Will) called out for Pip. Mr. Pembroke had sent Pip on an errand outside the building, and he was not within earshot. They both called out again for Pip then realizing Pip was gone they looked at me.

"Pratt, come over here."

I ran to where they were working and took hold of what they asked me to, while the men fitted a metal ring around the staves. Just then Pip entered the room and, incensed at seeing me helping Will and Bill ran over and knocked me down. The barrel we were working on fell to pieces as Pip, and I wrestled on the floor. When Mr. Pembroke entered Pip jumped up and pointed at the mess and shouted, "Look what Pratt done, Mr. Pembroke."

Mr. Pembroke rushed over and started beating me with his cane, shouting, "Damn you, Pratt, I told you to stay away from the workmen."

That was the point that I realized I was not cut out for cooperage. I continued working obediently, doing all and only what Mr. Pembroke requested. As much as possible I gave Pip a wide berth; I wanted no more trouble. Every waking hour I spent searching my mind for a way out of my situation but nothing came to me save packing my bag and walking away and that, for many reasons, seemed impossible. Then destiny took a hand.

I was rolling a finished barrel out the side door—the largest were kept on the north wall, near the door (fear of theft, I believe)—when I heard some music playing through the trees and across the road. A circus, I thought, or a traveling medicine man drumming up business. But I recognized the tune as a hymn I had sung in church. Why would a circus or a salesman play a hymn? I climbed atop a barrel to try and get a look. Through the trees, I could barely make out a wagon standing in an empty lot across Water Street. Behind the wagon was a platform upon which stood a man in a black coat and behind him sat a young woman dressed in white playing a lap organ. A crowd had gathered around them and some in the crowd were singing along. The woman's voice thought was the purest and strongest, sailing above the rest on the high notes.

My vision was still obstructed by the trees on this side of the road, and I wanted a better view. I hefted another large barrel atop the first then rolled another over to use as a step. I climbed to the top and there, standing easily eight feet above the ground, I could see them quite clearly. They were itinerant preachers— trouble-makers my father would call them.

The girl put the organ on the chair then stood by the man's side as he led his flock in prayer. He was tall and gaunt, clean shaven, wearing a black suit and white shirt. The girl stood next to him, as tall as his shoulders, wearing a simple white dress—father and daughter I guessed. Her light brown hair was long, tied back with a white ribbon and dancing in the ocean breezes. I could not take my eyes off of her; even from such a distance, she was the most beautiful sight I had ever seen.

Then something knocked the bottom barrel shaking the whole tower supporting me. I waved my arms trying to keep my balance, but in an instant, there was nothing under my feet. I dropped like a rock to the ground below. The barrels upon which I had stood were now rolling swiftly down the pier, knocking down others like nine-pins. The chaos continued until a good half-dozen barrels ended up in Salem harbor. I tried to get up, but Mr. Pembroke was soon on me with his cane. He knocked me back to the ground and continued to pummel me until I lost my senses.

When I opened my eyes again, Mr. Pembroke had his cane raised to strike once more, but his arm was stayed by the grip of an angel in a white gown, no doubt sent by God to save me. Her hair was the color of a fawn in spring, and her eyes were blue flames.

"You'll not strike this boy again!" the angel cried.

As my eyes regained focus, I saw that the preacher was there too, and all those who had been praying with him had gathered around me. Then I realized it was not an angel, but someone just as heavenly— the girl who played the organ and sang.

"I thought you were an angel from God," I said to her.

"Hear that Mirabile?" the preacher said, "an angel from God." Then he turned and spoke to me loudly, as if speaking to a young child, "Tell us boy, what happened here, why was this man beating you?"

"I was standing on the barrels," I said, "trying to see across the street."

"Trying to hear my words?" he asked.

"Yes, sir."

"Brothers and sisters," the preacher looked up to the crowd, "the boy was beaten for trying to hear the word of the Lord."

"He was beaten for being an ignorant fool." Mr. Pembroke said.

"Let's give him a taste of his own medicine." Said a voice from the crowd and several others concurred.

Mr. Pembroke raised his cane against the crowd, "He is my servant, and I'll treat him as I will."

One of the men tried to grab Mr. Pembroke, but the preacher raised his hand. "Jesus said 'turn the other cheek.' We will not resort to violence." Then to Mr. Pembroke, he said, "And neither shall you, sir."

Mr. Pembroke saw how close he was to being torn apart by the crowd and pondered his options. The men from the workshop had gathered at the door; most were bigger than anyone in the crowd. But could they be counted on? Was a fight worth starting?

"You take him then; he's no damned good to me." Mr. Pembroke said and walked back into the cooperage.

The preacher and the girl helped me to my feet, and with an arm around each of their shoulders, I hobbled to their wagon.

CHAPTER 2

The Gospel According to Travis; The Fruit of Deception; A Hasty Retreat.

The Reverend Isaiah Travis and his daughter Mirabile introduced themselves to me as they readied their covered wagon to leave. They were headed for the western end of New York State, they told me, where the people were notoriously welcoming to the word of God.

"The 'burned-over district' some call it," Travis said, "for the number of times their souls have been set ablaze. But a soul is never burned over; once set on fire, it will always retain a spark."

I could join them, they said, offering me food, shelter and paying work if I did, but I had to decide fast. They were leaving Salem immediately and did not intend to return. I was reluctant to leave my home, but I saw nothing but trouble if I stayed, so I agreed to go with them to New York.

We headed west out of Salem, passing farms, first familiar than strange to me, then into woodland, farther from home than I had ever been. That night I slept outside, under a blanket, while Mirabile and the Reverend slept inside the wagon. It was frightening at first, but soon it became routine. I slept under the stars when the night was clear and under the wagon when it rained.

As we traveled, my days were spent studying scripture—learning the Bible randomly, verse by verse. Sometimes I would sit next to Reverend Travis as he drove the horse, and he taught me the hellfire verses. Other times I would ride in the wagon and Mirabile taught me the merciful ones. She taught me Bible stories, most I already knew, but her voice was like music as she read. I loved the time I spent with Mirabile; she was so kind and beautiful. I hoped she might begin to feel a similar affection for me, but she showed no interest beyond that of a teacher to a student.

It was a lot to learn, and they wanted me to know each verse by heart.

"You'll thank me, Jonathan," said Reverend Travis, "an aptly chosen bible verse will win any argument."

But I still had trouble remembering; there seemed to be no common thread connecting the verses. I thought maybe if I just read the whole book it might make more sense. When I suggested this to Reverend Travis and Mirabile, they just looked at me strangely.

Reverend Travis said, "That would only confuse you, boy. It is a tonic best taken in small doses."

So I continued struggling with the recitations without the help of the written word.

The first big town we came to was Worcester, Massachusettes; the Reverend wanted to hold a service there. I thought my role would be limited to setting up the stage and handing out tracts and the like, but as we ate breakfast around the fire outside of town, Reverend Travis told us he had other plans for me.

"I can't stop thinking about that crowd back in Salem." He said, "They had so much sympathy for Jonathan that they would have done anything for him. They would have murdered that cooper had I but said the word. I wonder if we could make that work again."

"How do you mean?" Mirabile asked.

"What if Jonathan came before the crowd and testified? Limping to the front, his face bruised and cut, telling how his master knocked him down and beat him."

"I think it was the other boy knocked me down," I said.

"Beaten by his master for desiring to hear the word of God." The Reverend said, in the tone he had used that day in Salem.

"He beat me for knocking down his barrels."

"Beaten senseless for the Lord's sake. Rescued by an angel of God, isn't that what he said? An angel of God in the form of our beautiful Mirabile. Yes, I think that could work."

"That's not really the way it happened," I said.

"It doesn't matter, Jonathan, the details don't matter. All that matters is you were listening to the word of God and you were beaten for it. That is all they want to hear, and that is what we will tell them."

"Like the parables," Mirabile said. "You don't think Jesus actually knew that prodigal son, do you?"

I thought not, and I got the point. With some misgivings I rehearsed that simple story and, while somewhat less than the truth, it was much easier to learn than the Bible verses, and by the end, I nearly believed it myself. I especially like the ending where the angelic Mirabile stayed the hand of the aggressor and shamed him into freeing me from bondage. It was a moving story.

We arrived in Worcester on a fine spring afternoon, and it pleased me not to be working at the cooperage. Instead, we would go shopping in town. Reverend Travis had a billfold full of bank notes, which he kept separate from the offerings. He extracted a bill, said "this should do it," and, arm around my shoulder, took me to a tailor in downtown Worcester. He bought me a new suit of clothes, complete with a wool cap and a white cotton shirt. Though the bill no more than five dollars, the Reverend paid with a twenty dollar bank note, taking the change in gold coin. I was duly impressed—it looked as though there was money in this work after all.

We found a vacant lot near the main thoroughfare, and I helped set up the stage. There was some lifting but nothing hard, nothing like a day hefting barrels at the cooperage. One end of the stage rested on the back end of the wagon, the other end set upon two barrels. Mirabile and Revered Travis showed me how to set it straight. It went up easy but seeing the stage set up started me fretting about the role I was to play. Mirabile told me not to worry; it was better if I were nervous; it would be more natural. She told me to say the words as well as I could and let the Reverend handle the rest, she went on to the stage to ready the lap organ.

On the Reverend's signal, she began playing "A Mighty Fortress." People became curious—as I had been in Salem—and gradually a crowd had formed to listen to the music. When the crowd had reached a size he liked, Reverend Travis mounted the stage and began singing in a loud but melodious voice. Many in the crowd could not resist joining in. When the song was over, he led us in prayer, thanking the Lord for the beautiful day and for the opportunity to bring His word to the good people of Worcester. Then came the sermon. The text was all righteousness and forgiveness – the salvation for those who follow Christ; damnation and hellfire for those who did not. He spoke of the difficulty of preaching the gospel in these Godless times and talked especially of the wickedness in Salem.

"Brother Jonathan, come forward please." He motioned me toward him, and I climbed to the stage. He turned to the crowd and said to them. "Brother Jonathan was chastised, for trying to hear the word of God. He was beaten, as you can see, and driven from his livelihood."

The reverend had fairly well told the whole story before calling on me to speak, but as I spoke to the hushed crowd, they hung on every word. I was fearful at first, and my voice wavered, but as Mirabile had predicted, that only added to the effect. I had rehearsed well, and by the end, I was speaking with confidence. When I finished, Reverend Travis led us in prayer, praying for my health and praying for the soul of my tormentor. He said "Amen, " and Mirabile played the organ as we all sang "Rock of Ages" with great enthusiasm.

After the service, we passed a basket for donations, and it filled quickly. Many in the crowd came forward to congratulate Reverend Travis on a wonderful sermon and to praise my bravery and righteousness. A small group was standing around the two of us when a voice called out from behind.

"You owe me, Reverend! That bill you gave me is queer!" It was the tailor we had visited earlier in the day.

Reverend Travis turned and said with all meekness, "Pardon me, sir?"

"I took your twenty dollar note to the bank and was told the bill is counterfeit. I should have known better, but I thought I could trust a preacher."

"As did I trust the Salem man who donated it." Said the Reverend. "I assure you, sir, I had no idea that the bill was bad and I insist you take retribution from the offerings these good people gave for God's work. And of course, the boy will relinquish his new suit."

But the crowd would not have it; as they had in Salem, the gathered multitudes sided with the preacher. They chastised the poor tailor and shamed him until in confusion he left without his money. Some of the people were so moved by this that they gave a second donation to prove how unlike the tailor they were.

So that day I got a new suit of clothes, and the Reverend a pocketful of gold and the collection basket was augmented, while the poor Worcester tailor took a serious loss. And in the back of my mind, I was more than half sure that the tailor was right.

As Mirabile so often told me, "The Lord works in mysterious ways."

*

As we traveled further west, we presented our service in town after town. My addition was well received by the people of western Massachusetts, and the Travises were extremely pleased by the increased contributions I was generating.

"For the Lord's work," the Reverend said, "We'll need money to establish ourselves when we reach the burned-over district."

He went on about how we would use the money to gather a huge flock of converted souls and reap a magnificent bounty in the name of the Lord, and on and on, in like terms until by the end I couldn't always tell when he was talking about souls and when about money. But I sensed we would not go hungry as we benefitted God and our fellow man. Any doubts I may have had were allayed by Mirabile; her goodness shone like the sun, how could she be anything but righteous?

By the time we got to Northampton, my cuts and bruises had completely healed. Even in the early days, the wounds looked much worse than they really they were, now they were barely visible at all. Mirabile applied some paint to my face and made me look as hurt as the day of the fall, if not more so.

"For the parable." She told me.

By Pittsfield, my leg had healed as well. I no longer walked with a limp, and the Travises were not happy about that either. They gave me a crutch to walk with whenever I was to appear in front of a crowd. In the back of the wagon was a trunk filled with costumes, makeup and the like. This seemed odd to me at first; then I remembered the minister at the Congregational Church wore a costume as well—a long black robe trimmed in white. There was more to this business than I yet understood.

Following each service, Mirabile would continue playing hymns while the Reverend and I passed through the crowd with baskets to receive donations. It was not easy for me with a crutch and a basket moving among well-wishers intent on shaking my hand, but my infirmity brought out the best in people, and I always returned to the wagon with a full basket. Often Reverend Travis would curtail his collection duties midway through so he could stop and talk with one or more of the fashionable ladies who came to hear the word. Sometimes he would go off with one of them, leaving word with Mirabile or me where and when we should later meet him. In Pittsfield, he left with a fine looking woman, impeccably dressed and not as old as his usual hosts. He told me to come by in two hours and gave me an address on Fenn Street.

Mirabile and I took the opportunity to do some shopping. We would be going to Albany next and thought it best to buy our groceries while still in farm country. As we shopped for vegetables, I asked Mirabile why her father always left with the ladies.

"He ministers to widows and old maids." she said, "He gives them comfort, and they make sizeable donations."

Her tone with me was short; I didn't know if it was the answer or my asking that bothered her, so I asked no more on the subject.

It was nearly sundown when we finished shopping and, though we were at least half an hour early, we took the wagon to the Fenn Street address and waited there for the Reverend. Mirabile was silent, and I was feeling blue. Something about the twilight in a strange town made me lonely. I longed to be back in the home that was no longer mine.

"Do you ever get tired of traveling, Mirabile?" I asked.

"What's the matter, Jonathan? Do you miss your mother?"

"I never knew my mother." I had told her this before; she had not remembered.

"I'm sorry." She said, softening now. "I've been traveling so long it's all I know. I don't know where I would light if I stopped."

"I'm afraid that's happening to me."

"Don't worry, Jonathan, you're young yet, you could end up anywhere. You are good in front of a crowd; that could be your fortune."

"I try to be as good as you."

She smiled for the first time all day, then leaned over and kissed my cheek. "If that's your ambition, you needn't try so hard."

I was happy that she was speaking again, but a kiss from her soft lips had me in ecstasy. It was short-lived, though. From across the street, we watched a man hurry up the front walk in into the Fenn Street address the Reverend had given us.

"Uh oh." Said Mirabile.

I was not sure why this man meant trouble, but I knew he did. Someone lit a lamp in the front room, and we could hear a man and woman arguing. It was muffled but loud enough to hear from across the street. Then, in the shadows by the side of the house, I saw another man carefully emerging from a window. He hit the ground and ran toward the street. It was the Reverend; he was not wearing pants.

He saw the wagon and ran to it, climbed into the box, grabbed the reins and with a snap we left that house as fast as the horse could travel.

"What happened?" Mirabile demanded.

"There was a misunderstanding." The Reverend said, "You remember that nice lady I was speaking with this afternoon?"

"I remember."

"Well, she told me her husband was away. She was lonely and asked if I would come to dinner and tell her about the gospel. I would never miss an opportunity to spread the word, and I thought she might be good for a large donation, so I said yes. As it happened, her husband decided to come home early, and when he saw us together in an attitude of prayer, well he jumped to the wrong conclusion."

"What happened to your breeches?"

"Another unfortunate confluence of events, I had spilled gravy on them during dinner and the dear lady offered to soak them for me and remove the stain. They were hanging to dry when the husband came in. Fortunately for me, he chose to express his displeasure to his wife and not to me, so I took the opportunity to flee through the window, sans breeches."

"We are away; why the haste now?" She asked. We had reached the outskirts of town, and the Reverend was still driving the horse at breakneck speed.

"This woman's husband, as I learned upon his arrival—wearing his badge of office and a pistol in his belt— is the sheriff of Berkshire County. I won't feel safe until we cross into New York, and maybe not even then."

CHAPTER 3

A Floating Hotel; The Canalers' One Rule; Peace Disrupted; God's Will Revealed.

We did not stop until we reached Albany and even then the Reverend was fearful. At the nearest livery, with the same sense of urgency as our departure from Pittsfield, he negotiated the sale of the horse and wagon and went thence to a ticket agency, where we booked passage on an Erie Canal packet. We were bound for Syracuse.

The boat was advertised as a "floating hotel," providing food and lodging, a seasoned crew, and the company of fellow travelers of the highest quality. The whole proposition sounded like a jolly adventure to me and a welcome change from the wagon. I was anxious to get on board, but as it happened, we sold the wagon too soon. Going from the Hudson River to the canal, the boat must pass through a series of twelve locks, like steps on a stairway, to reach the proper elevation. It would take a full day, maybe longer if other boats are ahead of ours. Better, they told us, to go by land to Troy and board the packet there.

So we traveled by stage to Troy, and while the coach was more comfortable than the wagon in which I rode through Massachusetts, it was not a pleasant ride. The coach was crowded with passengers bypassing the locks as we were and there was not an inch to spare. In addition to the three of us, the stage carried a dour old Scotsman and a husband and wife with two young boys. The Scotsman spoke not a word, but the boys prattled incessantly, moving as often as they could between their parents' laps and the floor of the stage. By Troy, I was quite anxious for the luxury of the packet.

That's how green I was then.

We boarded the *Mary Claire*, a somewhat careworn canal boat about 70 odd feet long and maybe 18 feet wide. It had once been red and blue but was now so chipped and faded that a coat of any color paint would be welcome. It was a fat, squat affair, but long enough, we were told, to accommodate at least five dozen passengers.

The captain greeted each of us on the gangplank as we entered the boat In Troy. "Greeted" is not the right word; he scrutinized each as if to determine how much trouble he would endure by hauling this person down the canal. He was especially keen at identifying men of the cloth. The old Scotsman we had met on the coach, wearing a long black coat and carrying a portmanteau, was halfway down the plank when Captain Horne raised his hand to stop him.

"You a preacher?"

"I am a Presbyterian minister if it's any of your business." Said the old man.

"I'm telling you now, so there'll be no trouble." The captain said, "I'll have no sermonizing, no hymn singing, and no public praying on board this boat."

The old man spat back, "I'll not cast my pearls before swine."

"Make sure you keep your word on that," The captain said, and let the man board. Then he muttered, "but I never met a preacher wouldn't lie."

Reverend Travis and I were next down the plank, carrying the trunk between us.

"You ain't Presbyterian." The captain said.

"No sir, I am not." said the Reverend.

The captain closed one eye and grimaced. "But you are a preacher."

"I preach the gospel, in the proper place."

"I knew it. You heard what I told your brother, no preaching. And don't be comparing theologies with the Presbyterian; I don't want a holy war." He gave me a quizzical look then said, "You neither."

Reverend Travis assured him we wished only to travel, and the captain reluctantly let us, board. He did not challenge Mirabile.

We carried our belongings below deck where we would be sleeping—men in one section women in another, separated by curtains to preserve modesty. The Women slept in cots, small but no doubt comfortable compared to the bedrolls on the floor of the men's side. The smaller and more adventurous of us slept on shelves, suspended, one above the other, by ropes from the ceiling. I tried it one night but fear of falling kept me awake all night, and I opted for the floor from then on.

A table ran down the center of the cabin, where those who purchased meals could dine. When it rained, we all sat inside at this table but in warm weather, must and mildew, mingling with smells from the kitchen and privy, drove us all onto the deck on the roof of the cabin. If this was a "floating hotel," then my notion of hotels needed revision.

The *Mary Claire* was operated by the Hornes, three brothers who looked alike, dressed alike— in dirty canvas pants and chambray shirts— and shared the same hostile disposition. They all had stringy black hair under big straw hats; all had dark, deep-set eyes and each had the same distinctive aquiline nose. If I were to see one of their faces peering through a window, I would be hard-pressed to tell you which it was (though I would be equally frightened regardless.) Moving about the deck of a canal boat, however, they were easy to tell apart. Jason Horne, the captain whom we met when boarding, was the oldest, around thirty years old I would guess. He was tall and burly, walked with a swagger, spoke in commanding curses— it was quite clear, he was boss. Captain Horne left the hard work to his brothers, spending most of his time on the tiller and the rest staring ahead smoking his pipe. When we came to a blind curve in the canal, he would stand up and blow two or three blasts from a long brass trumpet to alert any boat coming the other way. When not on the trumpet he would sing the foulest, most objectionable songs imaginable in a deep baritone voice.

Caleb Horne, early twenties, was shorter and stockier; just as strong as the captain but slower and not so bright. The youngest, Jack Horne, was lean, lanky, and hostile; clearly fighting to hold his own among the other two. Jack was about my age, with a gravelly voice that would sometimes crack when screaming at his brothers— something which he did constantly.

The afternoon we boarded was sunny and comfortable, and as the passengers became situated, most chose to sit on the chairs atop the cabin hoping to view the scenery once we cast off. As the crew prepared—Jack manning the tiller, Caleb busy with the ropes—the captain stood in the bow and addressed us loudly.

"There is but one rule on the canal." He pronounced it "canawl" as did both his brothers and within two days so did all the passengers. The Hornes also had a way to pronounce "Erie" that somehow had more syllables than letters—none of us duplicated that.

"Just one rule: when we come to a bridge, duck down. If you are sitting down and don't duck, the bridge will yank yer head off by the chin, and if you are standing erect, you won't be so for long. A bridge will abide no argument, it wins every fight, and there's a hunerd bridges between here and Rome alone. When a bridge is imminent, the helmsman will holler "bridge!" that way you won't need to trust your eyes. Even a blind man will escape injury if he listens to the helmsman. And that, my friends, is the one rule on the canal."

We sat on the cabin roof as the boat departed the dock. Mirabile was still angry with her father and not speaking to him. Reverend Travis was lost in thought; I knew he was disappointed by the captain's no-preaching order; he had planned to hold services on the canal boat, hoping to defray costs. Including meals, the trip would cost four cents a mile for each of us, and we were going at least 200 miles. I sat between them, hoping for Mirabile's attention— I could still feel her kiss upon my cheek. But Mirabile was noticeably preoccupied with the manly form of Captain Horne as he sang and smoked his pipe at the bow of the boat.

I got up and walked around the top of the cabin. Once we cast off, Captain took over the helm from his brother Jack, and Jack took to surveying the state of the boat. He was full of energy, walking the length of the boat along the gunwale, checking this and that. He stopped at the front of the boat to holler at Caleb for stowing the ropes too slowly. Caleb rose and hollered back. I could barely understand the fight through their peculiar accent and canalers' vocabulary, but I could tell the anger was real. Sheathed on his belt, Jack wore a wide-bladed hunting knife with a bone handle. As the fight intensified, his hand moved to the butt of the knife. This had a quieting effect on Caleb, who just shook his head and turned back to the ropes.

Jack climbed up to the cabin roof and saw that I had been watching.

"Hey, sport," he said to me, "you planning to stand all the way to Rome?"

"I'm just walking around," I said, trying to sound friendly. I did not want to incur his wrath.

"What's your name?" He asked, looking at me with one eye closed, as his brother had on the gangplank.

"Jonathan Pratt."

"Jack Horne, Howdja do." He said and shook my hand. Well, this fellow is all right, I thought. How good it would be to have a friend on the boat.

Jack walked over to me, looked me up and down, walked around behind me and said, "Fancy cap you're wearing, Jonathan Pratt."

"Thank you," I said turning around.

"Ever seen a hat like this?" He asked, pointing to the straw hat he wore. It was broad-brimmed, and the crown rose to a point, his brothers each wore one like it, as did all the canal workers I had seen in Troy.

"I never have," I said, to facilitate conversation.

"Look," Jack took off his hat and held it out to his side and explained loudly and with enthusiasm. "See how tall it is? We soak 'em in water overnight then stretch 'em out."

"Why?" I asked.

"Why what?" Jack shouted.

"Why do you stretch them out?"

"Why, so they'll look like canalers' hats, ya idjit."

At that point I felt a hard push in the middle of my back; it was not sharp, but strong and unyielding and quickly knocked me off my feet and flat onto the deck. Jack was rolling with laughter, sprawled across a chair. Several of the passengers were laughing as well, politely covering their mouths as they resumed upright positions on the benches.

*

I had broken the only rule of the canal; I had let a low bridge knock me down.

No, canal travel was not the adventure I had hoped for. It was slow; often I was tempted to jump out and walk on ahead and meet the boat at the next lock. In sunny weather, I sat on the cabin roof, as did most of the passengers, and watched the scenery (albeit lush, green and beautiful) ever so gradually reveal itself. Once or twice an hour we would hear the cry of "bridge! Low bridge!" and all would prostrate ourselves to the oncoming viaduct. I never again failed to heed the helmsman's warning or allowed a bridge to take me by surprise after the day Jack had so fully diverted my attention that a low bridge very nearly broke my back.

And he tried again—often. When a bridge wasn't imminent, he would trip me as I passed on deck, or try to knock my cap into the canal. In fact, Jack never missed an opportunity to make me look the fool, ridiculing my clothes and my speech until I could barely stand it. It was no different than Pip at the cooperage; where I had sought friendship and camaraderie and found only misery. And once again, I had to find a way out.

It wasn't just Jack, either; the Travises were terrible traveling companions. Mirabile and the Reverend remained at odds, and though she would half-heartedly drill me in scripture (much to the amusement of Jack), Mirabile spoke very little to me. Instead, she used every free minute to giggle and chat with Captain Horne. The joy I had experienced from Mirabile's kiss was now just a brief and fading memory.

I was glad, in a way, that the Travises were preoccupied with other matters because I knew that soon enough they would be back to planning their "harvest of souls" and I feared I could longer tolerate my role in it. It seemed to have more to do with taking money than saving souls, and I was ashamed of the deception. Besides, I still hadn't seen a penny of it.

The boat would stop, from time to time, at locks to raise us up to a higher stretch of canal and at towns along the way where we would stop to take on supplies and passengers. It gave us all a chance to step onto dry land and stretch our legs. I thought of bolting during one of these stops, but where would I go in the middle of New York, a state that seemed to be nothing but primeval forest and canal towns, so new they still smelled of sawdust? How would I survive in either?

We stopped just east of Canajoharie, and I saw another preacher giving advice to some of the hoggees—the boys who lead the mules pulling the packet. The Horne brothers employed two of them who, like the mules that they walked down the towpath, worked six-hour shifts, around the clock, sleeping in the bowstable—a little stall in the front of the boat—when not working. Mostly orphans, with no homes but the canal, the hoggees had atrocious reputations, drinking and smoking at a young age and swearing like sailors at sea. I had grown used to the blasphemy and vulgar language of the Horne brothers, but to hear it from the lips of a boy of nine or ten was still shocking. The minister was admonishing them gently, trying to shame them into dropping the curses from their vocabularies. He left the boys with a tract entitled "The Swearer's Prayer." They seemed attentive and happy to take the tract though I doubted any could read. When the preacher turned away, I heard one mutter, "Goddam fool." and the rest laughed.

The preacher then moved to enter our boat but of course Capt. Horne spotted him right away as a man of the cloth. This one was especially exuberant holding a Bible in one hand and a bag of religious tracts in the other as he strode up the gangplank.

"Stop right there, Reverend." The Captain said. "I haven't room for another passenger."

"Oh I won't take much room, sir and I won't be with you long. Just long enough to lead your passengers in prayer, talk with those who profess Christianity, and minister to you and your crew."

"Oh no, you won't." Said the captain.

"This is the *Mary Claire*, is it not? And you would be Captain…" he pulled paper from his coat, unfolded it and scanned the contents, "Horne, Captain Horne. Am I correct?"

"What is that to you?"

"I have a letter here, Captain Horne, from Mr. John Allen of Rochester, New York, giving me free passage at any time on any of his canal packets for the purpose of edifying passengers and crew on the word of God." He handed the letter to the captain. "That includes the *Mary Claire*."

Captain Horne took the letter and grimaced at the content; I sensed that reading was a laborious task for him, but he got the gist. "Jesus Christ, that son of a bitch Allen has been a thorn in my side since I set foot on this boat." He thrust the letter back. "Alright, Reverend, come aboard and do what you must but cause no trouble and don't try to convert the crew."

"Thank you Captain, but I not an ordained minister. I am Deacon Eaton of the American Bethel Society. Our mission is to bring the gospel to men of the sea, including canalers, so I am afraid I must speak with you and your men before I leave. In the meantime, it would please me if you refrained from cursing or taking the Lord's name in vain in my presence."

"Best of luck ta ya." The Captain said as the man passed.

True to his word, Deacon Eaton brought the word of the Lord to the canal, insisting we say grace before meals and as he got to know the passengers, calling on some of them to say it. In the evening he held prayer services in the cabin with larger attendance each day. During the day passengers would seek him out for heart-to-heart talks that often ended in tears. When no one sought him, he would seek them. The *Mary Claire* was awash in the glory of God.

The afternoon of Deacon Eaton's second day aboard was hot and still as we all sat lazily on deck. Nothing was moving, and there was no sound, but the Captain singing as he stood on the bow, watching for God knows what, in the canal ahead of us. Mirabile was watching him just as intently, and Captain Horne knew it; his song was not as shocking as his usual fare but still saucy enough to hold her interest. The deep baritone rolled through the otherwise tranquil afternoon.

> Our cook she was a grand old gal,
> She wore a tattered dress
> We hoisted her upon a pole
> As a signal of distress.
>
> Oh the E-ri-e was risin'
> And the gin was getting' low
> I scarcely think we'll get a drink
> Till we get to Buffalo-o-o,
> Till we get to Buffalo.

Someone had caught Reverend Travis's attention as well; a handsome and well-dressed lady passenger, not too many years older than he, was listening intently as the Reverend earnestly, but quietly, revealed the word. With the captain busy singing, he thought his preaching would go unnoticed, but he had not counted on Deacon Eaton who had been standing quietly behind him the whole time.

"Pardon me, sir," the Deacon said in his exuberant fashion, nearly startling Reverend Travis off of his chair, "but I could not help but overhear you spreading the gospel to this fine lady. We haven't been introduced; I am Deacon Eaton of the Bethel Society, and they tell me you are Reverend Travis, a minister of the Lord. Is that correct sir?"

"It is," said the Reverend, rising to shake the Deacon's hand.

"I came to ask you Reverend, why do you hide your light? Will you not lead this boat in worship?"

Reverend Travis had been watching the deacon closely since he boarded; studying him, I thought. Though he was called to lead, Travis knew he was not the leader here, and that did not suit him. And he was still, very wisely, afraid of angering Captain Horne.

"I have made a promise to the captain of this vessel that I would do no preaching. I am a man of my word and will not break that promise."

"How fortunate we are that Paul made no such promise to the Romans."

"Render unto Caesar, that which is Caesar's." Said Travis.

"How does that apply, sir? No, the captain is lost, and it is for us to redeem him. 'What man of you, having a hundred sheep, if he loses one of them, does not leave the ninety-nine in the wilderness, and go after the one which is lost until he finds it?'"

The old Scotsman (whose name I never learned), sat nearby, trying to stay out of the fray, but could not resist turning to see who was quoting scripture. Mr. Eaton caught his eye and said, "And what about you sir, wasn't I told that you, too are a Presbyterian minister?"

"And what if you was?" said the Scotsman.

"Don't you agree that we should be tending to the souls on board this boat? Shouldn't we be professing our Christianity? Shouldn't we be spreading the Word, and leading these people in worship of our Lord?"

"Ach," he said with a sweeping gesture to the towpath, "Why not go lead them mules in worship? It amounts to the same."

"Sir, if you are implying that the people on this boat are no more Christians than mules are, then I must heartily disagree. I have prayed with them, and I daresay each one is a better Christian than you show yourself to be."

"It takes more than folding your hands and mouthing the words." The Scotsman spat back, "You are either saved, or you're not saved. The Lord has already chosen, nothing you do or say can change that. It doesn't take much to see that none here but myself is saved, the rest of you are among the non-elect with no hope of salvation."

"Are you saying that only the Presbyterians are saved?"

"No, no, of course not." Shaking his head, "Ach, the Presbyterians in this country have gone so far astray they can never be saved. Only the members of the Anti-burgher Secession Church have a hope and not all of them, to my mind, are truly righteous."

"'For whosoever shall call upon the name of the Lord shall be saved.' - Romans 10:13" said the deacon.

"'For those whom he foreknew he also predestined to be conformed to the image of his Son,' Romans 8:29" shouted the Scotsman, turning red with anger.

The two fought each other verse for verse, often, as in the first case, drawing contradictory sentiments from the same book. These were not hellfire verses of Reverend Travis, nor were they Mirabile's merciful ones; they were strange and mysterious, fraught with heavy and unfathomable meaning. It was hard to follow, but I could see the crux of the argument: we were either free to choose salvation or that that decision had already been made for us, long before we were born. They each argued well, but I was beginning to favor the Scotsman's view—everything that happened was preordained, and each of us came into the world either saved or damned. It would explain so much.

Reverend Travis started out taking Eaton's side but realized early that he was outclassed and by the end seemed to be waiting for a winner before committing himself.

As the intensity of the argument increased, with verses hurled in angry shouts, the fight got the attention of the Hornes. Two of the brothers, Jack and the Captain, came running to the deck.

"I told you, gentlemen, I would have no fights over religion and I damn well meant it." The captain said. Then he grabbed Eaton while Jack grabbed the old Scotsman and each pushed his man toward the edge of the boat. Eaton went flying into the canal, but hard as Jack pushed, the Scotsman held his ground. Captain Horne turned his eyes toward Travis, and the Reverend jumped off the boat himself without need of further coaxing. It seemed to me like jolly fun now, and I rushed to help Jack with the Scotsman and together we had him over the edge and into the canal. Then Jack hollered, "All preachers in." and a push of his shoulder knocked me into the canal as well.

I stood up and found that the water was shallow enough to walk through. The canal water stank of sewage and I scrambled toward the boat, anxious to get out as soon as possible. Soon we were back on board, and having a good laugh over it, even Deacon Eaton. But the Scotsman was still in the canal, floundering and crying for help.

"I canna swim! I canna swim!"

The captain called down, "Stand up, ya fool, the water's only four foot deep."

But the Scotsman could not find the bottom, and still, he floundered, no longer calling for help, his head under the water. Then the struggling stopped, and he lay still in the water, just a big mass of dark, sodden wool floating in the canal. The Scotsman had drowned.

CHAPTER 4

Labor, Guilt, and Cider; In Vino Veritas; A Metamorphosis Unforeseen.

The labor of bringing the drowned Scotsman back on board the canal boat was the hardest work I had done since leaving the cooperage, but it was almost a blessing, for a time taking my mind off my role in his death. I worked with the three Horne brothers for what must have been hours, trying to leverage three hundred odd pounds of flesh and fabric out of the water and over the gunwales. Deacon Eaton took to praying, but if he was praying for our success, it did not seem to help. I did not see what engaged Reverend Travis, but I am sure it was neither labor nor prayer. The Hornes finally decided on using a block and tackle, and with a rope around the old man's neck, we hauled him aboard like a prize catch.

The import of the event did not fully hit me until I lay down to sleep—a man had died, and I was at least partially to blame. The guilt would have kept me awake had I not been so fatigued. I slept soundly and would have slept until lunch if Captain Horne had not awakened everyone at first light for the purpose of addressing all aboard.

The sun was barely visible above the trees behind of us when the captain assembled us all atop the cabin. With a brother on either side of him, Captain Horne spoke.

"Everyone now listen to me." He began in his most authoritarian voice, "Listen to me now and listen good. Yesterday, as we all know, we lost a passenger. It was a tragedy; the worst you can have aboard a canal boat. You prayin' folks, I know you prayed last night for the dead man, and I thank you for it. But it's morning now, and we must take care of earthly matters. We will soon be in Canajoharie, and I have no choice but to inform the magistrates. The canal is not like the ocean; we can't just leave our dead behind. This man's death must be reported, and it is best to get this business done and behind us.

"There will be questions, and if all our answers are the same, we will be on our way all the faster. For those of you who did not see what happened yesterday, let me tell the story. Several of the men of the cloth, that we are so, so, fortunate to have on board the *Mary Claire*, were engaged in a Biblical discussion—you may have heard them loudly citing chapter and verse. My brothers and myself, heathens that we are, did not understand the playful nature of their disputes and went up top to try and cool them down. These jolly men decided to take our advice and cool down by jumping into the canal. Now, ninety-nine times out of a hundred, or even ten times that, jumping into the canal does no permanent damage. This time, though—well, maybe the Scotsman should have removed his coat first.

"In any case, between the locks and the lawmen, we stand to be in Canajoharie one night at least. There is a fine inn in town for those tired of canal boat sleeping. And that's all, except if any man remembers yesterday different than I told it, please talk to me before talking to the sheriff."

Reverend Travis and Mirabile were already gone. They had left a note on my pillow saying that they planned to hold a service in town if they could find a willing church, far enough away from the passengers that they would not attract their attention. I was to meet them at the inn at 6:00. No doubt it would be the usual service, crutches and all. I wasn't sure I could do it now, still harboring the guilt of killing the Scotsman. It seemed like so much mockery, more than my soul could bear.

Most of the passengers had already left the boat, and the Horne brothers seemed just as happy. The body was laid out on the grass near the lock, covered with a canvas tarpaulin. They were waiting for the arrival of the sheriff and the coroner. I had no place to go and decided to wait as well. Maybe if I talked to the sheriff, it would ease my guilt. I hadn't yet decided if I would relate the incidents as I remembered them or as Captain Horne remembered them.

Jack Horne came striding up to me saying, "Why so glum Pratt? We've a whole day in front of us with nothing to do. You ain't planning to spend the whole day here are you?"

"Leave me alone," I said.

"Don't be like that, Pratt. You were such a jolly fellow yesterday."

"You mean when we killed the Scotsman?"

Jack grabbed me by the shirt and pulled me behind the locksman's house. Quietly, through clenched teeth, he said, "We didn't kill the Scotsman; don't say that, even in jest."

"I wasn't jesting, we threw him off the boat, and he drowned. We killed him."

He rolled his eyes and scolded me like a child. "First of all, nobody drowns in the canal. How in hell could we know he wouldn't have sense enough to stand up? And second, weren't you listening to him? By his religion, nothing happens unless God wills it. We done God's will and nothing more."

It surprised me that Jack had been listening, but yes, I had been listening too. Not only was the Scotsman beating Deacon Eaton at the scripture game before his demise, but he had begun to sway me to his way of thinking. I saw that I was already beyond saving, already damned, why was I even reading from that wretched book?

"You see what I am saying, Pratt. I can tell you agree."

"We still pushed him," I said.

"But we didn't kill him. And if we stay around here today, we'll be answering questions from coroners and magistrates, and one false word will have us stalled here for days."

"If that's God's will there's nothing we can do about it."

"Maybe it's God's will and maybe it ain't, and maybe there's nothing I can do about it, but I'm sure as hell going to try. And for both of our sakes, so are you."

He led me into the woods beyond Canajoharie, and I didn't resist. "I know this place, Pratt. We can have some fun here if you let yourself. I can show you things you've never seen before."

The forest grew thick and deep very quickly, and I was soon lost. I asked Jack if he was sure he could find his way back. He said he knew his way around the full length of the canal and could never get lost. But Canajoharie he knew especially well because he had grown up nearby. I asked if he still had a home here.

"My home is the canal." He said.

We came to the end of the woods and on to a farmer's freshly plowed field—a good sized piece of land.

"Must be planting spinach or peas," I said," they like to go in early."

Jack looked at me. "You a farmer? I thought you was a preacher."

"I don't know what I am now," I said, "Might as well say I'm a canaller; it's as true as anything else."

This sent Jack into a fit of laughter. "You are a funny lad, Pratt. C'mon, if you like growing things, you 'll love this."

He took off through the plowed field, cutting across the left corner towards another stand of trees. I started running too and caught up with him.

I hadn't run since I left my father's farm; in fact, I had a barely moved. It felt great to stretch my legs, and breathe air not tainted by canal water or the human stench of the sleeping cabin. We ran into a huge apple orchard. The trees were just beginning to bud, but they already smelled sweet to me.

"Too bad it's not apple season," I said.

"Well, it's always cider season," said Jack.

We walked through the orchard and into the farmyard. Jack led me to a shed behind the barn. The door was tied shut with a piece of cord; Jack pulled out his knife to cut it.

"Are you sure that's wise?" I said.

"If he really cared about his goods he'd put a proper lock on them," Jack said, and with one stroke of the knife, the door was open. Inside were dozens of earthenware jugs, of all shapes and sizes.

"This one ought to do us," Jack said, taking a heavy looking gallon jug. "We'll return the jug when we're done; he won't know the difference."

Jack made a half-hearted attempt to retie the shed door then we hurried away. I followed him into the woods again to a stream about a hundred yards beyond the farm. I now had faith that Jack meant me no harm, but if he left me here, I would never find my way back to the boat. We followed the stream a ways then around a bend I could see a waterfall, about ten feet tall, not too wide, with a pool below it. We walked almost to the falls then up the bank into a mossy patch beneath the trees and sat down. Jack pulled the cork out of the jug, took a drink then handed it to me.

I took a sip. It tasted bitter, strangely burning. "I think this cider is spoiled," I said.

Jack started laughing again. "Oh no, Pratt, you've never had real cider before. Take another drink, the second taste is not so bitter."

Then I realized what he meant—hard cider. My father was a teetotaler, as was everyone we knew. The Pratts did not drink alcohol. But I was no longer in my father's house, and I had less and less use for his morals. I took another drink. It still burned but Jack was right; it tasted better the more I drank. In fact, everything got better. I soon forgot the Scotsman, and I was happier than I could ever remember being. Jack and I were laughing and talking like old friends, and I could not remember why I had been frightened.

*

So we passed the jug, and Jack told stories of the canal; famous fights, collisions, exploits of legendary canallers. He had a way of telling the most horrifying tales in a way that had me rolling with laughter. Even when he described the tricks he played on passengers it all seemed like harmless sport, and downright funny when played upon someone other than me. It was clear that Jack loved life on the canal; it was his home;

"But it ain't gonna last," he said, "my brothers want me off the boat, the end of this trip or sooner. I been a hoggee since I could hold a rope, leading the mules down the towpath, hauling the *Mary Claire* back and forth from Troy to Buffalo, for more years than I can say. This year I said no more; I'm not a child leading mules; I am part of the crew on board.

"Well, because of family, and because of a hundred reasons I can't begin to tell you, they agreed. And for just as many reasons, it will not last beyond this trip. Jason is going to buy the boat from that man in Rochester; he has the money saved and ready. By Jason's reckoning, the *Mary Claire* will earn enough to support him and Caleb, and no more. I'm off the boat. They'll hire me season by season, as a hoggee or a cook, if I want. I told him, 'Goddam that, I want my share of the boat,' but there's no use. "

This touched me deeply. It wasn't so long ago I was forced to leave the only home I had ever known for the good of the family. "What will you do?" I asked.

"Oh, I have plans," Jack said, grabbing the jug from me and taking several large gulps. "I've been up and down this canal enough time to know it ain't the canalers making the money. Listen, Pratt, come fall I can buy all the apples I want for a nickel a bushel. Take'em down to New York City, where people buy apples for two cents apiece. That's real profit."

This was unexpected. I followed the logic, but it did not feel right. "Is no one doing this now?" I asked.

"Sure," he said, "farmers and merchants, spending all the profit on transportation, but I know how to move cargo; I can get apples to New York for next to nothing. Then when I have the apple business running I'll branch out— apple butter, apple pies," He lifted the jug, "And what about cider? See, up here we have too many apples; in New York City, not enough. That's how you make your fortune. Now I just need enough money to buy the damned apples and a cart in New York."

Jack got quiet then. Maybe he was thinking about apples, I know I was.

"What about you, Pratt?" Jack said at last. "If you ain't a preacher, why're you traveling with one?"

So I told him the story of leaving the farm escaping the cooperage and my role in the religious revivals. I did not have Jack's flair for storytelling, but I had him laughing once or twice.

"Why you're just a will-o-the-wisp, Pratt, going wherever the wind blows you."

"I suppose you're right."

"But it don't make you happy. Why don't you blow in your own direction? You in love with that Bible girl?"

This brought on a wave of melancholy. I didn't know how I felt about Mirabile anymore. She was so delicate but so strong; so comforting but so elusive. Nights alone I still felt her kiss upon my check, but there would be no more kisses, how could there be?

"C'mon sport, have another drink. I didn't mean to make you downhearted. Say, why don't we go swimming, cool down a bit?"

It was unseasonably hot, and the cider had warmed me to the bone. The water did look awfully inviting. "Can we swim here?" I asked.

"Who says we can't?"

Jack went up behind the trees. I thought it funny that the tough canal boy was too modest to undress in front of me. As I stood up to disrobe the world seemed to swirl around me, I thought I was going to fall back down. I was dizzy from the cider; it was not a disagreeable feeling but certainly disorienting. With some difficulty, I removed all my clothes and started toward the water.

"Hey, Pratt," Jack called from behind me.

I turned to see Jack standing before me, arms akimbo, stark naked. And miraculously transformed.

"My God! You're a girl!"

I was aghast; had the cider made me delusional? Beneath layers of rough and dirty canaller's clothing had emerged the body of a lithe and slender young woman, like a butterfly from a cocoon. I didn't know whether to stare or look away. I stared. I tried to cover my manhood with my hand, but it had grown beyond covering. Jack moved closer and replaced my hand with her own.

"You don't seem to mind it that much," she said.

So that afternoon, on the mossy bank of a stream, near a waterfall, somewhere in the great state of New York, I learned more about life than I had in weeks of Bible study.

CHAPTER 5

Driven from the Garden; Descent into hell; Miraculous ascension.

I had never seen a woman naked before. The closest I had come was a china statuette—a Grecian goddess standing nude on a pedestal –that my mother's family had brought with them from England. As a child, I had been fascinated by that unclad beauty, but the porcelain ideal was no match for flesh and blood.

I knew the mechanics of procreation; growing up on a farm I had seen every class of animal in the act of copulation. I had even imagined myself in the act, with some handsome girl from school, or one of my sisters' friends or even the low women on Water Street that I had seen as I rode with my father to the Salem docks. But even my wildest dreams could not hold a candle to the splendor I experienced that warm spring afternoon in Canajoharie. I could not understand why human beings did not spend every waking minute making love, as Jack and I did that afternoon.

Once beyond the shock of Jack's transformation from rough canaler to alluring wood sprite, I realized I should have seen it from the start. In the face I had taken for just a duplicate Horne brothers' face I now saw delicate nuances not common to the males of that clan. Yes, it was from the same mold, and Jack was no beauty. The Horne family nose remained the prominent feature, but I now saw a curl in the lips I hadn't seen before, and the eyes, wide and feline, had a sparkle and depth where the brothers' were little more than vacant slits. Even her hair, still as shaggy and rough-cut as her brother's, was soft and fine as silken threads.

"I'm sorry I took you for a boy, Jack."

"Never mind, Pratt, that's what I want to be took for." She said. "I fool everyone but my brothers. I think sometimes Caleb isn't really sure."

"But why? Why not just be a girl?"

"Stay home and bake pies, you mean? It ain't my nature; I'd rather be a canaler. My brothers wouldn't let me on the boat if I was a girl. But I just do what comes natural. Makes Caleb mad that I am more the man than he is. Jason takes if for a lark and likes to see people fooled, but if I didn't pull my weight, he'd drop me on the shore and leave me there.

"Besides, I can be a girl anytime I need to be." She rolled over and kissed me, and we were at it again.

We never did go swimming. The afternoon seemed endless, drinking cider and talking when we weren't making love. At one point Jack pulled a clay pipe and a satchel of tobacco from a shirt pocket, and I added sot weed to my litany of newly acquired vices.

With the sun low in the sky and the jug nearly empty, we sat naked by the stream, unwilling to move until we heard a rustling in the woods behind us and a voice calling out, "There ya be! Thieves! Fornicators!"

We turned to see a farmer, no doubt the cider maker, heading towards us carrying a hunting rifle. We gathered our clothes as quickly as we could.

"Leave the jug.," said Jack.

Following the banks of the stream, we ran, naked, as fast as we could, away from the crazed farmer.

"What if he shoots?" I said.

"It won't get his cider back so he won't waste the lead." She said.

When we were far enough away and could see the farmer had stopped pursuing us, we stopped to dress. Though I had outrun the farmer, I could not outrun the cider which overtook me then and knocked me senseless.

I had lost control of my legs, when I spoke my words sounded strange, and my memory of what happened next is spotty at best. At some point the sun had set, Jack had left me, and I was standing, fully clothed again, outside the inn.

In a panic, I remembered I was to meet the Travises there at 6:00, and I knew I was late. The clerk eyed me with suspicion as I entered the inn. I told my story, and with some reluctance, he told me the Travises had left me a message. They had gone to the Congregational church, and if I arrived in time, I should meet them there. I have no idea how I got there, but somehow

I made it to the church and knowing the service had already started, I looked for the back door. Inside I saw the Reverend standing behind the lectern, leading the flock in prayer. Mirabile sat behind him ready to play a hymn when he finished. The scene was illuminated by candles on the altar and on both sides of the room. It was quite beautiful.

I saw the crutch lying on the floor near Reverend Travis's coat, and I picked it up and hobbled out onto the dais. The church was packed with the righteous, but not all had their heads bowed, and they started to murmur as they saw me limp toward the pulpit. Revered Travis turned and saw me coming; by the look on his face, I could tell he knew my condition and knew he could not stop me.

He a-mened his prayer and introduced me as Brother Jonathan. He called me to him—making it clear I was not to open my mouth—then began telling my story himself. Walking with the crutch was hard in my condition, and it grew ever harder; I couldn't seem to get a grip on the thing, and I nearly tripped myself with every step. Finally, I threw the crutch behind me saying, "I don't need this."

The crowd gasped. Reverend Travis was horrified, but the man was nothing if not quick on his feet.

"Halleluiah" He called out, "Praise Jesus, the boy's been healed. He was crippled, and now he can walk."

"That's right," I said, "I can walk."

"Mirabile, please help Brother Jonathan to a chair, he's healed but still week. Brothers and sisters, I am full of the Holy Spirit. Let us pray in Jesus's name."

Mirabile led me out of view, out the back door and into a wagon. I fell asleep then, and that is my last recollection of the evening.

*

I woke up the next morning on the canal boat. The sun was high, and the table had already been cleared from breakfast. It was just as well, I was hungry, but the mere thought of food made me gag. I still had the taste of cider in my mouth, and like the first sip, the taste was bitter.

If my afternoon in the woods with Jack had been paradise, the following day was hell itself. My head was throbbing with pain, and when I left the cabin, I thought the sunlight would blind me. The boat approached a curve, and the blast from the captain's trumpet was like a punch to my already tender head. I slouched towards an empty chair, but just as I was about to sit down, someone yanked it away and fell on my back, writhing in agony. I couldn't believe it; Jack had done it. She stood above me, now a boy again, dressed in her rough canal clothes.

"You look uncomfortable, Pratt, sprawled across the deck like that." She said, then walked away laughing.

Had I dreamed it all? Had Jack really transformed into a sweet young girl who seduced me, or had I been plied with demon rum and left deluded? Nothing had changed on board the *Mary Claire*; Jack was still the ugly bullyboy I had always known.

Reverend Travis helped me up and said, "Come inside the cabin, Jonathan, I need to talk to you."

Once inside his tone was less than gentle, "What the hell were you doing yesterday?"

"I had some cider," I said, barely able to say the word without getting sick.

"Never again come to a service drunk, Jonathan. To the people we minister, alcohol is as bad than the devil himself. I had to tell them that you were so full of the spirit of the Lord it made you stagger and babble like an idiot."

He continued to berate me about the cider until the pain in my head pulsed in rhythm with his words. And he scolded me at length about coming onstage unexpectedly and for running an act we had not rehearsed. Going forth, I was to stick to the script. It was the first time I had heard him speak in these theatrical terms; it confirmed my own views on the venture.

"But as it turns out," he said, relaxing his tone somewhat, "your improvisation was well received. These people are hungrier than I thought; they believed I healed your legs through the Holy Spirit. We are going to build the whole act around healing by faith.

"But Jonathan, you must never catch me unaware again." He chuckled, slapping me on the back. "Oh, and the sheriff will be by today, asking about the Scotsman. You must echo the captain's story, or we will never leave this place."

He left me more confused than ever. The cabin was close and stuffy; I needed fresh air. I wished the Reverend really could heal me. Maybe if I sat in the sun without moving or thinking the heat and light would purify my soul and relieve my aching head. As I stepped out of the cabin, Jack slipped a foot under mine, and I stumbled almost going head first over the gunwale.

Jack was walking away. I got up and chased after her, grabbing her arm.

She turned and said, "What?"

"What are you doing to me? Didn't you tell me you'd stop?" Maybe she didn't; I had no clear memory of what she told me.

Jack glanced around quickly, then pulled me back into the cabin. She grabbed my shirt and led me into the crew's cabin and shut the door. In an excited whisper, she said, "I can't treat you different now, my brothers'll notice."

"You aren't treating me same; you're treating me worse. I feel like I'm dying as it is, and now I have to watch out for you."

"Cider got you, huh?"

I nodded.

"Well, I can make you feel better. Drop your britches, Pratt."

"What here?" I couldn't believe what I heard. "No, I can't. I have to talk to the sheriff. "

"Alright Pratt, if all goes well, we'll be out of here soon. Listen for my brother's horn; he'll blow it as we approach Little Falls. When you hear the horn, make sure you are up top. "

"What?"

Jack headed up on deck, then turned and said, "And don't give nothing to the sheriff. Lay it all on the deacon."

The sheriff of Montgomery County arrived that afternoon. He and the coroner had been around the day before and had removed the Scotsman's body and taken statements from everyone on the boat—everyone but Jack and myself.

I waited above deck while the sheriff interviewed Jack below. After all of it, I was still unsure how I would answer the sheriff's questions. There was the captain's truth: we had been roughhousing atop the boat, and all had jumped in. But I knew the real truth, Jack and I had pushed the old man in, and it had not been easy. Still, I could not avoid what Jack had reminded me; by his religion, God already knew when he would die, and who would push him overboard. It was written; it was not something we could change.

Jack came back on deck, giving me the high sign, as the sheriff called me below. The sheriff was as nervous as I was, murder and suspicious death being as rare as it was in Montgomery County.

"Mr. Jonathan Pratt," he said, "You are traveling with Reverend Travis, are you not?"

"Yes, sir," I said. "We are spreading the word of God."

"And you were there at the time of the drowning?"

"Yes sir, one minute he was there, the next he was gone."

"And was there an argument before the, uh..."

"Yes, sir," I said, "a most educational ecclesiastical argument. The Scotsman was arguing predestination against Deacon Eaton's belief in man's free will."

"And did the argument turn violent?"

"No," I said, "it was all in fun. We all jumped into the canal, then we all got back on board—all but the Scotsman."

"That is what so many have told me, but I cannot ignore Deacon Eaton's testimony. He said it was you, along with a member of Captain Horne's crew who pushed the Reverend off the boat."

I had expected this, and I was ready. "I hate to speak against a man of the cloth, Sheriff, but I wonder if Deacon Eaton was not as much to blame as anyone. He did nothing but pray and preach upon boarding the boat, in violation of the captain's wishes. It was Deacon Eaton who started the argument and he who stoked the flame. We who jumped into the canal—and I include the Scotsman—did so to douse a fire that could not end well. I bear no ill will toward the deacon, but I'm afraid that what he tells you now comes from guilt and nothing more."

The sheriff sighed, closed his notebook and said, "I have heard that story too. Perhaps it is just as well for all concerned if this matter were treated as the unfortunate accident it no doubt was."

I concurred.

As Jack had predicted, late in the morning we came to a bend in the canal, and the captain blew his trumpet. With no idea what to expect, I did as Jack had told me and made my way to the top of the cabin. There stood Jack with a stuffed haversack across one shoulder and what looked like my carpetbag on the end of a loop of rope around the other.

"Now what?" I asked. She just smiled and pointed to the front of the boat and an approaching bridge.

"Low bridge!" shouted Caleb from the helm. I started to duck as everyone else did, but Jack caught me under the arm and kept me upright. With her other hand, she caught the bridge as it came toward us.

"Grab the bridge, Pratt." She said, pulling herself upward. I had no choice but to comply, and we both pulled ourselves up as the boat drifted beneath us. We scrabbled through the railing and onto the surface of the bridge. I realized then that this was Jack's dramatic escape and I started running down the bridge expecting her to follow.

"Wait a minute, Pratt." She said. "Let's see what they do."

We stood at the railing watching the boat where eighty, or so, wide eyes stared back at us. The boat moved slowly and without stopping, someone— a Horne brother, maybe, or Mirabile Travis— could have easily jumped off the boat and run to the bridge and grabbed me, if not us both. But nothing happened, nobody moved, the boat just kept floating west.

CHAPTER 6

Another Change of Habit; Entering Watervliet; The Partnership Torn Asunder.

We stood on the bridge and watched as the boat moved on slowly. At first, we could see them, all the passengers standing at the rear of the boat, gawking at us, then it was hard to tell if they were looking or not. The boat floated off in the distance, then the canal banked to the right, and it moved out of sight behind a stand of trees.

"Why didn't we just jump off the side, on to the towpath?" I asked Jack.

"Then they would have had to chase us," Jack said. "And probably would have caught one of us. Besides, you wouldn't have come if asked ya."

"I might have," I said.

Jack nodded and smiled at me. "Anyways, I always wanted to try that—hangin' from a bridge. They'll remember us. They'll tell stories about us."

We crossed the bridge and started walking east. I quietly pondered my new situation. I knew I had to leave the Travises; I couldn't do that work anymore. It wasn't God's work, I knew we were selling lies, and people lined up to buy them. But, for all that, I never went hungry with the Travises.

"How will we eat, Jack?"

Jack laughed, "Oh we'll eat Pratt, "she punched my shoulder, "We'll eat like kings."

"But how?"

Jack stopped and pulled a leather pouch from her shirt; it was filled with gold coins and banknotes.

"Where did you get that?"

Jack closed the bag and stuck it inside her shirt. "I told you my brothers were saving up to buy the boat—for themselves, not including me. I been leading them mules long as I can remember and they weren't going to give me a share when they bought the boat. So I just took the money. I've been planning it all season."

"You took it all?"

"I helped earn it all."

"But wouldn't a third be fairest?"

"Well Pratt, you're the preacher, so you would know what's fair," I knew that attitude; if I didn't watch she would have me on the ground. "But they were going to leave me with nothing, so I left them with nothing. That's fair enough for me."

As it turns out, it was fair enough for me too. That night we slept in at an inn with a feather bed; the first real bed I had slept in since leaving the farm.

Our plan was to tell the world we were trappers, come down from the Adirondacks to sell our winter pelts. To that end, we went first to an outfitter in Little Falls who sold me a pair of canvas trousers, a chambray shirt, some boots and a jacket of buckskin. Jack, with some reluctance, exchanged her canal hat for a trapper's woolen cap and bought herself a blanket coat. I put on the new clothes, but when Jack saw me in full array, she thought me too natty. To take the shine off it, we took my new suit to the banks of the canal and in the mud and sand, we stomped on each piece—the breeches, the shirt, and the coat—until they were thoroughly soiled and somewhat tattered, then we washed them in the canal and hung them on tree limbs. Once dried, they looked and smelled nearly as bad as Jack's attire, and then she was satisfied that, if I kept my mouth shut, I could pass for a trapper.

We followed the canal east, and during that time we lived a life that was next to ideal. By day we were two carefree trappers, young men from the hills looking for adventure. But at night, whether in a room at an inn or in the woods off the road, we were husband and wife, and Jack, back to her proper sex, all but overwhelmed me with her passion.

Once I had become accustomed to the standard mode of lovemaking, Jack taught me some variations. There were ways, she explained, where both parties could experience pleasure, without the possibility of conceiving a child. This was a possibility that, in the throes of lust, had not even occurred to me. I could not imagine what might happen to Jack, or to me, or to the child if Jack were to bear one. Needless to say, I listened to every word.

The easiest way, she told me, was a method she had learned from a boy in Oneida. "Male continence" his people had called it, and it involved ending the process just prior to the man ejaculating. In practice, though not completely satisfying to either of us, it was a fairly good compromise. She had other methods, though, more effective at both goals—some she had learned from other boys along the canal some she had surmised herself. Many of the tricks she proposed were—at least by my unstructured reading of the bible—so abhorrent to the Lord that their practice had led Him to destroy entire cities.

I know, dear reader, you are saying to yourself, "He has taken up with a doxy, he deserves what he gets." Yes, it is true, I had started down the road to hell, but it is a winding road, through wilderness unimaginable. Follow me to the end before pronouncing the rope a fitting destination.

In fact, I knew full well I was living a life of sin, but I had, by now, fully accepted the religion of the dead Scotsman. Not the righteous assurance of my place in heaven, quite the contrary; I believed my damnation was certain and irreversible. The Lord knew before creation who would be sheep and who would be goats; why should I feign righteousness when the Lord and I both already knew which herd I was in. To be sure, there were nights, well past midnight, with all others asleep, when I was kept awake by the horrors of hell awaiting me. But morning always came, and in the earthly plane, the life of sin has much to recommend it.

We had a destination. We were heading for New York City to put Jack's simple dream to the test—buying apples upstate at five cents a bushel and selling them on the street for two cents apiece. The profit seemed good, but how many apples could New York eat? Apples were just the start, Jack said, Once the apples were flowing, we would add cider to the mix. New York would drink all the cider the Mohawk Valley could produce, Jack speculated, and the profit then would be astronomical. We would be the Vanderbilts of cider.

I was all for it; things were going so well for me (ignoring, of course, the damnation), I could believe it was just a stepping stone to even greater times. But here is some advice to those as young as I was: when everything is green grass and blue skies, by all means, enjoy it; but don't spend your time dreaming of the next harvest, instead prepare for the coming storm.

We headed east toward Albany, there to take a steamboat down the Hudson River to New York. Along the way, I believe we stopped at every tavern and roadhouse on the canal. I had even regained my taste for cider, though I had vowed, after the first binge, to never touch another drop. I had also developed a taste for ale and rye whiskey. I had resigned myself to a life of sin, and it seemed that every corner held an opportunity to pursue that life. I tried to express this sentiment to Jack, and she just nodded, saying, "Wait 'till we hit Watervliet."

Watervliet was on the west side of Troy, the eastern end of the canal—

end of the line for the men and boys moving the boats. The canal boats would continue down the locks to Albany and there unloaded, but canalers took their pay in Troy, and all but the most conscientious took the money to Watervliet.

I had grown used to the canal towns, each had a tavern or two, but for the most part, they were serious drinking establishments. I expected no entertainment beyond Jack's often quite entertaining yarns, and the bottle itself. Watervliet was not like any place I had ever seen. The town was nothing but taverns; I saw no dwelling there that did not serve spirits. Jack led me the wildest dives—with names like The Black Rag, The Pigs Ear, and The Tub of Blood—who were fighting tooth and nail for that canaler pay, offering music, loose women, gambling, blood sport, prizefighting, and all else that might be appealing to a man numbed by weeks of monotonous travel down the big ditch.

It was after dark when we arrived, and I was completely lost in this place, but Jack knew where she was going and led us into a tavern called The Peg Leg House. I heard the muffled noise of the crowd before we opened the door, but once inside we found a raucous celebration that, to my mind, we were only two drinks away from joining. Music from a fiddle and a button-box had driven the boys to the dance floor. A few had partners, but most of the men were just tapping their heels and gyrating to the rhythm. Jack and I bought ale at the bar and stood there laughing at the spectacle.

"Jack Horne," a voice boomed from across the tavern, "Is that Jack Horne?"

Jack tensed at the sound of her name, and looked around for a quick exit; there was none, and the man was coming closer.

"Lukas Ramsey," Jack called back, "You still on the canal?"

"I'm still canallin'" In girth, the man was as wide as Jack and I together, and in height, perhaps a foot taller. "But I see you surely ain't."

"I've had enough of the canal, Lukas, I'm following other pursuits."

"Your brother's looking for you, Jack," said the giant with a sneer, "He's really anxious to see you."

"Tell my brother to go to hell, and you go chase after him."

The big man paused for a moment, breathing heavily, then said, "I will relay those sentiments, and best of luck to you, Jack Horne."

He turned around and walked out of The Peg Leg.

"Who is Lucas Ramsey?" I asked.

"He's captain of the Queen of the Mohawk," said Jack. "and he's big trouble. I'm going to go see how big."

And she followed Lukas Ramsey out the door.

*

39

I had never seen Jack as troubled as she was when she left the Peg Leg House. It was clear from the man's tone that Jason Horne—by now somewhere west of Syracuse—was already aware that his money was missing. The news had traveled up the canal all the way to Troy, and that had to be bad for us. Just how bad, I would not know until Jack returned. I could do nothing but sit in the tavern and fret over the possibility that Jack and Lukas Ramsey were outside locked in battle. And even if that were the case, what help would I be?

The din and confusion inside The Peg Leg made it difficult to keep my mind focused on the problem. One of the boys thought he recognized the tune being fiddled; he stood up and started singing in a voice as loud as it was dissonant, driving the dancers off the floor. Some of his friends joined in while others began booing and hooting for them to stop.

Another group of men had entered the tavern, each carrying a caged rooster, and began setting up a pit in the corner for the bantams to fight. The birds seemed ready, flapping and crowing as they angrily eyed each other.

The fiddler had found another tune, unfamiliar to the erstwhile singer, and the dancing resumed. A lady approached me then and asked why I was not on the dance floor. I told her I did not know how to dance.

"Well, it's not too late to learn." She said and pulled me out of my seat. She tried to show me how to place my feet, lifting her skirts to show the movements of her own, but I ended up just haphazardly jumping as I watched her dance. It was a jig or a reel—something fast and bouncy—and, as the girl was wearing a blouse cut low enough to show the cleft of her breasts, my focus was drawn to her bosom more than her feet. When the fiddle played a slow song, she held me close and, once again, her astounding bosom was the center of my attention. After another fast tune and some more exuberant movement, we sat down, winded.

"That was a fine lesson," I laughed, "how can I repay you?"

"How about a glass of ale?" she said, smiling back at me.

I purchased two pints of ale, and we spoke amiably as we drank them. Her name was Elsie, and even in the dim light, I could see that she was somewhat older than I but very pretty, with fair skin and rosy cheeks, red lips and a head of wild black curls that fell to her shoulders. She asked what I did, and I told her I was a trapper, who had just sold his winter catch.

"And did the furs bring you much?" she asked.

"A bounty," I replied.

She seemed much interested now in making me aware of the gambling opportunities offered by the Peg Leg. There were men playing cards, with much intensity, at tables throughout the room. Of course, the cockfights would start soon, but those who could not wait were wagering on which of two cockroaches would be the first to walk outside a prescribed circle.

I told her I was not keen on gambling, but she persisted. Later that night there would be prizefights with the Bully of Rochester. Having recently defeated the Bully of Buffalo, he had declared himself invincible and would take on all comers. Some of the local boys thought the declaration premature and were prepared to challenge.

"Surely, you'll wager on the fights." She implored.

I was intrigued by the thought, but I knew nothing of fighting and had never before wagered on anything.

"Why don't I just take you upstairs, then?" she said with a wink, "That's something you can't refuse."

I wondered what was being played upstairs, but before I could ask, the fiddler announced that the entertainment was about to commence. A lithe looking man stood next to him bouncing on his toes; the fiddler introduced him as Davey, and the crowd went wild.

"What is this?" I asked Elsie.

"He's wonderful," she said, "you'll love the show."

Behind the musicians was a staircase to the rooms on the second floor. Davey, in trousers and shirtsleeves, took his bows at the foot of the stairs, as the crowd cheered. With flair, he bolted up the staircase but, when he reached the landing, a man came from the shadows and dealt him, what to me appeared to be a sound blow to the head with a hammer. Davey came tumbling down the staircase, arse over teakettle, landing flat on the ground. I thought him unconscious if not outright dead. But Davey arose, took his bows and the patrons of the Peg Leg cheered loudly and threw coins onto the floor at his feet. He bowed again, and with all humility, picked the coins off the floor. Then he queued up to do it again; once more up the stairs, once more a blow from the hammer, and another wildly dangerous tumble down the stairs. He bowed to the accolades, scooped up the coins and prepared for another ascent.

Again and again, he ascended the stairs, meeting the hammer each time and tumbling wildly back down. Each time is bowing to the crowd and gathering up the tossed coins. After the fifth tumble, Davey picked up his hat and ran out the back door. The crowd went wild, cheering, stomping their feet, and throwing even more coins. But it looked like Davey was not coming back.

"He never does more than five." Elsie told me, "He leaves the coins for the house."

The shouting and stomping continued, the crowd wanted more from their star and would not abate until the fiddler raised his arms and shouted that Davey had left the building.

Elsie grabbed my arm, and instinctively I put mine around her waist. "Have you ever seen anything like Davey?" she asked.

The whole show had me laughing, and as I was about to tell Elsie what I thought of Davey, When I saw Jack, from the corner of my eye, storming back into the tavern.

"Pratt, you idjit, I'm not gone ten minutes, and you're taking up with whores?" If there had been a fight, it appeared Jack fared well. I was, at least, glad of that.

"No Jack," I said, "this is Elsie. She taught me some dance steps and told me about the Peg Leg. There'll be prizefighting later."

"Sorry, missy," Jack said to Elsie, "but Mr. Pratt will not be available for prizefighting tonight."

"No, Jack, it's no trouble. Elsie and I were just dancing and talking."

"Whataya say, Miss Elsie," said Jack, with blood in her eyes, "can we let the boy down easy?"

Elsie, with a cold smile, stared at Jack for the longest time then said, "I'll do you both for a cut price."

"Not tonight, Missy we have ground to cover."

And as Jack pulled me out of the Peg Leg, I could hear Elsie call back, "That is a pity."

Jack hurried me through the darkness, away from the Peg Leg.

"My God, Pratt, " she said, "are you trying to tell me you didn't know you were consorting with a painted whore?"

"I'm sorry Jack, I thought she was just being friendly."

"I know you can't help being stupid, Pratt, but this ain't the kind of town where folks are friendly."

Jack was walking so fast I nearly had to run to keep up. She slowed down a bit to explain where we were going, or rather what we were running from. She had seen some of Ramsey's men at the Tub of Blood and heard them loudly discussing their plans to waylay a pair of canal thieves. Jason Horne had offered a reward for the return of his money, and the men were discussing whether to claim the reward or tell Jason to go to hell and keep the money.

"Fortunately for us," Jack said, "Ramsey's crew is just as stupid as you are. They're planning to get drunk and visit some ladies before venturing out against us. If we head down this road a little further, then into the woods, we'll be safe."

But she had no sooner said this when we were grabbed from behind by two of Ramsey's men, each as burly and strong as their captain. They held us fast while Ramsey came forward and met us head-on.

"Stupid, is it?" Ramsey spit, "Well who's stupid now, Jack Horne?"

"I know you're after Jason's money, Ramsey, and it ain't worth me getting kilt over," Jack said. "Let me hand it over peaceful."

Ramsey nodded to his man, and he let loose of Jack's arm enough for her to reach into her coat for the pouch. She handed it to Ramsey, who hefted it and appeared satisfied with the weight.

"Now let us go," Jack said.

"Not so fast, hoggee," Ramsey said. "That ain't the deal. Your brother wants the money and you too."

"Well, let this feller go at least." Jack nodded toward me. "He has nothing to do with this."

"Jason said there was two a ya. "

"No, no, that other poor fool was just a passenger running away from his people. After we jumped, he went one way, I went t'other."

"Who's this then?"

"Just some fool from the Peg Leg come out to ask me about employment on the canal."

"Why, this scarecrow wouldn't last a day on the canal."

"Exactly what I told him," Jack said. "He's got a whore waiting back inside the Peg Leg. He'll want to get back to that."

"Well if Jason Horne ain't gonna pay for him, I ain't gonna haul him. Let him go, Butch."

My captor freed my arms. I solemnly tipped my hat to Captain Ramsey and hurried back to the Peg Leg.

"Now let's find some suitable accommodations for Jack Horne on our return trip." Said Ramsey as his men led Jack away.

CHAPTER 7
A Midnight Search; A Hand from the Dark; Fit to be Tied.

Inside the Peg Leg House, the chaos and confusion had increased in my absence. The cockfights had commenced in earnest with all the ensuing cries and calls of man and animal. Bettors were waving banknotes in clenched fists and wagers were made with such speed that I could not believe that all would be honored at the close of the match. But sure enough, as the losing cock lay bleeding on the sawdust floor debts were paid with a civility I would have thought impossible in the Peg Leg.

I knew that Jack had not been serious about me returning to my whore; it was just part of the rouse to persuade Lukas Ramsey to release me. I looked for Elsie anyway and saw her sitting with an old canaller who was well aware of Elsie's occupation and just as happy for it.

The Bully of Rochester had arrived and had stripped to the waist, preparing to fight his Watervliet challengers. He looked frighteningly strong; a man would have to be very drunk to enter a boxing ring with this brute— and of course, quite a few were. The Bully was the only man I had seen in town who might be a match for Lukas Ramsey. But even if I could convince him to fight the good fight, and help me free Jack, he had a lot of business to take care of first.

I would need a plan much more clever and realistic than recruiting the Bully of Rochester as hero. There was no point in trying to follow Ramsey and his men, they would be vigilant, and I was unlikely to get close enough to achieve anything. I believed they would take her to the *Queen of the Mohawk*. I would need to find that boat, then determine how to free Jack, all while trying to navigate a town I did not know, with neither friends nor finances.

Fortunately, some of *Queen of the Mohawk*'s crew were drinking at the Peg Leg House, and as Jack had observed, they had a tendency to very loudly announce their intentions. The Queen was third in line to enter the locks for Albany the following morning. There was not a power on earth, they boasted, capable of preventing Lukas Ramsey from pulling his boat to the head of the line and entering the locks first. I now, at least, had direction—I must find the canal, find the locks, and count back three boats to the *Queen of the Mohawk*. There I would find Jack.

For someone familiar with the city of Troy, or someone conversant in the lore of canals, the goal would, no doubt, be easily attained. In my brief time on the canal, though I had traversed several locks, I did not pay close enough attention to now be able to distinguish a lock from any other structure on the canal. But well before that, walking in the dark with no point of reference, I could not even find the canal. I must have walked for an hour before asking a man on the road. He thought me daft and told me the canal was through the trees, just two rods to my right. I had been walking parallel to the canal the whole time and in the wrong direction.

I went through the woods and easily found the canal, then walked back along the tow path. Eventually, I could see the canal boats tied up for the night, waiting for sunrise, and the slow travel through the locks. I Walked further, past the boats, to the point where they could go no further, shut out by a huge wooden gate. This, of course, was the first lock. I counted back, and sure enough, the third boat back was *Queen of the Mohawk*.

At first, I thought the boat was quiet, and all aboard were asleep, but as I got closer, I realized a group of men were sitting on the roof, taking and passing a jug. They were extremely drunk, and I could not make out all of what was said, they seemed to be arguing over what was to be done with the money and what was to be done with Jack. They would be traveling through the locks all day, then unloading their cargo, then taking another day back through the locks, all before they started their journey back down the canal. They did not want Jack Horne on their boat that long; thought the prisoner too difficult to guard and too annoying to listen to. One didn't trust Jason Horne to pay the reward; wanted to leave Jack in Troy, split the money with no one the wiser. Another thought that plan would fail unless they murdered Jack Horne, and left no witnesses.

Between the drinking and the arguing, the men were too preoccupied to notice me climb aboard the boat go down below looking for Jack. The Queen was hauling grain, barrels and barrels of grain backed tightly side by side throughout the boat. Unless she was inside a barrel, there was no room for Jack here. I had read a story once about a man who hid underwater in a swamp, breathing through a hollow reed. Could Ramsey have Jack tied up in a barrel of wheat, breathing through a straw? No, that was far too clever and involved too much work for the crew of the *Queen of the Mohawk*.

I looked through the crew's quarters, under filthy bedding and among their wretched possessions, she wasn't there, and she wasn't in the galley either. When I was convinced that Jack was not below deck, I went above. There was very little room between the cabin and the gunwales, and I made sure Jack was not occupying any of it. Finally, I peeked up to see if the men on the roof had her with them. I saw all of them now passed out, sprawled around the jug, but I saw no sign of Jack.

I was starting to think they had her somewhere on shore and I would never find her. Then I remembered the perfect place to hide a captive on a canal boat. In the front of each boat was a small stable where the mules slept when they weren't hauling. On the *Mary Claire*, many times I saw the Horne brothers pulling the mules out of there, holding their tails so they wouldn't get skittish. Jack was in the stable or she was nowhere.

I hurried to the front of the boat; the stable door was bolted but not locked. As quietly as I could, I unbolted the door and opened it. Careful not to awaken the mules, I ventured forward to look inside. A hand shot out from the shadows, grabbed my collar pulling me inside. I lost my balance then; my legs were useless as my arms flailed about for something to grasp as my head was bashed soundly into the timbers. For an instant I saw stars shooting from behind my eyes, then all sensation was gone.

*

I awoke lying wedged between two restlessly sleeping mules. All was dark, and I was sure Ramsey and his crew were now holding me captive until I saw it was Jack wiping the blood from my wounded skull.

"Jack, what did you do?"

She held her finger to her lips and whispered. "Sorry Pratt, I thought you was one of Ramsey's men."

"Do I look like one of Ramsey's men?" I said as loudly as I could without breaking a whisper.

"I was cocked and loaded, Pratt. The next man through that door was going into the wall. Sorry it had to be you, but that decision had been made."

"Am I bleeding?" I asked, touching the sore spot.

"You'll survive," Jack said, pulling my hand away. "What's going on with Ramsey?"

"They're all up top, drunk, sleeping soundly."

"How many?"

"Three."

"Ramsey, Butch, and Stubbs Hennessey —he's got more, but they're probably drunk somewhere else," Jack said. "My plan was to take out the man who opened the door, then run away. But the man turned out to be you. With you here, Pratt, and them all asleep, maybe we'll stick around. Has Ramsey still got the money?"

"No doubt." I said, "I was surprised you gave it up so easily back at the Peg Leg."

"He would have found it anyway. I didn't want them big sausage fingers groping around under my coat."

"He doesn't know you're a girl?"

"I told you, Pratt, no one knows. Just you and my brothers. If Ramsey had found out, this night would have had a much different ending, much different."

"Well, how will this night end?" I asked.

"We're going to leave with our money."

"No," I said, "It's too dangerous."

Jack assured me it wasn't. They had been too drunk to tie her up properly when they put her in the stable, and if they had continued to drink—which I was able to confirm—nothing on earth would wake them. She coiled the rope they had used to tie her and hung it from her shoulder. It was much more rope than they needed to tie Jack up, which may have been part of the problem. We left the stable and climbed back on to the human part of the boat, then quickly and quietly, climbed to the top of the cabin. They were sleeping alright, all three of them loudly sawing wood.

"You get the pouch from Ramsey's coat," she told me, "while I make sure these fools will never catch us."

Jack got busy tying the rope around the sleeping bodies, while I crept, on hands and knees towards the largest of the three.

Ramsey was snoring so loudly; I was sure that any minute he would awaken himself or one of his slumbering crew. He looked, for all the world, like a sleeping giant from a fairy tale. I was wishing I had a beanstalk to slide down, as I reached my hand inside the giant's coat, looking for his gold.

Jack was making quick work of the rope, tying one end around Ramsey's leg, then threading it through each piece of stray furniture on deck, around the neck of Stubbs Hennessy, then tied the other end around Butch's leg. Done with her work, Jack stood over my shoulder as I gingerly felt around under Ramsey's coat. Not finding it on his left side, I switched to the right side and soon had my hand around the fat leather purse.

"Got it!" I whispered.

But no sooner had I spoken when the giant awoke and jerked upright.

"No you ain't, you son-of-a-bitch."

I held fast to the purse, ran to the bow and leaped to the ground below as Ramsey scrambled to his feet and tried to chase me. Jack ran to the rear of the boat, calling them a bunch of drunken cowards; Butch, now awake as well, rose to chase her. As he got to his feet, the rope pulled the leg from under him and with a thud, he landed flat on his face. The rope around his neck was strangling Stubbs; he tried to scream, but the cries were choked off as they left his throat. Ramsey was still on his feet, but when he tried to follow my leap, the rope caught his leg in midair and stopped him short. I heard the sound of breaking glass as his head hit the window of the cabin.

Jack and I ran from the scene followed by the screams and groans of the crew of the *Queen of the Mohawk* still tightly tethered to their vessel. We ran until we could hear them no more.

"We've killed them," I said when Jack and I had stopped to get our breath.

"Nah," Jack said, "they're alright."

But I was not consoled. I still had their screams in my ears as we lay down to sleep in the woods outside of Troy. We had left them in a bad state, and I was still afraid that one or more of the men might die. I was still under a cloud over the Scotsman's death; another death would seal my fate. It was the canal; I had to put it behind me.

CHAPTER 8

The Legend of the Canal Pirates; Judgment Day; Waiting for the End of the World;
A Burden Transferred.

"Ramsey and his boys go through trials like that on a daily basis." Jacks said when I expressed my concerns the next morning. "If what happened last night kilt any one of them, well, they was never a canaler, to begin with."

I would not have argued with that logic, even if I had any idea where to get a foothold. I was still afraid that I would be a murderer once more but saw no point in expressing my fears. Jack was not worried about stealing the money yet again, as long as we moved far away from the canal. It would be "towrope news," she said, traveling up and down the canal and it was best if got ourselves as far away as possible. We amended our plans; instead of heading straight to Albany to catch a steamboat to New York City, we would go north, into the Adirondacks, where no one would be looking for a canal thief.

We headed off on foot, at first through towns no less wild than Watervliet—Cohoes had a fine array of taverns for a town its size, Halfmoon, smaller still, was also a wonderful place to get a drink. Then further into the country, where a town was just a name given to the crossing of two roads, with a tavern or an inn or a general store, someplace a farmer might travel to buy provisions, have a drink with his friends, or share a bed with someone other than his wife. Each crossroads was smaller than the one before, and we stocked up with as much food and grog as we could carry, not knowing which crossroad would be the last.

A day north of Halfmoon we came across a copy of a newspaper from Troy, wrapped around a recent catch from the Mohawk River. We dined on trout and read the news. One headline stood out, and could not be ignored:

Pirates Strike in Troy
Lives Nearly Lost as Marauding Gang Loots Canal Boat

The captain of the canal boat, *Queen of the Mohawk*, reported to sheriff Malone, Thursday morning, that on the previous night his vessel was attacked by a gang of canal pirates who absconded with all the money on board, an estimated $400. Captain Ramsey said that the gang attacked the boat sometime after midnight and overpowered those on the boat. Only three men were aboard; the remaining crewmembers men were sleeping in Watervliet at the time of the attack.

"Had we been at full strength," Captain Ramsey explained, "we would have repelled the attack. But the thieves had us outnumbered, two to one, and our defense was not sufficient."

Captain Ramsey suffered server lacerations to the face when his head went through a cabin window, another crewman, Stubbs Hennessey very nearly strangled when the pirates attempted to hang him.

It is believed that these are the same marauders who robbed a canal boat near Canajoharie earlier in the season. Captain Ramsey speculated that they were likely headed westward again.

Jack couldn't stop laughing after reading the story. "Imagine, Pratt." She said catching her breath. "We've become a gang of six pirates, and tough as we are, we did not manage to murder Ramsey and his brave crew. Since we're now headed westward, I don't think anyone will be looking for us up here."

I thought it might be safe now to head back toward Albany, but Jack wanted to continue north a few more days, just to be sure. I think she enjoyed being away from civilization and was not anxious to go back. I was not so sanguine about the wilderness. The road we were on soon diminished to little more than a path through the woods and then, imperceptibly disappeared altogether, leaving us to find our own way through the forest. At night the hoots and howls of wild animals constantly interrupted my sleep, filling me with dread over the threat of pouncing wolves or wildcats. And I couldn't help but remember stories I had read about the forest Indians, who moved without sound, communicating by mimicking the calls of woodland creatures, and who had no mercy for white intruders.

The animals are harmless, Jack told me, and the Indians are long gone. But I still had doubts. I was glad when the rocks and ledge of the Adirondack foothills meant an end to the deep woods. We crossed a shallow stream, and a huge cliff of gray rock now blocked our way north and set our direction eastward. I felt somewhat safer with a wall on one side and increased visibility up and down the stream, though what I could do if I saw an adversarial man or beast, was still unknown.

As we walked along the flat rock embanking the stream, we came upon a depression in the stone, filled with ashes and burned wood; someone had recently built a fire there.

"Don't that beat it?" Jack said. "No matter how far you try to get from the human race, there's always someone just two steps in front of you."

We decided to build a fire there ourselves. The rocks and cliff would offer some protection, should the weather turn bad, and we had fresh water from the stream; it seemed like a good place to stop. I gathered wood while Jack took an inventory of our rations. We had nearly half a pound of bacon that would not survive another day's travel, and we had about a pint of rum that we had been saving for something—his appeared to be it. I used a flint to light the kindling and while we fed the fire, we passed the bottle.

"There's too many people in New York State, now; this proves it. Maybe Ohio is the place to go. That's where all the canal passengers are going—off to Ohio to start farming. Still a lot of cheap land out there without a lot of people."

"I thought we were going to New York City," I said. "There are more people there than anywhere in America."

"Well, you have to go where the people are if you want to make money." She said, "But once you've got the money, you want to get as far away from them as possible."

"You think you're going to get that kind of money selling apples?"

"Don't start with me, Pratt. I told you apples was just the beginning." She was shouting now. "We got to get the lay of the land first, find out who we can trust and who we can't, you know, who'll help us and who'll hurt us. When we know who's good and who ain't good, we'll know what to do."

Before I could respond, we heard a man's voice, thin but clear, echoing, apparently from within the cliff, "Hast thou come to judge me?"

Jack and I looked at each other in amazement; it was startling to think there had been someone within earshot our whole time there. While the voice didn't sound frightening, I was not convinced he wasn't a threat, and for lack of a better weapon, I armed myself with a large rock.

Jack stood up and called back to the rocks, "Who's there?"

"Hast thou come to judge me?" the voice was louder but still sounded distant.

She walked along the side of the cliff, looking for an opening and I followed. She came upon a fissure in the rock; narrow, but wide enough to admit a person. "I think he's in there." She whispered pointing at the crack.

"Hast thou come to judge me?"

"Come out here!" Jack shouted into the crack. "And speak English!"

What came out of that cave was more wraith than man. He was tall and exceedingly slender. His hair grew to his shoulders and his beard to the center of his chest, and each was so filthy and matted that the hair hung in rattails. Covering a body that was little more than skeleton and skin, was a long broadcloth nightshirt, which may have been white once, but was now frayed and blackened at the hem and stained and streaked from ankle to shoulder. But his eyes were the most starling—ivory orbs protruding from the shadowy depths of his skull, with pupil black as midnight; no color at all just huge black circles.

"Have you come to pass judgment on my soul?"

"Pass judgment on your soul?" Jack shouted. "Who do you think we are?"

He backed away, raising his hands. His motions were jerky and skittish, like a chipmunk's.

"You are that you are." He said solemnly.

"Come again?"

I said quietly to Jack, "He thinks we've been sent by the Lord."

*

We invited our new-found friend to be our guest for dinner, though, in fact, Jack and I were the guests in this hermit's home. He eschewed the rum but received the bacon as if it were manna from heaven—which he may have believed it to be.

Jack asked the man how long he had been living in the cave.

"Since the year of Our Lord, eighteen and forty-four." He said.

"You've been out here for four years?"

"Perhaps," he said, while enthusiastically cutting into a rasher of bacon, "but, since the Advent, I don't believe it is correct to reckon in earth years."

Jack closed one eye, and with tilted head scrutinized the man more fully. "That's it," she said, "it makes sense now. You're an Adventist. A disciple of Reverend Miller."

I had never heard of the Millerites—four years previous, I had little knowledge of anything outside the farm—but Jack remembered it full well and told me the story. Apparently, this Reverend Miller had used information gleaned from the Bible to calculate that the date of Christ's second coming was a day in March 1844. He took the knowledge to the people, with banners and tents shows, and on that fateful day, thousands of the faithful, a sizable majority of them living in the state of New York, who had sold their possessions and donned ascension gowns, gathered on hilltops waiting to righteously ascend into heaven.

As he heard it recounted, our guest hung his head in sorrow. "Yes, yes," he said, I was a Millerite, but as it came to pass, one of little faith." He raised his head and looked us over as if seeing Jack and me for the first time.

"My name is Hiram Abernathy, and I have waited a long time to tell my story." He had left off eating now and was intent on talking. In the evening twilight, Jack and I stoked the fire, and I for one was happy to keep the flames alive as something to look at beyond Abernathy's empty but imploring eyes.

"I owned a dry goods store in Halfmoon. I lived there with my wife and our daughter Grace. We were Methodists then, though we became something else, you may call it Millerite or Adventist, the truth needs no name. Some friends had acquainted us with the work of William Miller, who through faith and reason had used scripture to determine the date of Christ's second coming. My friends, my wife, myself, we all believed. We would sell our property, and on that day, gather together on the hilltops and await our ascension into heaven.

"It had all been worked out, I had agreed to sell the store for $1,200—though the inventory alone was worth more than that—and on that day we would all ascend into heaven together. On the morning of that great day, my wife and grace went along with all of our brethren to the hills outside of Halfmoon. I stayed behind to complete the sale and would follow when the property was liquidated. But when it came time to sign the papers, my faith did not hold. I could not sign the papers; I did not share the faith of my friends and family, not enough to lose my property. I went back home then and packed my bag. I knew that either the world would end today and I would be sent to hell, or the world would not end, and I could not face my wife and daughter.

"But as I walked home, I saw a rainbow to the north. And as I stopped to look, I could see that it was a double rainbow, and all around it was mist, and all the world was mist and fog but the for the astounding double rainbow. I saw myself, then, as a doubting Thomas, needing a sign from above, where others had faith that was pure. And now I had a sign.

"I went back to town to complete the sale of my store, but the buyer now offered only $600. But that only strengthened my belief in the world's sinfulness. I closed the deal, donned my ascension robe and went off to face my judgment. But I did not follow after my wife and brethren; partly out of shame for my lack of faith, and partly compelled by the heavenly sign, I instead walked north, toward the end of the rainbows. I walked north until I could walk no more, and here I have remained, awaiting the Lord."

"What do you suppose has taken him so long?" Jack asked.

"Oh, I suspect he started in places like China and Africa, to take care of Hindoos, Mohammedans, and other pagans first," Said Abernathy. "He will do the Christians last."

"What became of the $600?" I asked.

"It's hidden in the cave." He said.

"'It is easier for a camel to go through the eye of a needle than for a rich man to enter into the kingdom of God.' Mark 10:25," I said.

Mr. Abernathy gave me a look of sheer terror; his eyes grew extraordinarily wide. "Is that why the Lord has not come for me?"

"I don't know the mind of the Lord," I said. "only his scriptures."

Abernathy stood up and hurried back through his little crack in the cliff. He emerged a few minutes later with a thick leather wallet.

"Here," he said, handing me the wallet filled with banknotes, "Here is all my money. Take it; I no longer need it. Only my salvation is important."

"What of my salvation?" I said, feigning reluctance to take the money.

Jack grabbed the wallet from my hand, saying, "That's alright, we'll put this money to good use. You know, for the good of mankind in these final days."

"Yes, yes." Said Abernathy softly, but he had already lost interest in the money.

Jack and I thought it was a good time to take our leave. We packed up our belongings and said our goodbyes, leaving the bacon as a gift for Mr. Abernathy. He was appreciative for the bacon and also thanked us again for taking his money and removing a burden that he had not even been aware of carrying. We headed back through the woods then, knowing we would eventually hit a road that would take us to Albany.

You, good reader, who have followed my progress from Salem to Canajoharie and halfway back again, have, no doubt long ago passed judgment on my behavior and found my morality lacking. I have been living as a libertine, on stolen money, flaunting the laws of God and man, thinking of nothing but my personal comfort. And maybe your judgment is sound. But for me, it was not until I took that poor man's life savings, and made him glad to give it, that I began to see myself as truly bad. It was as if all the deception of Reverend Travis, all the violence of Ramsey and his men, all the larceny and meanness of Jack at her worst, came out of me in one simple Bible verse calculated to hoodwink the poor hermit. I was the devil quoting scripture, and I knew instinctively the effect it would have on Mr. Abernathy.

54

It was no longer a matter of theory and theology, it was beyond the old Scotsman and his unyielding predestination, I now truly walked with the damned.

CHAPTER 9

Return of the Canal Pirates; Yet Another Transformation;
Toil and Trouble, Sound and Fury.

Looking down upon the city of Albany from the hills to the west, brought to mind a beehive that one season hung under the eaves of the barn at our farm. The incessant activity in Albany, the people, on foot and in carriages, flitting from one place to the next, purposeful but without conceivable motive, was so like that hive; constant motion, an incomprehensible pattern that one interrupted at his peril. In the end, we knocked our hive down with a broomstick, into a barrel of water, killing all but the most restless of the bees. Albany did not fall so easily.

I was struck at how substantial the city felt. We walked through the downtown section down long straight streets with brick buildings on each side of the road, four and five stories tall. Jack was exuberant, talking without letup, revising her plans with every step.

"We've got the rhino, Pratt, let's go straight to cider. We'll go to New

York and surely find people ready to buy cider. That's where the big money is."

But before we did anything else, Jack wanted to find the best hotel in the city, take their best room and sleep on a featherbed for three or four days.

As we walked through the streets of Albany, the respectable people kept a safe distance away, sometimes crossing to the other side of the road to keep from passing us on the sidewalk. They seldom saw woodland creatures, such as we had become, on the streets of their city, and prudently kept a fair distance. As we moved through the city, I'm sure our smell preceded us; the personal funk of sleeping in our clothes on the forest floor combined with the smoke of so many nights of cooking fires had rendered us somewhat rank. I believe a blind man would have known enough to keep his distance.

Our outcast status made it difficult to ask for directions. Most shied away from us all together and those who stayed to listen thought their legs were being pulled when Jack asked after the best hotel in the city. Jack was starting to get angry, and I knew no good would come of that. When we passed in front of the post office, I was sure that would be our answer; if we asked in there they couldn't ignore us, and they had no place to run.

The post office was crowded with people doing their daily business. I counseled Jack on the virtue patience then left her waiting in line while I went to read the bills posted on the office wall. I scanned them quickly—horse for sale, temperance meeting, Mr. Johnson of Hamilton Street will no longer be responsible for debts incurred by his wife. Then one bill caught my eye, it was a wanted poster, offering a reward for the capture of the "Canal Pirates," including a drawing, from the waist up, of the two outlaws in question. The faces were too plain to recognize, but they were dressed as trappers; from the details of the clothing, especially the hats, they had to be Jack and myself. The dress that had rendered us anonymous in the taverns along the canal would mark us as outlaws in the city. I quickly but discretely pulled the bill from the wall lest some current postal patron might make the connection.

Then Jack came over saying, "Benment's American Hotel, on State Street, is what we want. And I also learned that Forrest is playing Macbeth at the Odeon."

I had no idea what the second part meant, and there wasn't time to ask. "Look at this," I said, showing Jack the poster.

"Damn me, if that ain't us," she said. "We have to get out of here."

The American Hotel was luxurious. The lobby had a high ceiling supported by Greek pillars; velvet drapes adorned the windows and around the room men in tailored suits sat in upholstered chairs reading newspapers or conversing with equally well-dressed ladies. In another room, I could see people pleasantly dining and men standing at the bar drinking. We somehow had to change our clothes and join them.

The clerk at the desk did not want to give us a room, for all the same reasons that no one on the street wanted to give us directions. He looked us up and down, and with his nose in the air flatly refused to serve us. But I have learned that in any business transaction, money will trump nearly any prejudice. Though we only intended to stay one night, we offered to pay for one week's stay in advance. He grudgingly gave us the key to a room on the second floor.

I thought our best course was to stay in the room all night, then leave before dawn and get out of Albany on the first steamboat. Jack had other ideas; she came back around to Forrest at the Odeon. Apparently the actor Edwin Forrest was performing at the Odeon Theatre in Shakespeare's play Macbeth. I had never seen a play in my life; theatres and theatrical people were not highly regarded in Salem. But Jack was quite enthusiastic about Shakespeare. She explained that when she was growing up, there were only two books in the house, The *King James Bible* and *The Plays of William Shakespeare*. That was how she learned to read.

"They both had good stories," she said, "but the people in Shakespeare, good or bad, always had reasons for what they did. That wasn't always true with the Bible. But both books use that high-tone English and if you can read that you can read anything. That's why I read better than Jason and Caleb can't read at all."

She explained that *Macbeth* was her favorite play and Forrest was the greatest actor in America, and she was damned if she was going to miss this. I was against it, but Jack was unyielding. Finally, I agreed but stressed that we must put on different clothing.

Jack had only one outfit, but I still had my preacher's suit and my work clothes from the cooperage in my carpetbag. My first thought was if I dressed the preacher and Jack the cooper, we could pass through the streets of Albany without being mistaken for canal bandits. But while Jack and I were both about the same size, her shape was considerably different. My clothes bound her so tightly in the hips and the breasts that she looked not like a man, but like what she was—a woman masquerading as a man. We could not go out on the street without drawing unwanted attention.

There seemed to be no solution; then I had a brilliant idea. "What if I go out and buy you a dress?"

"What?" she shouted, "You're insane Pratt."

"Think about it, Jack. What could be more natural than a man and a woman going to the theatre together? We can do whatever we want in Albany that way."

Jack fumed a bit but in the end, had to agree it was the only way she could safely leave the room. And I think she may have been more than a little intrigued by the idea.

"Get one with flowers on it." She said as I left to go shopping.

I wore my preacher's suit, and though it was terribly wrinkled, I did look somewhat more respectable. Believing it safer, Jack and I had divided up the money equally so I had plenty of cash to get whatever was necessary. I went to the shops on Market Street and State Street to see what they had.

Buying clothes for Jack was not as easy as I had anticipated. It seems that women who do not make their own dresses have them tailor made which would not work for me. I found one shop with readymade dresses, but the selection was small. I told the sales clerk (a man) that I was buying a dress for my sister. He frowned and told me to bring her into the store. I said I couldn't, but she was about my size. His frown grew deeper, and he told me there would be no refund if the dress did not fit. But in spite of it all, I found a dress I thought would work—striped but with flower trim.

I asked the clerk what a woman would wear under the dress, and he sent me to a store called the Temple of Fancy. It was huge, selling everything from furniture to soap. There I asked the same question of a female clerk who blushed but sold me a chemise, some petticoats, and a pair of drawers. I also bought a bonnet, a purse and a bottle of perfume. I was spending wads of money, but oddly enough, the strongest perfume cost the least, so I got a bargain there.

When I got back to the hotel, carrying an armful of parcels, I saw a policeman in uniform talking with the clerk. They were looking at a poster he had just hung behind the cigar counter—the Canal Pirates poster. It was not the same clerk who had checked us in, so I took a chance and went over to ask about it.

"Have you seen anyone who looks like this?" the policeman asked.

"Goodness, no," I said, "who are they?"

"Canal pirates, they've been robbing boats all season. They were seen in town this morning."

"Here in Albany?" I asked.

"Walking down State Street as if they owned the place. Post office said they were coming here."

"To this hotel?"

The clerk said "I didn't come on until this afternoon, so I don't know if they are here or not. They will have to ask Wilson."

Back at the room, I told Jack what I had heard, and she conceded that we were doing the right thing. She looked with bewilderment at what I had bought then commenced to putting it all on. When she was fully dressed, it produced another profound transformation in her. To this point, I had only known Jack as a women when she was stark naked. What stood before me now was a fully dressed full grown woman, a stranger that I did not recognize until she spoke.

"This is the nonsense I've been working my whole life to avoid." She said, adjusting her bodice in the mirror.

She doused herself with perfume and put on the bonnet. Then I put some perfume behind each ear. We walked arm-in-arm out of the hotel, and off to the theatre.

*

The Odeon Theatre was the largest building I had ever entered, and there were hundreds if not thousands of people milling around, waiting for the play to start. I could see why a secular crowd this size might make a city like Salem uneasy. There were people of every class there—had the streets not been so dangerous, our trapper clothes would have gone unnoticed in the theater—and I had the sense that violence could erupt at any moment.

But we were dressed well and had plenty of money so we took seats in the first balcony where we could safely look down on the restless rabble. The balcony was extremely disorienting for me, and I sat down as soon as I could. Above us was another balcony and protruding from the wall on either side were private balconies where the best dressed sat, safely isolated from the rest of us.

Before the play started, men walked the aisles hawking sandwiches and spirits, and I took the opportunity to try their wares. Painted whores in red satin, (yes, I could now identify them with ease), would saunter and sashay down the aisles, trying to catch the eye of any unattached man with some money in his pocket. I resisted of course, but I watched them in operation. They took the willing men somewhere in the back of the balcony and in a remarkably short time were back on the trail looking for another. This continued for the full length of the play, and I believe a few even visited the boxes where heads would occasionally disappear from view only to return moments later adjusting their collars.

They doused the lights in the house and lit them on the stage, and the play began. Three witches appeared on stage, and the crowd cheered wildly but I was a bit uneasy, witchcraft being a sore point to those from Salem. They cheered again when Forest made his appearance, dressed in an extravagant costume of some ancient nobleman. Throughout the play, the crowd would very vocally express their feelings towards the characters and the actors who portrayed them. If they did not like a character, they would hoot and hiss, but if they did not like an actor's performance they threw things at him— some, apparently, had brought fruit and other objects in with them for that express purpose. But Forest always commanded respect. He would strut across the stage and make his point, even when the language was, to me, somewhat obscure.

Forest was Macbeth, and the gist of the play was Macbeth murdering people around him so that he could become king. When Macbeth grew tired of killing people, his wife would get on him to continue. She was always making him do things he did not want to do, and I could not help but see a parallel between Macbeth's wife and Jack. Subsequent plays I have seen have had a similar effect—making one think of affairs in his own life. I believe this is intentional.

The play was quite exciting at first, but it soon fell into a pattern of speeches and murders, with the speeches becoming ever longer and more imponderable, and the murders less shocking. I left Jack engrossed in the drama and went downstairs where I had seen men drinking at a long bar as we came into the theatre. A number of men were standing there yet, no doubt as tired as I was of watching Macbeth's killing spree.

"It's not the murders I mind," said one man, it's just that Macbeth won't stop talking about it."

I asked for a glass of ale, and as it was being poured, I saw the canal pirates poster on the wall behind the bar.

"Haven't they caught those canal pirates yet?" I asked the man next to me.

"They must be in Albany somewhere; they were seen downtown this morning." He said, "I saw them myself. They must still be in town."

"Sure they're in town." Said another man, "They have a room at the American Hotel."

"How do you know that?" I asked.

"I have just come from there. The clerk remembers checking them in. They aren't there now, but the police are waiting for them to return. As soon as they walk through the door, those pirates will be arrested."

As I drank my ale, the men told me what they knew of the canal pirates. They had been robbing boats up and down the canal all season; got thousands of dollars. And they had committed at least two murders: drowned a preacher in Canajoharie and strangled a canaler in Watervliet. I knew we hadn't killed anyone in Watervliet, but it disturbed me that people were talking about the drowning. I thought that nightmare was behind us. I said that I didn't think they were killers.

"Oh they're killers, alright," Someone said, "When they catch those boys, the trial will be quick and the hanging soon."

I hurried back to the balcony and told Jack all that I had heard. We couldn't risk going back to the hotel; I said if they caught us, we would be in deep trouble. I thought we should go right away and find a place to hide all night near the dock, then catch the first boat out of Albany in the morning.

Jack was unconcerned. "There are two things I'm not going to do, Pratt: I'm not going to leave Albany without my real clothes, and I'm not going to leave this play 'til it's over."

So I sat there, for what seemed an eternity, completely oblivious to whatever Macbeth and his wife were doing, trying to figure out how in the world we would get our clothes out of the American Hotel while it was guarded by Albany police. The plan I came up with would require a little bit of acting on our parts, and a great deal of luck.

The first hurdle to overcome was just walking through the door. I wasn't sure how convincing our disguises would be in deceiving someone who was actively looking for us. But none of the police had actually seen the canal pirates, and they were counting on us to remain in our incriminating trappers' clothes. The police in the hotel—one in uniform behind the counter, one in regular clothes sitting in the lobby—looked at us quizzically as we entered the hotel, but did not recognize us as the pirates.

I suspected there was another officer upstairs watching our room, so we could not just go up and open the door. The plan was to check in again, this time as husband and wife. I tried my best to act older than my years, and Jack, in her exaggerated fashion—holding her purse with fingertips, waving a handkerchief with the other hand—was trying to act feminine. I told the clerk we needed a room for the night and would catch the steamboat to New York in the morning. He took a key from the rack for a room on the third floor.

"There is liable to be some commotion on the second floor tonight," He said, "but if you stay in your room, you won't be bothered."

"Oh, my goodness," said Jack, eyes wide, her voice concerned but sweetly timid, "will we be safe."

"Rest assured, madam; you are in no danger. We are expecting the arrival of two desperate canal pirates," the policeman said pointing the poster on the wall, "but we will have them in custody before they reach the stairs."

"Oh thank you, officer, you men are so brave."

The clerk handed me a pen, and I proceeded to sign my name in the register. I got as far as the "P" and realized that signing "Jonathan Pratt" would not be such a good idea, as I had foolishly used my real name the first time I checked in. Instead, I signed "Jonathan P. Travis" and for good measure added "Rev." to the front of the signature.

"Reverend Jonathan P. Travis," the clerk read from the book and frowned. "We had a Revered Travis here some time ago. He paid with counterfeit bank notes, took us for quite a bit."

This got the policeman's attention, and he scrutinized me closely.

"An unfortunate coincidence," I said, "I have been mistaken for this other Reverend Travis wherever I go. A common criminal, I don't believe he is truly a minister."

"You are rather young for a man of the cloth, aren't you Reverend Travis?" asked the policeman.

"I was called to the Lord at an early age," I said, "but I assure you I graduated first in my class at the seminary. My wife and I have been spreading the good news throughout the state, but it has sometimes been a trial having this criminal for a namesake."

They seemed to accept this, but I could tell that everyone was relieved when I paid for the room in gold.

As I had suspected, there was another policeman in a chair outside of our first room. He was reading a newspaper but put it down as we reached the top of the stairs. When he saw that we weren't the canal pirates, he tipped his hat and let us pass to the staircase at the other end of the hall.

We sat in the room for an hour or so before putting our plan into action. Jack had deliberately left her shawl down in the lobby as an excuse to go back downstairs. She went out to get it, and I followed behind, waited on the stairs out of sight from the second floor. The officer on the second floor had dozed off, but awoke when Jack passed. She explained her purpose, and he nodded as she passed.

Jack got her shawl from the lobby then started back up the stairs. When she reached a point where she knew she would be visible to the officer on the second floor, she made it appear that she had somehow gotten her petticoats caught on the banister. With her leg exposed well above the knee, Jack squealed for help. The policeman rushed to her aid, but it was a most chaotic rescue. As he reached to untangle the petticoat, Jack raised her leg, so the policeman's hand touched her thigh. She squealed and pushed his hand away, saying, "Keep your hands off me!"

"Please, Ma'am, if you'll stand still I can free your clothing."

But Jack did not stand still, and the scene replayed itself several times. Taking advantage of the confusion, I ran to our old room and quickly and quietly unlocked the door. Once inside, I rushed around the room picking up articles of Jack's clothing and stuffing them into her rucksack. Then grabbing my carpet bag as well, I hurried out of the room. Jack and the policeman, still working at cross-purposes, had not yet freed her petticoats from the banister. I quietly ran to the other staircase, up to the third floor and safely into our new room with all of our goods intact.

Seeing that I had made it safely upstairs, Jack allowed her petticoats to be freed from their restraint. The officer asked if she was alright. She told him, yes, but instead of thanking him, she chastised the policeman for taking liberties when she was in a helpless state. He stood back while she straightened her dress and walked haughtily to the third floor.

Jack and I congratulated ourselves on the well-played gambit, then quietly waited for first light when we left for the steamboat dock. The policeman on the second floor was sleeping soundly, and Jack could not resist taking the newspaper from his lap; he twitched a bit but did not waken. Downstairs all were gone or asleep but the uniformed officer. I hoped he would not notice that we were leaving with luggage we had not brought in.

"We're off to meet the steamboat," I said, quietly, with a tip of my hat.

"Safe trip." The officer said back.

CHAPTER 10

No Ladies at the Bar; An Elusive Queen; An Unscheduled Stop;
Rancor and Reflection.

"**I** have never been so happy to leave a place," I said, as we stood at the rail in the rear of the steamboat watching the buildings of Albany fade into the distance.

"They are mighty easy to fool, though," Jack said, "you have to admit that."

The boat left Albany at precisely 7:00 am. A great number of people, mostly well dressed, boarded along with Jack and me; even if the police had been looking for the Reverend Jonathan P. Travis and his wife—and I suspected they weren't—we could have easily hidden in that crowd. But I still did not breathe easily until they raised the gangplank and pulled away from the dock.

After bidding farewell to Albany, Jack and I went to the front of the boat and sat down to view the river scenery. The Hudson was at least a mile wide, and in the water around Albany it was filled with boats of all kinds—sloops, canoes, rowboats—but our steamer dwarfed them all. The engine loudly chugged along filling the air with smoke and soot, and sometimes the progress was not so smooth as blades churned up the water on both sides of the boat. But I got used to it all quite soon and began to enjoy the ride. Steamboats are preferable in every way to canal boats.

The scenery unfolding before us was monumental. Tree covered mountains sloped down to the shore on both sides of the river with thick

64

forest on each bank interrupted only occasionally by dock and landings of the smaller towns along the river. It all felt majestic and invigorating as if we truly were heading toward a glorious new beginning. We were dressed like all the rest of the passengers, looking just like an ordinary couple, taking an excursion down the Hudson to see the sights in New York City. And that is just how I felt.

I believe we could have sat there the entire journey viewing the splendor that was the Hudson Valley (and, as it turned out, it would have been the wisest course.) But the morning passed quickly, and Jack and I were hungry for lunch. We went inside to see what the restaurant was serving.

There was a bar along one side of the cabin, and Jack suggested we have a drink before lunch. I was amenable, so we found a place to stand. Jack put a foot on the rail and asked the bartender for a glass of whiskey.

"I'm sorry, ma'am, no ladies at the bar." He replied

"What are you talking about?" Jack growled.

"The bar is for men only."

"No ladies at the bar, Jack," I said, with a gesture towards her dress.

"Oh, sweet Jesus," Jack said and went off looking for a place to change her clothes.

I decided to do likewise and found a privy large enough to undress in. I was anxious to get out of my preacher duds, but I had no desire to become a trapper once again. I decided to put on my cooper's attire; a simple workman's shirt and trousers. It was a comfortable outfit with the additional benefit of not associating me with any crimes committed in the state of New York.

Back at the bar, I saw Jack dressed in her canal boy clothes. She wore her trapper's hat but left off all of the extras she had purchased in attempt to resemble a trapper. Jack had not made it all the way back to the bar; she had stopped to watch a man playing a peculiar card game. He had an umbrella open, resting on its side on the floor in front of him and was using the up-facing side of it for a table. I watched as he threw out three cards, face down. An old farmer who was playing the game picked one. Apparently it was the wrong one because he cursed and put up some more money to pick again. They played again, and again the farmer picked wrong. I asked Jack what it was about.

"It's simple. There's two black aces and a red queen. He mixes 'em up, and you have to pick the queen. This farmer can't get the hang of it, but I can find it every time. "

The farmer lost again and said, "That's it; I'm busted."

The card man looked at Jack, "What about you, sonny, think you can find the queen?"

Jack reached for a coin, and I said, "I don't think it's a good idea to start gambling, Jack."

"No time for religion, Pratt. I have an opportunity here."

Jack bet a quarter. The man showed us the queen, then started picking them up and throwing them down, attempting to mix us up, but I followed the queen, and so did Jack. She pointed to the card; the man turned it over and, sure enough, there was the queen.

"I told you it was easy, Pratt."

The man handed Jack a quarter. She bet again, and once again I knew where the queen was. Jack picked the right card and won. I could not believe how easy it was to win this game.

"Alright, two-bits, step aside now and let the men play." Said the dealer.

"You're not getting rid of me that easy," Jack said.

"Put up some real money then. "

"Does a dollar suit you?"

"That's more like it. Let's go." And he shuffled the cards again, and once again I was sure I knew where the queen was, and Jack picked the same card but when he flipped it over it was an ace.

"Another dollar," Jack said.

Once again Jack and I both picked the wrong card. The game seemed to get harder the higher you bet. This went on several more times I began to think we were not good enough for the dollar game.

"Come on, Jack, let's go get a drink."

"No, I'm going to beat him. He threw my timing off, but I almost had it that time."

They went again, and Jack lost again.

"I'm going to take all your money, boy, one dollar at a time." The man said.

"No sir, I'm going to get it all back at once." And Jack put up ten dollars.

Well, I could not find the queen, but I could predict the outcome of this. Jack continued to lose, but now at the rate of ten dollars a deal. I pleaded with Jack to cut her losses and come to the bar, but it was as if the cards had a spell over her. She had won before and would win again, and there was nothing I could say to change her mind. When she began betting twenty dollars a throw, I left her and went to the bar myself.

I drank whiskey and worried about how to get Jack away from that game. At twenty dollars a bet she would soon lose all of her money. I prepared for the fight we would have when she came asking for mine.

The old farmer who had been losing when I arrived at the card game came up to the bar and stood next to me.

"That your partner losing at cards back there?" he asked me.

"I don't know how much longer, though," I said.

"You know the man's cheatin' don't you?"

"That notion has crossed my mind."

"I don't know how he does it, but he can make those cards fall any way he wants and change them even after they're out there."

"It doesn't matter how he does it; I won't be able to convince my partner."

"Maybe you won't have to."

The farmer told me that although he had lost all of his money to the card man, he stayed nearby to watch. He said he had discovered a way to beat the cheater at his own game. He said there was a mark on the back of the queen, a smudge, maybe lampblack from someone's dirty finger, but worn away and faint enough to be invisible to all but the person who knew it was there. Using that mark, I could pick the queen with absolute certainty regardless of how he mixed them.

"It has to be one big bet, though." Said the farmer. "As soon as he loses he'll know something's up and stop the game."

"You're sure it's still there?"

"Sure it's there. I'd use it myself, but he already has my money. If I can't get it back, at least I'll have the satisfaction of seeing him lose."

I went back to the game. Jack was still so engrossed that she could not or would not acknowledge me. Ignoring the bets as must as possible, I looked closely at the cards. Sure enough one of them had a faint black smudge in the corner, and it was never the card that Jack chose.

Jack made her choice, and the man flipped the card to reveal an ace.

"I don't believe the queen is down there," I said.

"You insult me, sir." The card man flipped one of the cards and revealed the red queen. It was the card with the smudge on the back.

"Can you handle a three hundred dollar bet?"

Jack looked up then, "No Pratt."

"Have you three hundred dollars?" the man asked me.

"There is at least three hundred in this bag" I pulled out the bag that held all of my money, it was probably closer to four hundred.

"No Pratt," Jack shouted.

"I will cover all that is in the bag." The man said and started throwing the cards.

My heart was pounding, but I knew I could not lose. I would win back all the money Jack lost and put an end to this theft once and for all. The cards landed on the umbrella, and I scrutinized them closely.

"Take your time, lad. Don't act in haste."

And there it was. The card on the left had the smudge on the corner. I had seen that mark on the back of the queen, and none of the other cards had it. I could not lose. I pointed the card; he flipped it over.

"Ace of spades," he said, "what a tragedy."

"Pratt, you idjit!"

I was stunned. I could not lose, yet I did lose. I had trouble catching my breath. I thought I would faint.

"Pratt, what did you do?"

Then it came to me, all at once, like a flash of lightning.

"They were in it together," I said. "The dealer and the farmer were in it together from the beginning."

I looked around, but they were gone. There was no sign of the farmer. The card man had folded his umbrella and disappeared.

*

The tongue-lashing I received from Jack was, judging by the audience of gawking passengers, more extravagant and profane than the average steamboat debate. She called me every form of varmint I had ever heard spoken of on the canal and a few more I tried to remember to ask about later. She would not relent, and I could not respond. But eventually everyone has to breathe and on her inhale I took my opportunity.

"They cheated us both, Jack." I said rapidly, "The dealer and the farmer were in cahoots from the beginning."

This idea took hold. She was about to let loose another salvo but stopped, paused a moment then spit out, "Tell me what you mean!"

In a few words, I told her what the farmer had told me and why I did what I did. I told her it had all been a sham, played out by both men—from the farmer losing in the beginning to Jack losing in the middle, to me losing at the end; it had all been a script, played out by the two of them.

I could see Jack's blood rise and I was hoping the anger would not be directed at me. It wasn't.

"Then let's get those bastards!" she shouted.

They had disappeared from view, the dealer and the farmer, but we were, after all, on a boat in the middle of the Hudson River. Unless they had jumped overboard—and they were not that type—they were still on board. We agreed that they must have changed clothes and disguised themselves and we went looking for them amongst the passengers. To Jack this did not mean a quick look, she went eye-to-eye with everyone, interrupting meals and conversations, lifting hats and removing spectacles, making a nuisance of herself that could not be ignored by the officials of the boat.

We were confronted by one of the captain's men— I wouldn't know his title, but he wore a crisp white uniform with epaulets and gold ropes—who asked us to please stop annoying the passengers. This officer had the misfortune of coming upon Jack at the precise moment that she had decided that these men who cheated her could not have done so and escaped without the help of the captain of the boat. She pulled out her knife and demanded that he either produce the thieves that had taken her money or bring out the captain to pay back what was stolen.

He ran away then, but he did return with the captain, flanked by two surly men, each about the size of Lukas Ramsey. Jack sheathed the knife and began to relate what had happened to us, what I thought was the cause, and what she thought was the cause. Then she demanded that he return the six or seven hundred dollars that had been stolen from us.

The captain listened patiently and waited until Jack was finished. I think he was surprised by our youth and decided to give us some leeway.

"We have three choices here," he said when Jack had finished, "I can put you in chains and make you shovel coal until we get to New York, then turn you over to the police there; or you can jump overboard and swim away; or I can take the boat to Rhinebeck and let you walk ashore and we part company forever."

We took the third option. The boat pulled alongside the pier at Rhinebeck, lowered the gangplank, and we walked off the boat while the passengers stood at the railing and watched as if we were just another tourist attraction. They lifted the gangplank and chugged away.

Jack started walking up the pier, but I just sat down there on the edge, watching the steamboat sputter away.

Jack turned to look, "C'mon Pratt, let's get out of here."

"No, Jack, I'm staying. I'm just going to sit here, and stay sitting here, until I can think of a way to live my life where I won't be accused of theft or murder, where I won't have to disguise myself to go to the theatres or sneak down corridors to get my own clothes out of a hotel, and where I will never again have to worry about getting thrown off a steamboat."

Well, I guess Jack was curious as to what I would come up with because she sat down where she stood, about three paces behind me. We sat in silence for a long time, but I didn't even have to turn around to know that we had not yet reconciled.

"I still don't know what you thought you were doing, Pratt," she said at last, "bettin' all that money. There was more than three hundred in that bag, and now it's gone."

"I'd guess you lost about as much as I did, Jack," I said without turning around.

"But I was losing by degrees, how could you lose that much at once?"

"The game's over now, Jack, and I don't see the difference."

We were quiet again. I watched the steamboat as it turned out of sight behind an outcropping of rocks some ways south, leaving behind only the trail of black smoke that followed it down the river. Soon the smoke disappeared as well.

I don't know if I was serious about sitting there until the thought of a way to live, but I was surely not ready to stand up. In fact, I had no idea how to change my fate; it always came back to the dead Scotsman. The Lord got me here, and he could damn well get me out of here. And I guess, in his own imponderable way he did.

As I sat on the end of the pier running these things through my mind, again and again, I stared idly across the river. I noticed a sloop tacking lazily down the river, a small sailboat, one-masted, with a mainsail, a topsail, and a jib—yes, in Salem we know our boats. I had seen so many on the Hudson since Albany, like seabirds, lazily riding the river as if they had no purpose. But before long I saw that this one was purposeful, it was heading toward me. Time on a sailboat is not like time on a steamboat, and I knew it would be quite a while before I knew his intentions. Just as well because I had thoughts aplenty, off of the river, to occupy my mind.

Finally, the sloop came up to the pier, so close that I had to raise my legs to avoid getting hit. It was piloted by one old man who threw a loop of rope around a piling, pulled the boat close to the pier, then sat back and lit his pipe. He nodded hello to me, and I nodded back.

He smoked for several minutes in silence then said, loudly enough for us both to hear, "Did I see you fellers get off the steamboat here."

"Yes, sir, you did," I said.

He took a long puff from his pipe and said, "She don't usually stop at Rhinebeck."

"They stopped special to throw us off the boat if it's any of your business," Jack called out.

The old man nodded as if it all made sense now, and just continued enjoying his pipe. I returned to my thoughts; all the wrong turns that had brought me to this pier. How could I undo my steps? How far back would I have to go to find another course that would lead to salvation? The answer was easy; it was the moment that Mirabile kissed me. Had I then the boldness I later grew into, I would have taken her, at that moment, away from her father, off on our own to start a new life, away from blasphemy and treachery and all of the baseness that grows in the canal.

"What was you throwed off the steamboat for, if I might ask?" the boatman called up.

"For being robbed and cheated at cards," Jack answered, "and having the audacity to ask the steamboat operator for recompense."

"You played cards on the steamboat?" the man asked, and I nodded yes.

"There's blacklegs on those boats," he said, "you never want to gamble on a steamboat."

"Well thank you, mister," Jack said, "I wish you had told me that this morning before I got on the Goddamn steamboat."

The boatman was quiet again. I went back to my thoughts, but I could not get back to that fleeting moment where I saw a path to a more beautiful life. This was the hand I was dealt; there was no use in dreaming. I wondered if the Lord ever did lay out a life that traveled down a path of joy and beauty. At first, I thought, of course, there were many living a life of ease, but when it came down to cases, I could not think of any examples that did not come from storybooks. From what I have seen of the world, everyone, rich or poor, is struggling with something.

"I don't imagine that Rhinebeck was your intended destination." The boatman said at last.

"We were on our way to New York City," I said.

"As am I.," he said, "I am waiting now until the tide is in my favor."

This time I nodded back, nothing else to say.

"You boys seem to me honest lads down on your luck."

"That we are sir," I said.

"I have a proposition that may benefit us all. I have a considerable amount of cargo on board," he gestured to some wooden barrels on the deck, and I could see that there were more in the hold. "And I will need some help unloading it in New York. I will carry you to that place if you will help me unload."

I looked at a Jack.

"We ain't used to working for no pay." She said.

I looked back at the boatman.

"And I will pay you a dollar apiece." He said.

I looked at Jack again.

"Well let's go then."

CHAPTER 11

The Hole-in-the-Wall; Shanghaied; A Long Lost Relation.

.

he sailboat proved a much more agreeable mode of travel than the steamboat. The quiet alone had much to recommend it; the sailboat being free of both the incessant chugging of a steam engine and the inescapable and often dangerous babel of human passengers. There was no sound at all save that made by the wind in the sails. The boatman, laconic by nature, neither spoke nor sang as he worked the ropes and rudder. Even Jack was silent; no doubt she had as much on her mind as I did. We had not settled our differences, but there was nothing more to say.

The little boat sat low in the water, and it seemed to magnify the grandness of the wide river and the mountains to the east and west. It was a fairly straight route south down the Hudson, but the river did bend and turn around stone outcroppings, becoming narrower, then incredibly wide, past terrain that sometimes rolled gradually down from distant mountains and sometimes ended abruptly with tall cliffs at waters edge. We passed one such section of towering rocky cliff that looked as though an immense curtain had been drawn aside to reveal that the entirety of New York State was resting on massive stone pillars as if crafted by some great and ancient civilization.

"The Palisades," the boatman said, knowing that the scene required comment, but not very much.

The mountains and treetops to the west were so far above us that our sunset was hours earlier than normal and we traveled in twilight for the last leg of the trip to New York City. Eventually, the land flattened out, and the boatman told us we had reached Manhattan, with New Jersey on our right. At first, it was all farmland, but as we went further south, we saw more and more buildings until the Manhattan side was nothing but buildings, taller and more tightly packed than Albany. Even from the river, we could see carriages traveling under streetlamps already lit down the roads leading to the river. As we traveled further south, the buildings appeared to be older, with some badly in need of repair. We went almost to the end of Manhattan, stopping at the Liberty Street Dock.

"We will wait here until my customer arrives," said the boatman.

It was nearly dark; it seemed to me an odd time to unload cargo. The boatman explained that it was not hard unloading in the dark as long as he had his own men along.

"I can hire the dockhands here," he said, "but when I do, not all the barrels make it to the wagon. If I wait until morning to unload, the Daybreak Boys'll take a share. "

It was completely dark when the wagon arrived, pulled by a huge, heavy-footed workhorse. The teamster maneuvered the wagon to a position he liked and Jack, and I began moving barrels. They were quite heavy, and it took both of our attentions to roll the barrels down the plank without losing control. We then rolled them up another plank onto the wagon. The teamster gave us directions on how he wanted the barrels stacked, but would not lift a finger to help us. We worked by the light of a lantern, and in the shadows, we could see the dockworkers eyeing us with contempt, but we gave them no opportunity to steal a barrel.

When we had loaded the last barrel, the boatman came up to the wagon where he and the teamster slowly and meticulously counted each one. There were twenty-four in total, lying in rows of four: three rows on the bottom, two rows atop them, and one row atop the two. When both men were satisfied, the boatman signed his name, and the teamster handed him the money. While the teamster was securing his cargo, the boatman paid Jack and me the promised dollar apiece.

"Thank you boys, that was money well spent."

"Those barrels are heavy," Jack said, "can I ask you what's inside of 'em?"

"Cider." He said.

"Cider?" This got Jack's attention, "See, Pratt, I told you there was money in cider."

"No there ain't," said the boatman, "not for me anyway. They gauge me at both ends, and those in between rob me when they can. Besides, no one in the city wants cider these days. Anyway, I won't be bringing any more."

He lit his pipe and started walking back to the boat. "You boys want a ride back north?"

"No, we're going to stay in the city."

He stopped then, took some quick draws on his pipe to get the embers glowing, then took a deep puff. He looked at us both then said, "I couldn't help but notice some bad blood between you boys. What is it, a girl?"

"It ain't that," Jack said.

"Then whatever it is, I would recommend that you put it behind you. You're going to need each other's help here."

We thanked the boatman and bid him farewell, then started up Liberty Street.

"That wagon's moving mighty slow with all that cider," Jack said, "let's find out where he's taking it."

And just like that, without a word between us, Jack took the boatman's advice and buried the tomahawk. But I was still leery. We were in this strange and hostile city with just a dollar apiece (and whatever money Jack hadn't lost on the steamboat), and for the first time since leaving the canal boat, I had doubts about our chances. I got a bad feeling about the city of New York the moment I stepped ashore. The boatman was right, though, we would need each other.

The wagon was moving so slowly that we could follow it down Liberty Street at a walk. Jack was talking again, and she was talking about cider.

"I told you we could make money bringing cider down here," she said.

"Didn't you listen to that fellow?" I said, "He's not making any money. Everybody steals from him. Nobody here wants cider."

"Somebody just bought twenty-four barrels. That's who I want to talk to."

I said nothing. As far as I was concerned, unloading those twenty-four barrels was my first and last venture into the business of cider. I wished I had never left the Rhinebeck dock; for that matter, I wished I had never left the canal boat. I never should have left the Travises. Now that I knew I was damned anyway, theirs was a safer life of sin. And I could hear Mirabile sing again.

The wagon trundled down Liberty Street almost to the East River then up Water Street about five blocks before stopping at a resort called the Hole-in-the-Wall. We watched as men came from inside the tavern and rolled three barrels into the place.

Jack and I went inside. The Hole-in-the-Wall was so wild it made the dives of Watervliet look like church picnics in comparison. The people wore all manner of clothing, but with a sameness to it, like a rag-picker's attempt at fashion. There were sailors in uniform, and children in nightgowns, women lounging with their blouses open and breasts displayed to the world. All of them were extremely drunk, and everyone seemed to be in contention with someone else. Fights would break out sporadically and when they did a woman would come from behind the bar to stop them. She was easily six feet tall, and her skirts were held up with suspenders. She had a pistol tucked in her waist and had bludgeon on a strap hanging from her wrist. When a fight would break out, she would grab the bludgeon and strike one or both of the fighters. This was usually enough to break up the fight, but when it wasn't, she would get angry and take matters to another level. We watched in horror as she bit the ear off one rowdy before throwing him out the door. She received a rousing cheer as she returned to the bar and spat the piece of flesh into a jar already half filled with pickled ears.

"Who the hell is that?" Jack asked the drunk next to her.

"That's Gallus Maggie, and ye best not cross the line when she's watchin'."

Looking out on the hell on earth that was the Hole-in-the-Wall, I was hard-pressed to say where that line was. Just how did Gallus Maggie judge when someone had crossed it?

We purchased ale and found a table against the wall where there was little chance of attack from behind. Oblivious to the chaos all around us, Jack went on about the cider. The old man didn't matter, she said, what matters was that someone bought twenty-four barrels of cider. We knew we would have to make new plans when we hit New York, and that's what we were doing.

As she spoke, I saw a young man stride into the Hole-in-the-Wall. His dress was peculiar to me, but the clothing was clearly finer than that of everyone else in the place. He wore his hat at a jaunty angle and had a large sheathed knife in his belt. Many of the men at the bar hailed him as he entered and gathered around him like old friends. Just as many shied away, and left the bar for the shadows. Some even hurried out the door to avoid his eyes.

Jack noticed him too and watched as he called out to the man behind the bar who hurried to the call and stood nodding as the young man spoke. Then as if following orders, he and another man hoisted one of the new barrels to a shelf behind the bar. They taped the keg, pounding in a spout, then poured the first glass for the young man. He took a sip and nodded.

"That must be him." She said standing up, "That must be the man who bought the cider. I've got to talk to him."

"Oh, let it rest Jack, please," I said, "We're not going into the cider business. Now let's go get some food and talk about getting out of this wretched city."

"I don't care what you do, Pratt, you can go to hell for all I care. I'm going to do what I came here to do."

She walked up to the young man and got his attention. He looked amused at first, to be talking to this boy, half a head shorter than he. But soon I could see he took an interest to what Jack was telling him and before much longer they walked out of the place together.

I waited at the table, sipping my ale until it was gone. Jack had stormed off before but had always come back; by this time I thought maybe she wouldn't. I had not eaten all day and was exceedingly hungry. I still had the dollar, less the cost of one ale, and could probably find a place to eat, but I had to wait, I had to be sure she wasn't coming back. I had no idea how late it was, but the crowd at the Hole-in-the-Wall was down to half a dozen boys at the bar and a number of passed-out bodies at various points around the room.

"Well, me lad, ye must be new in town. Leastwise I never seen you at the Hole-in-the-Wall afore tonight." A man bellowed to me. I looked up to see a big man standing over me—big chest, big arms, fists on hips, but smiling. I felt he meant me no harm.

"Yes, sir," I said, "I just came to town tonight."

"Is that a fact? Are ye here all alone, then?"

It was the question I had been asking myself all night, and I was ready to answer, "Yes, I'm alone."

"Well now lad, have ye no family here in New York?"

"No sir, I have not."

"Why you sound like a poor orphan child." The giant said gently.

"I have never had a mother," I said, "and I have no father either, so yes, I believe I am an orphan."

He nodded then in sympathy then asked, "Have ye ever spent any time at sea?"

"I have been more than a week on a canal boat, and I rode two vessels down the Hudson this very day."

"Well that's more than most," he said quietly, then quite loudly said, "Young lad, I would like to buy you a drink to welcome you to the city of New York."

"Thank you sir," I said, "But I would rather have some food. I haven't eaten all day."

"Let me see what I can do." He said and walked to the bar.

The whole interchange felt peculiar, but I had a good feeling about the big man. He was the sort of fellow I would need on my side if was going to make it in this city.

"Sorry lad, there was no food. I brought you a pint of stout; that should be hearty enough for your appetites." He said, putting mug in front of me.

I took a drink. It was hearty, hearty and strong, but warming through and through.

"Drink up lad." He said, and I did as told.

But after only two draughts from the mug, I was dizzy and disoriented. For one brief moment, I was lucid enough to realize two things: there was more in that mug than stout, and I am a terrible judge of human character. In the next moment, I became another unconscious patron on the floor of the Hole-in-the-wall.

*

When I awoke, I was lying on a hard wooden floor. The room seemed to be swaying, and I thought I must still be drunk from the night before. But I had only drunk one glass of ale and just a few sips of stout; why did my head hurt so? And why was the sun so bright? I rolled over and saw there was no roof over my head; I was lying on the deck of a ship. The truth came rushing back—my drink had been drugged; I had been shanghaied. There were five or six other men lying on the deck as I was, and another man, a man I recognized right away as the man who had befriended me at the Hole-in-the-Wall, was kicking each sleeping soul awake.

"On your feet swabbies, your captain is coming to inspect you."

I was still trying to make sense of it, but the long and short of it was, I was on a sailing ship, and I could not get off. The man in charge was now herding us like animals, making us stand straight for the captain's approval.

When we were lined up, the captain came down to review us. Our captain was something to behold; tall and beefy, with a long black beard, and piercing blue eyes. His uniform was blue serge with red lining and trim, with gold piping on the lapel, and gold epaulets on the shoulders He wore a visored cap that was similarly decked out. But even without the uniform, there would be no question who was in charge.

He walked once around us, slowly as if reading each man's worth from what he saw, then said to our captor, "McDougal, this is the worst lot yet."

"There is a lack of quality men available sir." The big man was cowering before the captain; I took some joy in that.

"Yet quality men is what I requested, McDougal, able-bodied seamen. I hope you do not think you are the only man in New York upon whom I can call.

"No, sir. If you will look on these men and tell me who you will keep, I will replace the others tomorrow."

The captain walked around us again, then coming around the front he singled me out.

"Look at this one, McDougal, does this look like a sailor to you?"

"Sometimes them small ones are good on the ropes, Captain," said McDougal.

"Good on the ropes, we'll see. What is your name lad?" the captain said to me.

"Jonathan Pratt," I said.

McDougal smacked the back of my head and said, "You'll address your captain as sir."

"Jonathan Pratt, sir," I said.

"McDougal is your boy mocking me?"

McDougal smacked me again, "Stop mocking the captain and tell him your name."

"My name is Jonathan Pratt, sir, and I mean no offense."

The captain stood in front of me now, looking me square in the eye. "Are you saying that you do not know that you are addressing Captain Samuel Pratt?"

"No sir," I said, "and I apologize for the coincidence, but my name is my name, sir."

"From where do you hail, Jonathan Pratt?" he stood in front of me now, scrutinizing closely.

"From Salem, Massachusetts, sir."

"And what does your family do in Salem?"

"They are farmers, sir."

He continued to look closely at my face for a time then said slowly, "And might your father be named Aaron Pratt?"

"Yes, sir, he is."

"Then allow me to introduce myself properly, Jonathan, I am your uncle, Samuel."

Was the captain now mocking me? My father's name is Aaron and, as I learned the day before my departure from the farm, he did have a brother Samuel, but Samuel went to sea when no older than I am, and was presumed by all to be dead. Was I to believe that same child had grown to be the captain of this ship?

"These men will do, McDougal. See the boson for your pay." The captain said, then turned to me, "Walk with me to my cabin, Jonathan, we have much to talk about."

The captain's cabin was small but comfortable, outfitted all around with dark wood and decorated with exotic artifacts—statues and masks, weaponry from pagan races—no doubt accumulated on his voyages. He had me sit at a small table, and he sat down across from me.

"I sense that you still have doubts, Jonathan."

"I am sure you are right, sir, but it still seems unlikely that you are my uncle."

"Let me ask you this," said the captain with an air of confidence, "did your father marry Susan Heywood as has he had intended?"

This sealed it; how else could he have known. "She was my mother, sir. She died when I was born."

"I am sorry to hear that, Jonathan, Susan was a fine girl. And a boy should not grow up without a mother. Tell me, lad, did your father ever speak of me?"

"Only once, sir. He said you were sent to sea to save the farm. He thought you were long dead."

The captain laughed heartily at this. "And yet I survived. Yes, they sold me into seven years bondage aboard a Salem merchantman to save the precious farm. How they must have lamented to think me dead. A year at sea would be the death of many boys, but I had a knack for sailing. I realized from the start that your common sailor is a stupid lout which is why a captain's iron hand is required to move a ship. I knew that I was not stupid, and I used that year to learn every trade aboard the ship, from cook to navigator. How those men taunted me for trying to rise above my station, but by the end of that voyage I had become an officer, and those same men bloody well took orders from me. At the end of my seven years, though my master begged me to continue with them, I shipped out as first mate on another man's ship. The following year, as a young man, not yet in his prime, I became captain of a schooner bound for China. I saved my money and invested wisely when the opportunity arose, and today I own four merchantmen of my own. Though I am wealthy enough to retire, I love the sea so much I still captain my favorite of the four, the Eastern Star, the ship we are on now. So no," he laughed again, "I have not yet died at sea."

"But still, you must hate them for sending you away," I said.

"No, Jonathan, as I said, I was never stupid. I was the third of three sons; what was there for me. Even without saving the farm, my choices were few. I could have gone west as a freebooter or gone off to sea. That the choice was made for me matters little today."

As interested as I was in the captain's story, I was beginning to nod off, and he couldn't help but notice.

"Well Jonathan, I have business to attend, for tomorrow at dawn we set sail for the South Pacific. I can see you need time to recover from Mr. McDougal's mickey finn. It would please me if you slept in my cabin while I tend to the ship's business, then joined me for dinner. I am anxious to hear your story.

I accepted the captain's offer, lay down in his bunk and slept as soundly as I ever had.

CHAPTER 12

A Glorious Proposition; Moses' Law; An Unwelcome Guest; Thy Will Be Done.

We dined early that day, in the captain's quarters. When I awoke, I was ravenous. The captain, sitting at his writing desk, asked me how I felt, and when I explained that I had not eaten since the previous day he immediately sent for our dinner. The meal was splendid: beefsteak, potatoes, bread and red wine.

"I like to eat well when in port," the captain said, "At sea, soon enough, even the captain's meal is little better than salt beef and hardtack."

I devoured that meal as an animal would. Then, sated and renewed, I leaned back in my chair and profusely thanked my benefactor. It was his pleasure, he said, but asked in payment that I tell him my story.

And so I related to my uncle, the great Captain Samuel Pratt, the entire tale that I have related to you, dear reader, from the day I left my childhood home in Salem to the night I landed on the floor of the Hole-in-the-Wall. As can be imagined, he sympathized with my indenture to the cooper; it so mirrored his own beginnings. And he applauded my pluck at leaving that cruel establishment. But most of the rest just drove him to laughter. The man had the most wonderful laugh; it would well up from somewhere deep inside and pour out in an abundance of pure joy that he could barely contain. He was especially amused by the incidents involving Jack, even the ones that still frighten me. He was duly impressed at how we had hoodwinked the Adirondack hermit but thought it only fair that we were then hoodwinked ourselves on the steamboat. The Hole-in-the-Wall was a familiar story to him, but it pleased him to learn how I had arrived there.

"Tell me, Jonathan," he said after sustaining another round of laughter, "is your Jack waiting for you ashore?"

"She's not my Jack," I said, then thought for a moment, "and she is not waiting. I suppose I shall never see jack again."

"Then let me make you a proposition, lad." His voice taking a serious tone now, "I would not hold you as one of McDougal's men, and you are free to leave at will, but I would like to offer you a position on my ship. Not as a common sailor, but as an officer; I will make you my second mate. I do not usually carry a second mate, so you will not be pushing another man aside—though pushing a man aside is a good way to get ahead on a ship; pushing him overboard if necessary, but that is off my point. As second mate you can learn what you need to know quickly and I can teach you in the proper order. Though a man can learn all as a seaman, it is the long way around, and a hard life while learning. Not a life I would impose on any kin of mine. Starting out as second mate will save you years of trouble—should you aspire to a life at sea."

"I accept with gratitude," I said without hesitation. What was there to hold me in New York? What was there to bind me to land at all? This was my first opportunity for a life with clear direction, and I was going to grab it.

"Then let's drink on it." The captain said with laughter, pouring dark rum into two pewter tankards.

"How I envy you, boy, seeing the world for the first time." He said, looking wistfully up at nothing in particular. "I went first to Liverpool on my maiden voyage. Ah, the Liverpool girls love a sailor. And Hamburg and Amsterdam and Marseilles."

He had a hearty chuckle for each city as if remembering some pleasant moments.

"And Barcelona, the dark-eyed girls of Barcelona." Then he broke into song,

> Farewell and adieu to you Spanish ladies,
> Farewell and adieu to you ladies of Spain.

The song dissolved into rolls of laughter and could see the man's thought were an ocean away. I would have given anything for one glimpse through his mind's eye.

"But you'll be going to the Pacific, Jonathan," He said, turning to me then, "to Maui, the closest place to paradise on earth. The girls of Maui are not yet Christianized; they're just as God made them. They'll bring you fish and fruit, and dance wearing nothing but flowers and skirts of grass. And the slightest of nods will persuade them to shed their vegetation." And he was laughing again.

The captain went to his closet then and pulled out an old coat of his for me to wear. Though too small for him it was too big for me. No matter, he said, a tailor on board would make it fit and affix the proper stripes, and I would soon look part of second mate. The captain then wanted to show me where I would sleep.

Though it felt as if we had drunk and laughed all night, it was still daylight when we went out on deck. The men I had come aboard with were still working, down on their knees scrubbing the deck.

As I walked by in my oversized officer's coat, one of the men called out loudly, "Look at the captain's new pet."

This stopped the captain in his tracks, and all of his joy disappeared. He started baking orders all around, "Bosun, prepare that man for a flogging. Mr. Jenkins, fetch me the cat."

As the men were obeying, he said quietly to me, "The insult was on you, Jonathan. If you let it go unpunished, it will fester and grow, and you will never have the men's respect. You must flog him."

For myself, I bore the man no ill will. It was an afternoon for jokes; how did one more hurt? But the captain was adamant on this. The man must be punished, and I must do the punishing.

The sailor was stripped to the waist and tied around a pole with his arms in front. His legs were tied as well so that he was unable to move. The "cat" was presented to me in a bucket of salt water. It was a fearsome thing with a wooden handle covered with braided leather from which protruded nine leather "tails" each one about twenty inches long and knotted at the end. I was to use it to flog the sailor.

The entire crew was mustered on deck, and the captain addressed them loudly and ceremoniously, "For gross insubordination towards an officer, this seaman will be given Moses' law, the blows to be administrated by your new second mate, Mr. Pratt."

To me, he said quietly, "You are to give him thirty-nine lashes, Jonathan, and do not hold back."

Having never flogged a man before, and bearing no malice towards this one, my first lash was somewhat weak. The captain took me aside then to talk about it.

"Jonathan, that will never do," he said with quiet urgency, "you are to punish the man not caress him."

"But I did not really feel the sting of the insult," I replied.

"It's gone beyond that, lad. It is about discipline now, and there will be no peace aboard this ship until that man's back is bleeding. As you whip him, don't think of this man, think of someone who did insult you, someone who deserves the lash. Make his the back you bloody."

I took my stance and gave it another try, but this time, in my mind, it was Mr. McDougal, the man who had shanghaied me, who I was flogging. I hit with full force applying the blow that McDougal deserved, and I heard my target grunt with pain. I looked at the captain, and he gave me a nod.

I continued flogging the man as if he were McDougal for several more lashes then, changing the victim in my mind, I applied a few lashes to the steamboat captain who had thrown us off. Now I was getting into a rhythm. I switched my target again, to the men who had cheated us on the steamboat. I was in a frenzy of anger giving each man the beating he deserved. Then everyone I could think of who had impeded me since leaving home tasted my fury; the Albany police, Ramsey and his crew, everyone aboard the *Mary Claire*—the Scotsman especially for dying so stupidly. Reverend Travis for setting me to the bad. Pembroke, the cooper, and Pip for their cruelty. Then my father and my brother and the whole Pratt family for turning out me and my uncle for the sake of the goddamn farm. And finally Jack, for stubbornly and selfishly leading me down the wrong road at every turn received lash after punishing lash.

Then the captain stayed my hand. "Whoa boy, that's thirty-nine, Moses' law. We don't want to kill him."

I woke as if from a dream. The sailor in front of me was no longer standing on his own. He had been beaten senseless, his back cut and bloody, the flesh torn away in spots. Two sailors untied him and carried him away between them, his feet dragging behind across the deck.

Through it all, it was as if I had been in a trance seeing nothing of the sailor or the ship or the water or the sky, only the image of whichever blackguard was receiving my wrath.

"Well, Jonathan, that should belay any notion of your weakness," Said the captain, "You have done well on your first day."

He showed me to my cabin then. It was much smaller than his, just a bunk a chest, a table, and a small chair, but to me it was beauteous. I sat down on the bunk. I had thought that when my mind cleared, I would feel remorse for what I had done to the sailor, but I felt nothing for him. Instead, I felt safe and cleansed as if I had beaten back and defeated the vile beasts that had been chasing me and I was now ready to begin a new life.

I was the Second Mate of the *Eastern Star*, and I was on my way to Maui.

*

My sleep was fitful that night. I was so anxious for daylight and our departure that every creak of the ship's timber and every unfamiliar noise on deck would awaken me. But they were just stray sounds and each time, disappointed that it was still dark, I would roll over and try to sleep. Then I was jolted awake by a sharp sound within the room as if the door had closed. I sat up in bed, sure that there was someone in the room with me.

"Who is there?" I said into the darkness. There was no reply, but as my eye adjusted to the darkness, I could see a shadow moving in front of me. I said again, "Who is there?"

"Are you Jonathan Pratt?" a whisper came from the dark.

"Who are you? What do you want?"

"Shhh. Be quiet now and come with me. I'm here to rescue you."

"You're what?"

"I'm here to rescue you. Your mate, Jack Horne sent me."

Then I understood; it was Jack trying to take control of my life once more, and I would have none of it. "Tell Jack thank you, but I don't need rescuing."

"Come on. Look at you, boyo, you won't last a week on this ship. Get up now, and let's go."

"I'll have you know I am the Second Mate of the *Eastern Star*, and I don't need to be rescued by you or Jack or anyone."

"Yes, and I'm James K. Polk come for tea." He grabbed my arm, "Now let's go. It weren't easy coming aboard this ship and I ain't leaving it empty-handed."

I knocked his hand away. "I'm not going anywhere."

"Well, he said you might give me trouble, so here's some back." From the darkness, his other hand swung a bludgeon down on my skull, and I was out again.

When I awoke, I was once again lying on a wooden floor. It was a dark room that smelled of urine and mildew; not at all like the *Eastern Star*. I sat up and tried to get my bearings. My head was throbbing. I reached up and felt a huge lump, still sore to the touch.

"Pratt, thank God you're alive," It was Jack. She came to my side, squatted down to peer into my eyes and feel my wounded skull. "I didn't tell him to hit you, Pratt, just bring you back. I was afraid you weren't going to revive."

"What is this Jack? Where am I?"

"You're on land Pratt; you're safe now."

"My God," I jumped to my feet, 'is it morning?"

"The sun's been up for an hour," Jack said, "I'll take you for some breakfast."

I ran for the door, then out into a hallway no brighter than the room had been. I had to maneuver around sleeping bodies lying randomly around the hall, then down a stairway also strewn with sleepers. I ran down another flight of stairs and through another crowded hallway until I finally found a door to the outside.

I had no idea where I was or where I would find the ship, but I had to make it back. If there was any chance that they had not already set sail, I had to make sure I was on board when they did. I ran towards the rising sun, knowing that if I went far enough, I would eventually hit water. When I reached the piers, I looked for landmarks I may have seen from the ship. I saw a flag pole that looked familiar, but no ships docked there. An old man was stowing some gear in the shed, and I asked him if the *Eastern Star* was still in port. He turned and pointed out to sea. I looked and saw the *Eastern Star*, already halfway to the horizon. Frantic, I asked the man if it was possible for me to row out in a dingy and intercept the ship.

"Well," he said slowly as if pondering my odds of catching the *Eastern Star*, "if you start rowing towards that ship now, by the time yer halfway there, she'll be in dockin' in Chiny." He exploded into a derisive cackle, laughing at me far longer than I felt was warranted.

Completely discouraged, I sat down on the dock, leaning my back against a piling, and watched the *Eastern Star* heading out to sea. From my vantage, the progress of the ship was imperceptible as if she were stationary in the water. It seemed like the easiest thing in the world, just to row, or even swim out to that object in the water, but I knew the old man was right. It was like watching a clock; the stillness was an illusion. Though I couldn't see the motion, I could not stop that ship any more than I could, I could prevent a clock's hands from circling its face.

After a while, Jack came running up to me. "There you are, Pratt, I didn't know where the hell you went. What're you doing here on the dock?"

"Watching my only chance at happiness on this earth slowly sail away forever."

"What, that ship?" Jack said, "Listen, Pratt, you're no sailor. You may not believe it but I done you a great favor getting you off that ship."

Then slowly and dispassionately I told Jack about my uncle, Captain Samuel Pratt, who had risen to his high position from the same wretched start as mine, and who had promised to be my protector, benefactor, and teacher on this voyage so that I might someday become a great captain myself.

"But now it is out of reach," I said, "soon to disappear forever, beyond the horizon."

Jack sat down next to me, and put an arm around my shoulder, "Then I apologize, Pratt, truly. But how could I know? I only wanted to rescue you, as you did in me in Watervliet. How could I possibly know I was wrong?"

"It's alright, Jack, I hold no grudge. It is just another reminder of what I have known all along—there is no point in trying to improve my fortunes, the Lord has marked me as damned and in his wisdom has decided to begin the punishment before I even reach hell. You are just the agent, not the author of my misfortune."

"C'mon, Pratt, buck up. Everyone has opportunities in New York; let's grab ours and make some noise here."

I heaved a great sight, "No, Jack, I'm not staying in this city. I'm going back north to Albany, and I am hoping that, if I'm not arrested there for theft and murder, the Lord will somehow signal me whether to go east or west. That is the extent of my future plans."

"I can see how that might have some appeal," Jack said, "but, ya know Pratt, even the simplest of plans will encounter impediments."

"What do you mean?"

Jack scratched her neck, looked to the sky, closed her eyes as if searching for the right words. Then she said, "That fellow who rescued you—Slasher Dugan—has a policy of never doing nothing for free. In exchange for rescuing you, I had to promise that both of us would go to work for him, at least until the debt is paid off."

"What's his line of work?"

"He's a criminal; he runs a band of thieves. He thinks we're canal pirates and wants us to join."

"He can't make us steal," I said, "Come with me Jack, we'll get out of the wretched place."

"It ain't that easy," she said, "Slasher Dugan is a Dead Rabbit."

"What does that mean?"

"The Dead Rabbits is the gang that controls everything around here. If we try to leave, every eye on the street will be looking for us. We won't get two blocks."

Much of this did not make sense to me then, but when you are being beaten down by so many, it hardly matters who is throwing the blows.

"Well, there's my sign from God." I said, "I will stay here and be a thief until, in his infinite wisdom, he chooses to send me somewhere else."

"We'll get along." She said.

I nodded slowly. "Tell me, Jack, does this fellow know you're a girl?"

"Slasher Dugan is good at what he does," Jack said, "and in the criminal world, he appears to be a man of great vision. But like most men, he has trouble seeing what is right in front of him. Slasher Dugan thinks I am a tough canal pirate from upstate. That I was anything but a boy would never cross his mind."

CHAPTER 13

The Five Points Gangster; In The Tombs; A Lesson in Civics; And One in Theology.

Dugan was the epitome of a Five Points gangster—words that meant nothing to me when I first heard them but which soon took on great significance in my life. As Jack had told me, Dugan was a member of the Dead Rabbits, a gang of rowdies

THE TOMBS.

who controlled Five Points, the neighborhood where we now lived. He wanted us to call him "Slasher," an appellation he earned by slashing a rival's face with a razor, but everyone else just called him Dugan, and soon Jack and I did likewise. Dugan was about twenty-five years old, with side whiskers nearly to his chin. He wore a soft hat, cocked at an angle; his sleeves were always rolled to the elbow as if too narrow to house his massive forearms. Red suspenders held up his trousers and on his feet were hobnailed boots. Tall, strong, and quick to anger—as I can readily attest—Dugan liked nothing more than a good fight and would indulge in that pastime quite frequently, either man to man, or in gang fights joined by other Dead Rabbits.

He told us we could live with him, until we got settled elsewhere, in a building known as the Old Brewery. If there is any structure on earth more filthy, more vile, more vermin-infested; with more degenerates, thieves, and libertines calling it home, I pray that I will never see it. In earlier times the huge three-story building had served as a brewery, but now it was divided into single, windowless rooms. Sometimes three or four families would inhabit one room, their cook fires filling the halls with smoke, and their wailing babies interrupting our sleep. Young men ran wild through the halls, entering any unlocked door, and stealing anything not clutched tightly by its owner. From fights, beatings and rampant promiscuity, screams would resonate through the halls at all hours. Dugan had one room to himself and even had a straw tick to sleep on, making him part of the Old Brewery's aristocracy. Jack and I slept on the floor of his room.

When in a bright mood Dugan was not such a bad fellow. He shook my hand when I returned to his room with Jack, and he forgave me for putting up a struggle aboard the ship. Jack had convinced him that we were notorious pirates from the Erie Canal, and he was duly impressed by our reputation. It was clear that he hadn't the slightest notion that Jack was a girl; in fact, he no doubt thought her more a man than I was.

"Jack tells me you're a good man to have in a tight spot, Jonathan." Dugan said to me, "I don't see it meself, but I'll take Jack's word."

Dugan explained his business to us. He had a crew of four or five thieves, tough as he was, but not as smart, who would bring him a cut of everything they stole. Every week he or one of his men would visit the local merchants and offer them the opportunity to pay him tribute rather than have their businesses destroyed. He also managed three prostitutes.

"You'll see 'em stopping by at odd hours to pay me my due." He said, "You boys keep your hands off of 'em unless you're payin'."

"What about the cider?" I asked, wondering where that fit into his business.

He laughed. "The cider was but a whim. I got a cravin' one night for cider, having not tasted a glass since I left Ireland, but nary a dive nor tavern nor grogshop in Five Points offered cider for sale. I sensed an opportunity so arranged with some men upstate for two deliveries. Well, you've seen the second delivery, and we haven't yet drunk up the first. Sure they'll take the barrels as a favor to me, but there is a limit even to that. It was me own mistake, I'll admit. The city has thirteen breweries and at least three distilleries. When yer aflood with barley who wants apples? Still, if I ever gets the cravin' again, I'll have me cider."

He had somewhat less forgiveness for the mistakes of others.

We soon got down to business and Dugan explained what he expected of Jack and me. We were both in his debt for the rescue and for the privilege of sleeping in his room. We were to repay him by stealing and bringing him the proceeds; it was only natural, robbery being our professed occupation.

"How much must we steal to be out of your debt?" I asked.

He scowled at this. "Oh, you don't want me putting a number on it, boyo, it may be higher than you can count."

I could tell he had little faith in me and I was trying his patience. He proposed that Jack and I go out the following day but go our separate ways, each stealing what we can, then at the end of the day he would be better able to assess our worth. I'm sure he wanted to see what I could do without Jack's help.

So the following day Jack and I separated outside the Old Brewery and began our lives as Five Points thieves. It seemed an odd place to begin thieving with everyone in the neighborhood so poor. I thought of improving my chances by looking for a more prosperous neighborhood, but I remembered what Jack had said about the Dead Rabbits. If even half of the idle fellows standing on street corners, who eyed me suspiciously as I passed, were Dead Rabbits, I stood little chance of leaving Five Points.

I was not sure where to begin. Though by this point I could honestly say that I was a thief, my experience was really rather limited. In fact, the only thing I had ever taken from someone against his will was the money I took from Lucas Ramsey's vest. And that wasn't even his money. There were shops along Canal Street which had money and goods I might be able to grab. Occasionally I saw a well-dressed man walking down the street; I considered the prospect of snatching a watch chain and running. It all seemed too dangerous to undertake without a little planning.

I decided to start small, just to get the feel of the thing. As Jack had described so long ago when we first planned this trip, there were men selling vegetables and fruit from carts on the street. Crowds of people were everywhere, shopping or just walking briskly up and down the streets. I saw a cart piled high with apples and I thought it would be the easiest thing in the world just to grab one of them and blend into the crowd. I snatched an apple and turned away quickly, hoping to move unseen into the passing crowd, but I had not looked where I was going and bumped into a large man who pushed me away, into another man who knocked me back toward the cart. I lost my balance then and stumbled into the applecart, pushing the whole thing over, spilling apples into the street.

As I lay on the pavement, the owner of the cart began beating me with a cane and yelling at me in some foreign language. This got the attention of a police officer who had been chatting with a young lady by a dry goods store. He had a stick as well, and I was afraid he intended to take a turn at beating me. Instead, he pushed the vendor away and poked me in the ribs.

"On your feet, boy." He said, and I complied. "Did you do this?"

He pointed with his stick at the overturned cart. The apples on the ground had attracted the attention of dozens of barefoot children who grabbed as many as they could carry and rushed back into the alleys.

"He steal my apples!" the vendor shouted, with a thick accent.

"I'll take care of him." Said the policeman, and with an iron grip on my arm, he marched me to the police station.

"What have we here?" asked the desk sergeant when we entered the station.

"Stealing apples and me not five feet away." Said my captor, "Do you recognize him?"

Of course, the sergeant did not recognize me, nor did any of the boys in blue who seemed to be lounging idly at the police station.

"We've new ones arriving daily; brazen thieves, all of them," said the sergeant, "We should make an example of this one, thinking he can do his thieving within eyeshot of an officer. Take him to The Tombs."

They put me in a black police wagon, and we traveled just a few blocks to The Tombs prison. The Tombs was a huge building of grey stone, with four thick columns in front, looking like an ancient temple to a vengeful god. The policemen took me in a side door, signed some papers, and left me with a man of a different uniform who walked me to the second floor and down the aisle. The cells were against the walls of the building, and the narrow hallway in front of the cells had railings on the other side and overlooked the vast empty center of the building. The arrangement was such that a guard standing on the first floor could look up and see activity on any of the floors above him.

The guard took a ring of large keys from his belt and unlocked a cell door, shoved me inside and locked the door again. The cell was already occupied by a man in rags, sleeping soundly on the only bunk. I sat on the floor, my back against the cold stone, and waited.

Through it all, I had kept my mouth shut. I thought of asking the guard how many days I must stay in the cell, but I was afraid that, like Mr. Dugan, he would quote me a number higher than I could count.

*

Time, in the changeless world of a prison cell, very quickly loses all meaning. The scenery in the dark cell never varied. My cellmate slept silently, his face to the wall, as still as death. Through the iron grating of the cell door, I could see the other cells on the tier, a scene fixed and stationary like a painting on canvas. The random voices of the other prisoners, muted and unintelligible, were the only signs of life and soon faded into the background of my awareness becoming nothing more significant than crickets on a hot summer night.

How long did I sit in the cell? One hour? Three hours? A full day? I had no way to tell. Perhaps I had finally died and gone to hell and was experiencing eternity. In some ways, the timeless calm was preferable to the frantic and dangerous activity of my normal earthly existence, but not enough to mitigate the ponderous and unrelenting boredom.

At length, the jailer returned and took me from the cell and walked me out of the prison. We entered a narrow corridor with windows on both sides overlooking the city; "The Bridge of Sighs" the jailer called it. On the other side of the bridge was the criminal court building. We entered a crowded courtroom, and I was thrown back into the familiar din of worldly chaos. I sat on a bench to await my turn to appear before a judge who was meting out justice to a motley assortment of petty criminals. Drunks, brawlers, prostitutes, and thieves of every stripe were brought before the judge. Everyone seemed to speak at once until the judge pounded his gavel and read his sentence, which invariably sent the prisoner back into the Tombs.

When I was called, the officer who arrested me also stood before the judge while a city attorney read the charges against me. The judge asked me my name and where I lived. I told who I was and said I lived at the Old Brewery in the room of Mr. Dugan.

"Dugan of the Dead Rabbits?" asked the policeman, speaking for the first time.

"Yes, sir," I said, "I believe Mr. Dugan is a member of that organization."

The officer looked concerned, "And are you in the employ of Mr. Dugan?"

"You could say that, yes."

The policeman whispered something in the attorney's ear, and the attorney nodded.

"Your honor we would like to request a continuance of this case while we investigate the matter more fully." said the attorney.

"Granted." said the judge with a pound of the gavel. The next case was called, and I was returned to my timeless jail cell.

When next I was taken from my cell I did not cross the Bridge of Sighs, but was escorted out of the Tombs through the same side door I entered. Outside the door, the officer who arrested me was chatting with Dugan. The jailer handed me over to my arresting officer who handed me over to Dugan.

"Thanks again, Murphy," said Dugan.

"My pleasure," said the policeman, "just try to keep a shorter leash on this one, Dugan."

Dugan said not a word as he walked me back to the Old Brewery and into his room. He shut the door behind us, then smacked me across the face with the back of his hand with so much force that it knocked me onto the floor.

"What in the name of Chroist was ya thinkin', Jonathan?" he screamed at me, "stealin' in front of a copper. Didja even look to see if ya was safe? And stealin' apples? If there is any risk at all of getting caught, at least make sure the score is worth it."

Dugan continued to berate me loudly, and I could offer no defense. There was no way to hide my utter lack of experience in big city theft. Soon Dugan calmed down a bit and explained to me the complications my error had caused him.

"Dealing with the police is a tricky thing, Jonathan. They'll turn a blind eye to most anything if you make sure they get a cut, but there are some things they can't ignore. One is stealing right under their noses. Makes 'em look bad; makes the citizens restless. Complaints get filed, and the whole system gets a shakin'. I had to call in a favor to get you out of the Tombs, not to mention the embarrassment you caused me. Were the police so lax when you were on the Eire that you could practice theft in front of their eyes, or is there no law at all on the canal?"

I was tempted to say the latter, but I knew the question was rhetorical. I just stayed on the floor until I thought the storm had subsided. Dugan got quiet and, thinking the worst was over, I rose to my feet. It was premature; I was no sooner standing than he smacked me down again and continued screaming at me. This cycle might have gone on all afternoon had not Jack burst into the room.

"Look what I stole, I bet I outdone Pratt," Jack said. She was carrying a three foot tall painted statue; a woman in a light blue robe trimmed in gold. "Everything's locked up so tight in this town I was having no luck at all. Then I went inside the biggest church I ever seen, and it's just loaded with goods that no one is guarding. There's a box of money in there ripe for the taking, but I thought this statue would impress you more, the gold alone has to be worth something."

Dugan just stared at her, his mouth gaping nearly as wide as his eyes. He took the statue from Jack's arms and gently set it on the floor. Then with the back of his hand across her face, he knocked Jack onto the floor.

"Ya don't steal from the goddamn church, Jack." He screamed, "How big a fool are ya comin' in here carrying the Virgin Mary? J'ever stop to think there might be a reason the church ain't guarded? Everything inside there belongs to God and the priest and the parishioners and believe me; you don't want to get on the bad side of any of them."

"Well, I ain't Catholic," Jack said.

Dugan kicked her in the ribs.

"Shut up," he said. "Just when I'm thinkin' there's no one stupider in the world than Jonathan Pratt, you come through the door, Jack, with the Holy Mother under your arm. There is no way I can maintain my criminal operations in Five Points without the good graces of the police and the church; in one morning's work, you two half-wits have managed to queer me with both. Now I've got to go and make this right with Father Flynn, or none of us will be able to walk down the street in safety. You boys stay here till I get back."

Dugan picked up the statue and left.

CHAPTER 14

Students of Thievery; In Flagrante Delicto; The Badger Game.

The day after our disastrous first tries at stealing in Five Points, Dugan gave Jack and me lessons in big city thieving. He had come back from the church a changed man, ready to help us correct our errors rather than berating and punishing us for them.

"I had planned to come home and murder you both," he said, "and drag the corpses into the hall to be discovered someday by someone else. But Father Flynn was so

forgivin' of me, happy just to have his statue back, that I thought I should forgive as well. After all, it was me own fault, sending a couple of farm boys out to steal in the city."

He taught us then how to pick pockets. Putting on a coat and vest, he coached us on removing a wallet or watch from a pocket without being detected. We practiced doing a simple collision of pedestrians, taking advantage of the momentary confusion to dip into our mark's pocket. Working in pairs was also effective, with one asking the mark for directions and the other stealing his goods. When Dugan thought we were ready—and it wasn't long—he took us out to try it on the streets.

We boarded a Fifth Avenue horsecar—the car that carried the brokers and bankers between Wall Street and their homes uptown. When we were positioned in the full car, Dugan would announce loudly, "There are pickpockets aboard; my wallet and watch have been stolen!"

The men on the car would instinctually feel for their own wallets and watches to make sure they hadn't been robbed. With this information, Jack knew where to look for each man's valuables. She lifted a man's wallet, secretly handed it off to me, I got off the car at the next stop, and we were all safe from detection. Jack and Dugan got off then and took the next car back. I got on, and we played the trick again traveling in the other direction, this time with me stealing and Jack receiving. After several successful trips, Dugan took the wallets and left us on our own, satisfied that we were now competent thieves.

Jack and I soon became accomplished pickpockets, working sometimes together, sometimes alone. In addition to the horsecar, we practiced our trade at funerals, political rallies, restaurants, even outside the church on Sundays. Dugan had no problem with us robbing from churchgoers as long as we stayed out of the church itself. Whenever a crowd gathered, Jack and I would be there.

Dugan could not have been happier with us. We were bringing in so much money for him that he could let us keep a sizeable amount. We had earned his trust, and that of the other Dead Rabbits, and could now travel freely in and out of Five Points. Jack and I had grown close once more; we worked well as a team and also spent time together when not working. We would go to plays at the Bowery Theatre and sometimes the theatres on Broadway. Jack liked the Shakespeare plays best, but we saw melodramas as well, and variety shows that were little more than dancing and singing. They were just fine for me. Sometimes we would go for a drink in one of the big Bowery beer halls, or any of the Five Points dives. They provided plenty of entertainment, as long as we minded our own business and stayed out of people's way.

Things were going so well that I had lost my urge to leave the city. I enjoyed picking pockets and felt no moral qualms about doing so. It was like flogging that poor sailor on the *Eastern Star*, I was not stealing from these individuals, but from the world of people who prospered while pushing me down. I loved the danger of it as well. I was very careful about lifting the goods without getting caught. But in the unavoidable cases when I was caught, I was never again without an escape plan. I would disappear down dark alleys where no sane man would follow. I had become a professional thief, and it pleased me.

But if there is one thing I have learned from bitter experience, it's that when all is well, and your life seems nothing but clear skies and sunshine, take warning. The winds are about to change and storm clouds gather just beyond the horizon.

I came back to the room one evening to find Jack lying under the covers on Dugan's mattress.

"Jack,' I said, "what are you doing? Where's Dugan?"

"He's out," she said, "He won't be back for hours. The Dead Rabbits are fighting the Plug Uglies tonight."

The Plug Uglies were another Five Points gang, one of the toughest. They were all huge men, most over six feet tall, and distinguished by the tall plug hats they wore, stuffed with leather and rags, to protect their heads when fighting. They always went into battle heavily armed with clubs, brickbats, and pistols. Periodically they would fight with the Dead Rabbits, usually in Paradise Park, over some perceived insult or someone stealing a girl from an opposing gang member. The battle would likely rage for hours and, win or lose, the Dead Rabbits would spend the rest of the night drinking and recounting their exploits.

"Come lie with me, Pratt." Jack sat up and revealed herself to be naked under the covers.

"I don't think that is a good idea, Jack."

"Come on, Pratt, Dugan is gone for the night. It's been such a long time; don't you miss it?"

Well, it had been a long time, and I did miss it. And if Dugan was out fighting the Plug Uglies, we were not likely to see him until the following day. I took off my clothes and got under the covers with Jack on Dugan's straw tick.

Jack had been so thorough and studied in keeping her true gender a secret from Dugan that I, myself, had nearly forgotten that she was a girl. I remembered right quick. We had not shared a bed since our last night in Albany, and we went at it like alley cats. Jack's screams of pleasure as the passion mounted were so loud and forceful that, had we been anywhere but the Old Brewery I would have feared alarming the neighbors. Then, just moments later, we lay spent and sweating, side by side.

"We have to get out of here, get our own room somewhere," Jack said.

"Somewhere outside the Old Brewery," I said.

"Somewhere outside of Five Points, Pratt, in my opinion."

"I don't think Dugan will allow that."

"To hell with Dugan," she said, "We've repaid our debt—fivefold at least. If we don't leave him behind, he'll have us here forever. We ain't like those other idjits working for him; we're smart, we know the ropes. It's time to move."

"It won't be easy," I said, "It will take some care."

"I'll show you some care." She said, throwing a leg across mine and we were at it again.

Then, at the most inopportune time imaginable the door burst open, and Dugan bounded into the room. The sight of us lying together in his bed stopped him dead in his tracks.

"Jesus Chroist," he shouted, "What's this then? Me own men engaged in unnatural acts in me own bed!"

"It's not what you think," Jack said.

"I knew from the start there was something peculiar about you boys, but I didn't reckon on this. Just a couple of buggerin' sissies." Dugan came towards us with murder in his eyes.

"It's not you think, Dugan. It's nothing unnatural." Jack sat up then and threw off the covers. Dugan stopped short again, experiencing his second great shock of the evening.

"Sweet Mother of God, you're a girl!" He stood there aghast. "Ya been a girl the whole time, hain't ya? And I didn't see it. This changes things. This changes everything."

"It don't change nothin'," Jack said, "Tomorrow I'll be the same person I always was. Nothing changes."

"Shut up now, missy, I'm trying to think." Dugan stared at Jack, stroking his chin.

"Nothing needs to change, Dugan. I'm as good as any of your men, ain't I? Better in fact."

"That's what has me thinkin'."

"So I'll stay a boy; no one's the wiser."

"Lassie, will ya put your blouse on, please." Averting his eyes now, "We've business to discuss."

"I'm not whorin' for you, Dugan."

"Oh, there's plenty of ways for a smart lass bring in money short of whorin'. Plenty of ways."

*

As I have mentioned, Dugan had three prostitutes under his control. Red Maggie, Lily, and Bridget were all very nice girls, but each one was as different as imaginable from the other two. Red Maggie, plump and jolly, and so named because of the mass of wild red curls on her head. In the right light, you would swear that her head was on fire, and (as I would learn later) when her drawers were down you would swear the fire had spread between her legs. Lily was petite, under five foot I would say, with black hair and dark eyes. It was impossible to determine Lily's true age. She was probably at least as old as me but would dress as a schoolgirl or a flower girl on the street, appearing no older than twelve years. A surprising number of men—and wealthy men at that—are attracted to girls of that age. The third was Bridget—blonde, slender and stern to a frightening degree (there are men who fancy this as well.) Bridget was the oldest and managed the other two in Dugan's absence. She had known him back in Ireland and was the only person in Five Points to call him by his given name, Eamon. She saw herself as Dugan's girl, and would sometimes share Dugan's bed, sending Jack and me into the hall to sleep. They say Bridget had been very pretty before Dugan broke her nose, but I never learned the story behind that.

There was no fanfare when Jack's true gender was revealed; one day there was Jack, the boy, the next there was Jackie the girl. The whores were more upset about this than anyone, not knowing exactly how this change would impact their lives. They had always been sweet to me, but cool towards Jack, as if they sensed something was not right. Now that she was a girl, they were openly hostile towards her and even friendlier to me.

The night Dugan caught us in his bed was soon filled with shouting. Now that he had a new woman in his crew, Dugan began formulating plans for her. But Jack would not listen to any of his ideas; she was sure that whatever he proposed, however clever, would result in her ending up a whore and she would have none of it. Dugan pressed her to listen, but he had other matters to shout about as well. Now satisfied that no unnatural acts had been performed in his bed, Dugan became angry that we had used his bed for our natural sex acts and he wanted to slap us down again for even thinking of it. But in the end, all of these arguments led nowhere, so, leader that he was, Dugan suggested we all go to sleep and resume the discussion, with clear heads, in the morning.

The next day Dugan asked Jack if she had any female attire. Reluctantly she showed him the dress I had bought her in Albany. It had been balled up in her haversack since the steamboat.

"That will do nicely," he said.

"I ain't whorin'," Jack said.

Dugan patiently explained that what he had in mind was beyond the ability of an ordinary whore because it required intelligence and deception—qualities he knew Jack to possess. It was called the "badger game," and it involved a woman pretending to be a whore, and bringing a man back to her room. But before anything transpires, another man bursts into the room claiming to be the woman's husband. He threatens to expose the man to the police, or expose him to his wife, or just to beat him to death on the spot.

"Faced with those alternatives, you'd be surprised how receptive the man becomes to the notion of a large financial settlement," said Dugan.

"But I wouldn't do any actual whorin'?"

"Of course not, Jackie darlin'," Dugan said, "I've regular whores for that. What I need for this is a girl with brains."

Jack continued to resist, but Dugan was relentless. Finally, Jack agreed to try it once.

"Brilliant." said Dugan, "Now take that dress to the Chinaman to get washed and pressed. We'll get started tonight."

That evening Jack put on the dress, and we all went to a grogshop on Orange Street called the Diving Bell, where Dugan explained the details of the badger game. The game was very simple, but the hardest part for Jack was getting beyond her boyish ways. Though wearing a fancy dress, she would lounge in the most unladylike positions. Dugan had to school her on keeping her knees together and adopting a more feminine attitude.

"You don't have to be a proper lady, Jackie, but you don't want to scare them away either," he said.

Jack told him she had her own way of doing things and guaranteed she would have no trouble getting a man interested. In Dugan's plan, she was to find a man in Pete Williams's dance hall, further down Orange Street and bring him back to a room he had arranged in a nearby house of assignation. The dance hall was a popular spot among men who came from uptown to experience life in Five Points; "going slumming" they called it, and to Dugan, they meant easy money.

Dugan took me to a small and simple room on the second floor with just a bed, a chair and a little table with a lamp. In one of the walls was a sliding panel and Dugan showed me how to hide behind it to watch all that happened without being seen. Then he went downstairs to wait for Jack.

Jack was right; it wasn't long before she entered the room with a man. He appeared to be clean and well-dressed, at least by Five Points standards, and probably about fifty years of age. No sooner did he shut the door when he started embracing and kissing Jack. He had his hands all over her and was lifting her skirts, trying to get his hand under them. Then the door burst open and in came Dugan.

"What's this? What the hell are ya doin' to me wife?"

The man jumped in fright and pushed Jack away from him. "I didn't know she was your wife, mister."

"Did ya think she was your wife, the way ya were handlin' her? Maybe your wife would like to hear about this, or maybe I'll just kill you meself." Dugan raised a fist, and the man cowered in fear.

I think it was the gentleman who first mentioned money, offering Dugan a hundred dollars to forget the incident.

"I'll take all that's in your wallet." Dugan said, "Consider yourself lucky ya got off so easy for molesting a man's wife."

The man gave Dugan his money, showed him that his wallet was empty, then ran out of the room. He must have been a traveler, come to the city on business, for he left Dugan with at least two hundred dollars. Dugan had high praise for Jack's ability to hook a fish of this size. But lucrative as the game was, Dugan had no intention of spending his nights playacting; that time was already committed to drinking, fighting and carousing with the Dead Rabbits. He wanted to try the game with me playing the husband.

So I waited outside the house, and, once again in a surprisingly short time, Jack returned, arm in arm with a high-toned gentleman. He wore a tall hat and the diamonds on his watch fob sparkled in the light from the streetlamp;

I could already picture the size of the man's wallet. But when the time came for me to play the cuckold, I had neither Dugan's acting skill nor the imposing threat of his height and girth. I feigned anger and said all the same things that Dugan had, but rather than bargaining for his life and reputation, this man opted to shove me aside and bound down the stairs. I followed after, but by the time I reached the street, the man had disappeared, and I had no idea in which direction he had run.

"You just ain't got the stuff, Jonathan," Dugan said to me when I was back upstairs. "And there's nothin' more pathetic than watching a man attempt a job he ain't suited for. I'll get one of me other boys to play the husband."

"No," said Jack, "I won't work with any of them idjits."

Since revealing herself as a woman, Jack had been receiving unwanted advances from some of Dugan's men. She wanted no part of a venture that might encourage them further.

"Alright, we'll try another game," said Dugan, "Not so elegant as the badger game, but just as profitable. And well within Jonathan's ability."

Dugan taught us the panel game. I would hide behind the same panel in the wall that had shielded me before and wait until the man removed his clothing and got into bed with Jack. Then I would quietly sneak out of the wall, find his wallet, remove the contents, and return to the hole in the wall, sliding the panel back.

The game proved quite easy for me when we tried it; I came back with a nice wad of bank notes. But Jack did not like the panel game at all. In order for me to steal his money without being seen, Jack had to distract the naked man in the only way that made sense. And once my work was done, Jack would not be done with hers until her partner was done with his. What Dugan had failed to mention was, there is no way to play the panel game and avoid confrontation and violence unless Jack allowed the man to have his way with her—completely.

"I ain't doing that again," Jack said when Dugan came in to pick up the money.

"I don't know why not," Dugan said, "we're makin' some big scores here."

"You've got me fornicating with strangers, Dugan, and if that ain't whorin', I don't know what is."

"It ain't whorin' Jackie; it's stealin'."

"Well, they're still fuckin' me for money and I ain't doing it again."

"Sure," said Dugan, "I'll get Jimmy to play the badger game with ya."

"No," Jack shouted, "I told you I ain't working with any of your men. I want to go back to picking pockets. What do you say, Pratt?"

"I think it should be up to you, Jack," I said.

Dugan gave me a smack in the side of the head and said, "It's never up to the woman, Jonathan, you should know that. We're makin' too much money to stop."

"I ain't doing it anymore," Jack said.

"You are. That's final." Dugan said.

Jack gave me an imploring look as if I should stand up to Dugan and put a stop to this. Then Dugan looked at me too, standing with his fists on his hips, waiting to see what I might try. But what could I do? If I put up a fight, Dugan would just knock me down again and get what he wanted anyway. I just looked at the floor.

"Fine." Jack said at last, "But I'll do the stealing myself. I don't want you or Jimmy or Pratt or anyone else in the room with me."

And that was how it started. Though she always called it stealing, and she never associated with any of Dugan's prostitutes, Jack had become what she had vowed she would not. Dugan had made her a whore, and I had done nothing to stop it.

CHAPTER 15

New Accommodations; The Wall Street Speculator; Pipe Dreams; A Battle, Biblical.

My world turned upside down in the days that followed. Jack was so upset that she would not even speak to me; not like the other times, now it was real and final. And I was not surprised; I had let her down, I had not done anything to stop that brute from starting her down a road she vowed she would never take. What did astonish me was that, soon after, Jack took up with Dugan—she became his girl, and it appeared to be her idea. They began sleeping together most nights, and I was relegated to the hall, but I could still hear the lovemaking as well as the arguments which sometimes ended violently.

What I should have done that night on Orange Street, was tell Dugan that I would not let Jack be his whore. He would have knocked me down of course, but it probably would have ended with one blow. One blow would have been enough to keep Jack on my side, then the following day I would have taken her out of that wretched city forever. But I had been too frightened to take that one blow and consequently Jack began another life that could not include me.

Dugan's prostitutes were livid, of course. This woman who had come from nowhere, had been a boy just days before, was now in a position of power and intimate with their manager. Bridget always carried a razor and, without question, was ready to cut Jack's throat if they were ever alone together.

But the girls took pity on me, another victim of this situation, and allowed me to stay in the room they shared on the third floor of the Old Brewery. Their room was cleaner than Dugan's, with pictures on the wall, and flowers, sometimes, on the table. They had a pallet that they shared but very seldom were all three in the room at the same time. They never brought the customers back to their room, there were other rooms for that, and sometimes they just did their business in the ally. My schedule being the opposite of theirs, I usually got the mattress to myself. But not always, and in spite of Dugan's admonitions, whenever I shared the bed with one of them, she would graciously bestow her charms free of charge.

It took about a week of turmoil, but this new situation eventually became normal and, as much as possible, accepted by all involved. During that time I had no contact at all with Jack or Dugan, then one evening Dugan came to talk to me. He was sufficiently humble; knowing he had bested me and taken away something of value, he felt no need to lord it over me. He had come to ask me a favor which had nothing at all to do with Jack.

"I have a business associate on Wall Street," he said, "a Mr. Thayer who pays me to guarantee his establishment won't be robbed. Mr. Thayer lives up around 40th Street, and every day he passes Five Points on his way to work. Well, like so many of his class, Thayer is curious about what goes on here after the sun goes down. He wants to do a night of slummin', but he's afraid to come down here alone. I'd escort the man meself, but it's the same night we'll be fightin' the Bowery Boys. I was wonderin' you'd be available, Jonathan, to give Mr. Thayer a night on the town. He pays well, and it would all go to you."

A battle with the Bowery Boys (which everyone pronounced Bowery B'hoys) was a dire and momentous occasion. All of the Irish gangs, regardless of how they felt about each other, would band together to fight against their collective enemy, the Bowery Boys, who viewed themselves as true native-born Americans and resented the rising power of the immigrant gangs. For me as an outsider, there was not a nickel's worth of difference between these two groups of idlers, wastrels, and thieves, but each side kept a tally of the other's petty insults and transgressions, and when their cards were full there was nothing left but warfare. When Dugan mentioned the battle with the Bowery Boys, I was relieved that he had not come to enlist me to fight. I agreed to escort Thayer around Five Points, but I was unclear exactly what I was expected to do.

"Just the usual," Dugan said, "show him the dancehalls and the dives, get him drunk, get him fucked, then put him in a hack heading back uptown. Beyond that, just do whatever he asks for."

That evening I put on my preacher's suit, wanting to make a good impression on Mr. Thayer, who, judging from the addresses of his home and his place of business, was a man of means. I was to meet him on the corner of Cross and Orange at 7:00; it would be a long night, but I would be paid accordingly. Dugan said he would be wearing a carnation in his lapel so that I would recognize him. But I didn't need the flower; when I saw a man step out of the hackney, his impeccably dressed in a perfectly tailored suit and top hat, I knew it had to be Thayer. He was in his thirties, I would say, wearing a neatly trimmed beard and mustache, and carrying a walking stick. He seemed a bit flighty, I thought, but not out of fear; it was more as if he worried that in looking one direction he would miss something in the other.

When I went up and introduced myself, he was exuberantly glad to see me and shook my hand with both of his. He told me he was ready to experience all of Five Points, and I said I would do my best to make that happen.

I had in mind several local resorts to show Mr. Thayer, but he arrived already prepared with a full list of places he wanted to see. From reading the papers, and discussing with other men, he said, he was fully conversant in Five Points nightlife. When he suggested John Allen's dancehall on Water Street, I thought maybe he meant to make an early night of it, and bed down with one of the whores there. Allen had an army of cheap girls in fancy clothes—black satin bodices, and red silk stockings, red-tipped boots with bells on the ankles. Thayer took a couple of spins on the dance floor and had a jolly time at that, but after a few drinks there he suggested we go to Yankee Sullivan's, and maybe catch a glimpse of the famous pugilist.

Sullivan, of course, was not there, and with the Dead Rabbits off preparing for battle, his place was quiet that night. We stood at the bar and drank whiskey. Thayer asked me how I liked working for Dugan. I lied and said I liked it just fine. When he asked exactly what I did for Dugan, I turned it around and asked about his job, knowing that nine times out of ten a man would rather talk about his own work than someone else's. He told me he was a Wall Street broker and speculator.

"You're the man my father blames for all his troubles," I said.

Thayer chuckled. "He is not alone in that. What is your father's occupation?"

"He's a farmer."

"Ah." He said and nodded his head knowingly.

"Tell me something, Mr. Thayer," I said, "just how would someone like you in New York trouble my father in Massachusetts?"

"It's all misunderstanding." he said, "I'll put it simply; farming is risky business. To add some certainty, a farmer will sign a paper to sell his crops at a fixed price in the spring before they are even planted. He knows exactly what he'll get for his crops. But if the price is higher at harvest time, they feel we have cheated them. They want it both ways."

"Then what do you do with the crops?"

He chuckled again. "We never see the crops. We wait for a better price then sell the paper to someone who deals in that sort of thing,"

"I think I see," I said, "It balances out because if the price is lower at harvest time, you lose money."

This really made him laugh, "We never lose money, Jonathan."

He tried to explain the nature of the deals he did, putting things together and taking them apart and doing it all with someone else's money. I did not follow most of it, but I was left with the impression that maybe my father was right, and respectable as this man was, his dealings were no less shady than Dugan's.

All the talk of speculation had set his mind on gambling and Thayer suggested we go next to Kit Burn's Sportsmen's Hall. Kit Burn's place featured dog fighting and similar spectacles for the purpose of betting. My only attempt at gambling, the card game on the riverboat, had ended badly enough to cure me of that curse for life. Since I didn't gamble or share the typical Five Pointer's love of blood sport, I seldom went to Kit Burn's. But Dugan said to do what Thayer wanted, so that is where we went.

We joined a crowd packed tightly around the rat-pit, so called because the amusement there often involved betting on which of several terriers could kill the most rats while the crowd looked on. That night, though, it was straight dog fighting—betting on which of two dogs would win a fight to the death. When I told Thayer I didn't gamble, he gave me money to bet so I could join in the fun anyway. I just bet on the same dogs he did. Either Thayer was a very lucky man, or he had some knowledge of dogs, for we won every bet. I sensed that Thayer was not a man who relied on luck.

The sport was as brutal as you can imagine, and beyond the betting, the sight of two dogs tearing the flesh off of each other until one lay motionless in a pool of his own blood, seemed to rile the blood of all who watched. Arguments over wagers turned into fistfights, and when one bettor stabbed another, Thayer and I joined the crowd rushing out the door lest we were stuck inside when the guns came out.

When we were back on the street, I thought maybe it would be time to find Thayer a girl and finish off his adventure. We had been drinking whiskey all night and feared that if he drank much more, a girl would do him no good. But Thayer had his own ideas.

"There is something I have read about and have always been curious to try." He said, "I understand that opium is available somewhere in the Five Points."

This was a surprise. I knew less about opium than I did about gambling. I knew there were some Chinese in Five Points who dealt in the stuff, but I did not know where to look. Thayer knew the way, though. He led lead me straight to a door on Mott Street with a hand-drawn sign in Chinese characters. We went through the door and into a dark hall where we were met by a Chinaman in silk pajamas with a long black braid down his back. No words were spoken; little communication was necessary. Thayer paid some money, and the man pulled aside a curtain, gesturing us to walk through.

He wasn't fooling me; Thayer had been there before.

*

Of all the vile dives I entered in the City of New York, none was so hellish as the opium joint where Thayer led me. The room was dimly lit, but tiny oil lamps, seemly placed at random points, revealed tiers of smoke swirling throughout the room. The smell was thick and musky, unlike anything I had ever experienced. As my eyes adjusted to the light, I could see bodies lying on the floor and in shallow bunks, three high against the walls. There were men and women; Chinese, white and black all lying together, and each with a lamp and a long pipe.

Thayer and I sat down on mats on the floor, and the Chinaman brought us a tray with a lamp, a pipe and other tools, and gave each of us a small ball of a black, tar-like substance—the opium. Thayer showed me how to prepare it for smoking, holding it first over a flame, then into the bowl of a long wooden pipe—performing each step with a solemn intensity as if it were a sacred ritual.

I coughed on my first draw from the pipe but quickly took another. The amount of opium was not large, and in just a few puffs it was gone. The effects were dramatic and almost instantaneous. A warmth spread through all parts of my body, and I had a sense of relaxed well-being I had never felt before. The room and its occupants, which moments before had filled me with disgust, now appeared as a picture of earthly perfection. This was exactly where I was meant to be at this holy moment.

I closed my eyes, and the rolling of my thoughts soon became a ship rolling over the ocean. It was the *Eastern Star*, bound for Maui, and I had been shanghaied again. But now I was alone on the deck; there was no captain, no crew, just myself and the seabirds crying plaintively overhead. I turned to look for them and realized I was not on the *Eastern Star* at all, but on the *Mary Claire* traveling peacefully down the canal. And I was not alone,

Mirabile was there with me. My head was in her lap, and she was stroking my hair.

"My beautiful boy," she whispered, "my beautiful boy."

"Mirabile," I said, "is it too late? Can I yet be saved?"

"Shhh." She said and moved her hand slowly across my body. Very gently she began unbuttoning my trousers, then slid her hand inside. She grabbed me then, with such force that it woke me from my reverie. I was no longer in the canal boat, but back in the filthy hop joint. And it wasn't Mirabile's hand in my pants; it was Thayer's!

"What are you doing?" I said and pushed his hand away.

"Don't worry, Jonathan, I won't hurt you," Thayer said softly.

All at once I realized what had happened. It was Dugan's work; he set up the whole thing, and he knew it would end this way. Not content with making a whore of Jack, he was making one of me. Just when I thought I could sink no lower, Dugan showed me that his pit of degradation had no bottom.

I jumped up, buttoned my trousers and ran out into the street. The opium was still with me, but it wasn't well-being I felt now, it was stark terror. Death lurked in every ally and every person I passed meant to do me harm. I couldn't go back to the Old Brewery; I did not want to see Dugan or Jack or anyone I knew. I stopped at Paradise Park sat on a bench, put my head in my hands and sank into utter despair.

I could hear strains of organ music coming across the park from Union Mission. It was a hymn, one I didn't recognize, but it made me nostalgic nonetheless. I thought again of Mirabile, her pure voice, the purity of her spirit. What would she think of me now? I looked up, looked towards the lights of the mission, there for the reformation of whores, would the doors be open for me?

"They are Methodist you know," a voice came from my right, "a woman's religion."

I looked at him, and what I saw made me think I had fallen back into a dream. He was an old man with wild gray hair and beard, wearing what appeared to be a tattered uniform of a high-ranking officer in some foreign army. It was green with gold braiding, emblazoned with stars and sunbursts. It must have been exquisite years before, but now was filthy and torn. He held in his left hand, as if a scepter, a metal carpenter's rule.

"I tell you this because I fear you are planning to venture there and it would do you no good."

"You are right, sir, it would do me no good." I said, "For I am one of the damned, ordained so from before creation."

"You sound like a Presbyterian," he said, "As was I, before I realized that I was, in truth, a Hebrew. That was when I became the Prophet Mathias, who joined together with Elijah the Tishbite to found the Kingdom of Truth, a Kingdom of the Father, at Mount Zion, up the Hudson River. Yes, they tried to stop me, the gentiles, accusing me of killing the Tishbite but they failed. The Kingdom is not in one place; it is with me ever. As I told the Prophet of the Latter Day Saints (who I know is led by Satan) when we dined in Ohio, I preach the end of the Kingdom of the Son, the religion of women; and the reawakening of the Kingdom of the Father, the religion of men."

"You're crazy," I said.

"No, sir, I must read you this," he pulled from his coat a faded newspaper clipping and began reading. The article said, in effect, that a judge had ruled that he was entirely sane in all matters except religion.

"Which of course is wrong," he said, "I am just more intimate than most in the Truth of the Father."

Finding it too tedious to listen to the man talk more of his life and religion, I closed my eyes again and tried to shut him out. But the Prophet continued, now quoting scripture, relating some great Old Testament battle.

"And Sihon would not suffer Israel to pass through his border: but Sihon gathered all his people together, and went out against Israel into the wilderness: and he came to Jahaz, and fought against Israel."

Still under the opium's influence, I could hear the battle cries, and in my mind's eye, could see the swords clashing, the chariots charging against the enemy.

"And Israel smote him with the edge of the sword, and possessed his land from Arnon unto Jabbok, even unto the children of Ammon: for the border of the children of Ammon was strong."

Then I opened my eyes, and the battle cries did not fade. In front of me, in Paradise Park, a battle was raging—not Israel against the people of Sihon, but the Bowery Boys against the gangs of Five Points. The Dead Rabbits marched to battle behind their emblem, a dead rabbit on a pike. The Plug Uglies, looking like circus bears in human dress were charging forward. The Shirttails, so called because they wore their shirts outside their pants like Chinamen, had entered the fray. The Roach Guards were there and the Chichesters as well; it was the largest gathering of gangs I had yet seen.

And from the other direction came the Bowery Boys, with their tall hats and long coats, their trousers stuffed into huge hobnailed boots. They were armed with clubs and brickbats, and each man had a knife, and a pistol stuck in his belt. The engagements were swift and bloody, and the park was already strewn with the fallen wounded. Before long a third faction entered the battle; the police in blue uniforms, on foot and on horseback entered Paradise Park swinging their clubs indiscriminately. And now every man on the battlefield had two enemies.

As the battle raged in front of me, I saw Dugan in the thick of it. It angered me to see him, and I stood up and shouted as loudly as I could, "Eamon Dugan, I'm calling you out!"

Dugan turned his head, and seeing it was me; he walked over.

"Jonathan, what in hell are you doing here? Where's Thayer."

"I've had enough of you, Dugan, I don't like the way you treat me. I don't like the way you treat Jack."

"Nothing but trouble, that one," he said, "I liked her better as a hoyden."

"You're a coward and a bully, Dugan, you need to be brought down a peg." I assumed a fighting stance, knowing full well it would be a fight to the death that I could not possibly win. I just wanted to do some damage to the man before I left this world.

But Dugan didn't comprehend that I wanted to fight him; the notion too absurd for him to entertain.

"You seem agitated, Jonathan, we'll talk after the battle."

"We'll settle our business now," I said and shoved him in the chest.

This got Dugan's attention, and his eyes widened as he cocked his massive arm to let loose on my face. But at the crucial moment, a Bowery Boy, standing not five feet away, heaved a brickbat, with deadly force, at Dugan's head. The shock of impact was so strong that it knocked the life out of Dugan and he collapsed to the ground in a pathetic heap. A sharp edge of the brickbat had sliced a deep cut into Dugan's temple, but he was not even bleeding. His heart had stopped beating. Dugan was dead.

The Bowery Boy disappeared into the crowd, but a Dead Rabbit came over to see what had happened. "You've killed Dugan," he said, pointing at me, calling other Dead Rabbits to gather around. "He's killed Slasher Dugan."

Two policemen came to see what had happened and the Dead Rabbits tried to persuade them to arrest me for murdering Dugan. But the policemen were not interested in a single murder with bloody warfare all around them. They tried to disperse the Dead Rabbits, who were determined to see justice done one way or the other. Then the Prophet Mathias stepped forward and in his labored, Biblical manner gave his account of the death of Dugan.

The ensuing confusion gave me just enough cover to slip down Cross Street and away from Paradise Park. I got to Sixth Avenue unmolested, then walked north for miles, past the closed up shops and the darkened mansions of the high-numbered streets, then out of the city and into farmland until I reached the end of Manhattan. It was nearly dawn, and I sat at a ferry stop until the morning service commenced. I took the first boat across the Hudson and never looked back.

CHAPTER 16

A View of all Creation; The Farmer's Daughter; The Celebration of Pinkster.

I must hasten to explain, lest you think my story nearly done, that Dugan's was not the death for which I will unjustly hang. Though the Dead Rabbits were certain that I was guilty of Dugan's murder, the death of a gangster on the battlefield is not a crime that the New York City police are likely to pursue. I am sure that the coppers were just as happy to be done with that particular menace to society. In fact, I daresay that no one in New York will miss Dugan, save the rest of the Dead Rabbits, and I am sure there are many in their ranks who secretly rejoiced at his passing. I did not fear arrest in the city, and would not be hung there under color of law, but the Dead Rabbits are bound to take revenge for the death of a fallen comrade and, had I chosen to stay in the city, my life would have been in constant jeopardy.

After crossing the Hudson, I found a secluded wooded spot and slept there most of the day. When I awoke, I walked the main road until I found a roadhouse where I could get a meal. I had plenty of money; the dogfights at Kit Burn's had been quite rewarding. I walked some more, then found another place to sleep. Thus began a cycle where I did nothing but walk, eat and sleep for several days.

I was heading north, walking atop the cliffs and hills bounding the Hudson that had appeared so magnificent on our boat trips down the river. From this perspective, the sailboats and steamboats that dotted the river as far as the eye could see were utterly insignificant. The thought that they carried humans, burdened with all their toils and troubles, was almost laughable. Up here I could travel days with no sight of another person, and that suited me just fine.

My goal was vague. I would walk north as far as Albany—I had no desire to go further north and revisit the Adirondack wilderness—hopeful that in the course of the journey I would receive some inspiration to help me decide whether, then, to turn east or west. I entertained the notion of going back to Salem, like the Prodigal Son returning home, but I feared that my father would not slaughter the fatted calf upon my return, and I knew that any comfort I found there would be short-lived. Perhaps I would go west, heading toward the burned-over district, maybe even, once again, joining my beloved Mirabile. But I sensed that my presence would not be welcome in the Travis camp either.

I was still some ways from Albany when the road led quite steeply up the side of a mountain. I could have taken a low road, gone around the mountain, but I was determined to reach the summit. My progress was slow, and the climb took several hours, but when I finally reached the top, the view there rewarded my effort. It was as if I could see all of creation from that place, to the ends of the earth in all directions. To the north were the rocks and crags of mountains even taller than the one upon which I stood, but further north were distant ranges, tiers, and tiers of gray and purple, dimmed by haze, fading into the horizon. Across the river valley, now so steep that the river itself was not visible from where I stood, were more mountains, rolling again into the shadowy distance. To the southwest the mountains parted, revealing a lush green valley far below, and nestled between verdant forests I saw rectangular fields of a lighter green—a farmer's crop just beginning to grow.

As beautiful and enticing as the mountains were, it was the farmer's field that enthralled me. Even so tiny and far away the cultivated field brought on waves of nostalgia for the pure and ancient days of my childhood on the farm. It was impossible to go back, I knew that, but why couldn't I venture down to this farm? There is always work to be done on a farm, and I would be willing to work for very little pay; for no pay at all if it came to that.

So I started back down the mountain, trying to maintain my bearings even when the road did not go in my direction. I had to weave back down through roads and paths, trying to set my sights on a field I could no longer see. I continued down for miles, further down into the valley than I had been before I started up the mountain. When the land finally leveled out, I was surrounded by forest, still no sign of the field, and it was already nightfall.

Exhausted, I found a spot in the woods to sleep, confident that the morning light would show me the way.

I woke early, and I set off through the woods with the rising sun at my back, still confident that I was heading in the right direction. Before long I found a path through the woods and followed it to a dirt road with ruts from wagon wheels. Still heading east, I followed the road, first over one hill, then over a second until, through the trees at the side of the road, I spied a field of newly sprouted corn. I ran through the trees and reached the field—acres and acres of young corn plants. At the far corner, I saw a red barn, and I walked the perimeter of the field until I reached it.

There I saw the farmer loading sacks of grain into the barn. He wore knee-breeches a shirt and vest; he was clean-shaven with a tall, broad-brimmed hat on his head. I said hello, and he greeted me in a language I did not understand. I told him I was looking for work, explaining that I had been a farmer most of my life. He responded in a language that I recognized to be Dutch; it was clear that the farmer did not understand English and I, of course, could not speak his language. I tried by gesture to explain what I wanted. Unsure whether I was getting my message across, I picked up a sack of grain and vigorously helped him load the sacks into the barn.

He was grateful for the help, and I thought he might agree to hire me as a farmhand. The farmer led me into his house. The kitchen was bright and cheerfully decorated. He called out, "Grieta," and a young girl hurried into the kitchen. They spoke a few words, then Grieta commenced to frying eggs. He had sensed correctly that I was hungry.

While Grieta cooked the meal, the farmer, in his way, conveyed his willingness to hire me. He showed me to a small room with just a bed, and like the rest of the house, it was clean and tidy. This was where I would sleep. He brought me some clothing to wear while I worked, seeing at once that my suit was too good for farm labor and that I had no other clothes. He indicated too that I would be paid for my work, and, though the amount and frequency of the wages were unclear, I was more than grateful. He said his name was Hans Van der Voort; I told him I was Jonathan Pratt and shook his hand enthusiastically.

Herr Van der Voort and Grieta were the only ones in the household, and I surmised that he was a widower and she his daughter. It was a happy household nonetheless. The farmer's daughter was shy and innocent at first; she had ways like a child, but her form was plump and womanly. She was a pretty girl with blonde hair and a ready smile.

You, oh worldly reader, no doubt chuckle to yourself at the mention of a traveler and a farmer's daughter—a story as old as travel and cultivation themselves. If you think yourself too jaded to read this story once again, you may skip ahead, for you will find nothing new here. But recall that my only experience with sexual matters had been with New York City whores and an

Erie Canal tomboy; at the time I had not an inkling of the trouble they can cause.

Though we were unable to converse, Grieta was happy for my company. In the evenings, after dinner, I would help her bring the cows in from pasture. She would laugh merrily as we ran together to chase some wayward animal. Sometimes she would tease me, and I would chase her through the field. We played together as children, and in my mind, I would have been happy to continue this way forever. But my mind is seldom the ruler in these situations, and one evening behind the barn, succumbing to a joyful impulse, I pulled Grieta close and kissed firmly on the lips. Startled, Grieta pushed me away and started running. But as she left, she turned around and smiled broadly, letting me know that my advance had not really been unwelcome.

I could not know it at the time, but that first kiss had sown the seeds of my undoing.

*

The place where we lived was called Kaaterskill, and no one in that community spoke anything but Dutch. I soon found ways to communicate without speaking; farm work involves very little speech, and the few needs I had beyond food, Grieta was able to anticipate quite nicely. Sometimes young people, having heard that there was an English speaker in their midst, would come by and ask for my help in learning that language. I did not mind helping, but for the most part, I was pleased that the lack of a common language freed me from the burden of conversation.

The church services we attended on Sundays were, of course, also conducted in Dutch. It was Christian; I recognized the Lord's Prayer, the Beatitudes, and other familiar scriptures by the rhythm and meter of the words. But I felt like the Catholics at the Transfiguration Church, whose priest held the service in Latin, a language that none of them understood. After a time or two, I could appreciate the advantage in that as well.

The workdays were hard and long, but I have always enjoyed farm work. Herr Van der Voort was a hard worker as well, but I could see that he was beginning to feel the effects of age. He did not have the stamina he once had and was happy to have an extra set of hands.

Each day I worked up an enormous appetite which Grieta sated with wondrously sumptuous meals. We still went out after dinner to bring in the cows, but now wound up every time kissing behind the barn. That first kiss I stole had awakened such passion in Grieta that she could barely contain herself while attending the cows and as soon as the last was in its stall she would pull me behind the barn.

While still innocent, by the standards I was used to, each time was increasingly intimate—with me stroking her magnificent breasts through her dress, and she moving her hand over the crotch of my trousers— until I sometimes thought I would burst. As passionate as Grieta was, she was also deathly frightened of being caught by her father; at the slightest sound, she would pull away and look in all directions, making sure our embraces had not been witnessed. Her caution was not misplaced; while normally even-tempered, I knew that Herr Van der Voort could be very harsh towards his daughter and I had seen him strike her quite hard when she broke a plate while clearing the table. Catching Grieta in a compromising position with me would, no doubt incite him to violence. I wasn't sure which one of us would get the brunt of it.

A short time after I arrived at Kaaterskill, the community gathered for a festive celebration which they called Pinkster. There was some religious significance to it—though I never knew what—because we all put on our best clothes that Sunday and found the church brightly decorated and attended by many more people than usual. Following the service, we went to a field where booths had been set up selling baked goods and candy; toys and trinkets for the children. A whole pig was roasting on a spit, and a wagon arrived bearing barrels and barrels of bock beer. A fiddler and an accordion player struck up a lively tune and couples rushed onto the field to dance.

Several families of African descent lived in the area, apparently former slaves or the children of former slaves. With slavey abandoned in the State of New York, they now worked as paid field hands or tradesmen in town. They all spoke Dutch as well and enjoyed the festival of Pinkster as much as anyone. Their tradition on this day was to dress up like their Dutch masters and imitate their behaviors. Instead of being insulted by this mockery, the Dutch found great delight in it, and each man was especially pleased if he could recognize himself in this game. The black men were also the most energetic and eccentric of dancers. The Dutch merchants selling wares at the festival would hire these men to dance in front of their booths and attract crowds.

The beer flowed all afternoon, and everyone there became happily intoxicated. After my time at Five Points, I found it nothing short of a miracle to see so many drunks and none looking for a fight. The sun was shining, and the air was warm, and a feeling of good fellowship engulfed everyone and showed no sign of abating.

Grieta came to my side, and I was afraid she would want me to dance. She tilted her head toward the dancers but not in invitation, but to point my attention towards her father exuberantly doing the polka, or whatever it is they do, with widow Cortlandt who owned a farm on the other side of the valley—a woman quite a few years younger than he. Herr Van der Voort was lavishing his attention on the widow, and she appeared to be reciprocating.

Still using just the simplest of gestures, Grieta suggested that we go back home, leaving her father here. There was a twinkle of mischief in her big blue eyes, and I realized it was now or never. I nodded, and we hurried back to the farm.

Giggling the whole way, Grieta led me into the barn and up a wooden ladder to the hayloft where we would have a soft and relatively hidden bed of hay. We embraced then and kissed, but Grieta was too anxious to linger long at that. She pulled her dress off over her head, revealing breasts even more magnificent than I had anticipated, soft and snowy white with nipples like wild strawberries. I put my hands upon them as Grieta went to work unbuttoning trousers.

But just as I had stepped out of my trousers, we heard the loud creak of the barn door opening. Grieta and I jumped back into the shadows, hoping whoever it was would not look upward. It was Herr Van der Voort and the widow Cortlandt, and they were too busy with their own lovemaking to look up at the loft. I did not want to watch, but Grieta stood there fascinated by the scene. Her father maneuvered the widow against a stable door and with one hand raised her skirts while with the other was trying to unbutton his breeches. He was having difficulty with the pants, and the widow attempted to help. The tangle of anxious fingers trying to undo Herr Van der Voorts breeches made quite an amusing show, and Grieta could not suppress a loud chuckle.

They both stopped their work, then, and looked up to the loft, seeing Grieta standing there with nothing on but her drawers, and me just the opposite—naked below the waist, with my manhood still at attention outside my shirt. The widow screamed and ran from the barn. Grieta's father, red with anger started for the loft ladder. I grabbed my trousers and boots and jumped out of the open loft doors. The fall was about ten feet, but I knew there was a pile of hay below. They hay cushioned my landing, but I still twisted my ankle in the process.

I ran as fast as I could with a bad ankle. Looking back I saw no sign Herr Van der Voort; perhaps he had turned his wrath on his daughter and would let me be. But no, I soon saw him come from behind the barn carrying an ancient blunderbuss that he used to drive vermin from the vegetable garden. He kept it loaded with powder and gravel, and though the weapon was limited in range and accuracy, I knew that the spray of gravel it delivered covered a wide area and if he got close enough he could not help but hit me.

I redoubled my efforts then, but my ankle was slowing me down. The old man was soon within range and let loose with the blunderbuss. The sound of the explosion echoed through the valley as the gravel left the muzzle of the gun with tremendous force. I was fortunate that he hadn't time to aim, and the full force of the shot went wide, but a good handful of gravel caught my buttocks and thighs, embedding in the skin and knocking me off my feet.

I prepared myself then to be murdered, but Herr Van der Voort was too exhausted to continue. Happy that he had felled me and driven me forever from his farm, he turned and walked away. I managed to get back on my feet, then slowly headed for the road, each agonizing step taking me farther away from Kaaterskill.

CHAPTER 17
The Saugerties Bard; A Theft of Identity; The Poughkeepsie Seer; An Unexpected Excursion.

I walked on, in spite of searing pain, down a road whose direction and destination I did not know. When far enough away to be sure I was not still being chased I stopped to put my trousers back on. It increased the pain but rendered me more decent for travel on a public road—though how public I was not sure, as I hadn't seen a soul for miles. The shot had not been fatal, but with an arse full of gravel I feared I could die of infection if the wounds were left untreated. I needed to see a doctor, but had no way to know where to find one, or even if the road I was on led to somewhere that a doctor could be found. All I could do was keep walking in hope that I would come across someone who did know.

From behind me on the road, I heard the sound of a rickety old wagon approaching. The clatter of the wagon was augmented by the sound of bells, and I heard the thing long before I was able to spy it. As it came closer, I could see that the wagon as festooned with American flags and had cowbells hanging below, accounting for the sounds I had heard. I thought the driver must be a traveling peddler of some kind. He pulled the horse to a stop when he came alongside me.

"You appear to be in bad shape, young fellow," he said, "may I give you a ride somewhere?"

"Yes, sir, please," I replied.

I briefly told my story and explained why it would be impossible for me to sit down next to him on the wooden seat. He pulled a blanket from the back of the wagon and fashioned a cushion for me, and I found that if I put all my weight on an unwounded section of my left buttock, I could ride relatively free from pain.

"Tell me your story in detail," he said, "I may write a song about it."

"Why would you write a song about it?" I asked.

"Have you not heard of the Saugerties Bard?" He looked at me incredulously.

"I'm not from these parts," I said.

"The Saugerties Bard," he told me, was the name by which he was known as he traveled up and down the Hudson Valley, playing fiddle or flute and singing songs he had written. He wrote about notable local events—murders, fires, steamboat accidents—and thought my story might make a good song. In town after the town, he would sing a new song, then sell copies of the lyrics at a penny a sheet.

"Can you make much money at that?" I asked.

"I get by."

The Bard's real name was Henry Backus; he was short and squat with gray hair and beard, long but neatly trimmed; and he had a peg leg. He was nattily dressed in knee britches and a cutaway coat with a broad-brimmed hat on his head. He had been a teacher, he said, with a wife and several daughters, but his children were grown, and when his wife died he took first to drink then to religion, neither was effective at ending his grief, and he wound up in a lunatic asylum in Hudson.

"Now free from both grief and insanity I travel these hills and entertain people with my music and song, and I may wish to write one about your adventure."

I told him my story starting from my arrival at Kaaterskill; fearing that my entire story would take more than one song to capture. He took no notes, but I could tell he was mentally putting words to meter, beginning the songwriting process in his mind.

As flattered as I was to have my misfortune immortalized in song, I told the Bard that my immediate need was finding a doctor.

"You seem to me sick at heart; you might do better with a visit to the Poughkeepsie Seer." He looked at me closely then, "But you do look a mite pale, and I appreciate the value of timely medical treatment," he tapped his wooden leg on the floorboards. "I am bound for Poughkeepsie. I will do my show there; then help you find a doctor."

I would have preferred the doctor first, then the show, but when we arrived in Poughkeepsie I saw why we had to follow his order. As we entered the outskirts of town noise of the rickety wagon and its bells attracted the attention of dogs encountered on the way. They followed us and their barking, in turn, attracted other dogs as well as laughing children who followed alongside the bedecked wagon. We led a loud and joyful parade as we approached the center of town. There the Saugerties Bard stopped the wagon, stood up and began playing loudly, a familiar tune on the fiddle.

His playing was adequate, and the sound and sight were enough to draw a crowd of Poughkeepsie citizens away from their drudgeries. Dozens of men and women gathered around the wagon and applauded while he played them popular melodies on fiddle and flute. Then he began singing his own songs in a voice that was rough but pleasing. The melodies were familiar, but the words were intricate stories of events that were, no doubt, familiar to those in the crowd.

The sight of such a large and attentive crowd ignited a flame of larceny in my heart. It had become instinctual for me to view a gathering like this as so many sheep to be shorn and in spite of the pain, I jumped down from the wagon and walked through the crowd to see if I could come away with some wallets and watches.

I managed to lift a wallet from the coat of a gentleman who was listening intently to the Bard sing about a terrible powder mill explosion. I stuck the wallet inside my shirt, but as I hastened to the outside of the crowd, I realized that I had become feverish and was much sicker than I thought when sitting in the wagon. I became dizzy and had to go to my knees. Before I knew it, I was lying flat on the ground, going in and out of sleep, with much of the crowd now gathered around me.

The Bard and some other men loaded me into the wagon, and I passed out from the pain and fever. When next I woke, I was lying face down on a table in a doctor's office.

"Ah, Mr. Ridley, you're awake," said the doctor as he put on his spectacles and readied his tools, "I believe you will live, but we must remove these stones from your backside."

I concurred but wondered why he called me Mr. Ridley.

"This may hurt a bit." He said as he dug a knife into one of my wounds and used forceps to pull out a piece of gravel. It hurt like hell. I heard a clink as he dropped the stone into a tin pan. I heard that clink at least a dozen more times, and the pain, each time, was greater than the time before.

Finally, the doctor said, "That's the last, Mr. Ridley. I will bandage the wounds and let you sleep until the fever breaks."

Sleep I did. It was a deep and dreamless sleep that lasted into the following day. When I awoke, I felt refreshed and no longer feverish. I saw my clothes on a chair nearby, and as gently as I could, I dressed myself. The wallet I had stolen lay on the seat of the chair. Upon opening it, I learned why the doctor had called me Mr. Ridley. Inside was the calling card of Mr. George Ridley, Esq., with an address on Washington Street in Oneida, New York. Judging by the amount of cash Mr. Ridley's wallet, he was a very successful attorney.

The doctor came in and was pleased to see me up and dressed. He said all the things that doctors say—take it easy, don't put too much pressure on the wounds, come back if they start to infect—but I could tell by the tone of his voice that he was not worried about my chances. I paid my bill and gave him a little extra for his trouble.

After I paid, the doctor said, "It's not my place to inquire how you happened to get a backside full of grapeshot, but if you don't mind my saying, you appear to be a young man lacking in direction."

"That would be the truth, doctor," I said.

"I can help with your physical wellbeing," he said slowly, "but for the rest, I would recommend that you visit the Poughkeepsie Seer."

"Sorry doctor, but I've had my fill of religion."

"Oh, this is not religion as you know it, Mr. Ridley. The Seer will look into your very soul; tell you what you need to know."

I was anxious to leave the town before the real George Ridley got wind of someone traveling under his name. But after two recommendations, as I was already in Poughkeepsie, I decided to visit the Poughkeepsie Seer.

*

"Good afternoon, Mr. Ridley." The Poughkeepsie Seer greeted me at the door of his modest home in a pleasant neighborhood of that town, "I am Andrew Jackson Davis. Won't you come in?"

He showed me to a chair in his study then went off to fetch us some tea. The room was dark; heavy curtains blocking the afternoon sun, and a single oil lamp on a table by the wall provided dim light. Mr. Davis returned, poured me a cup of tea, then one for himself. He sat down across from me, the tea on a low table between us.

"I'm sure you know me by reputation." He said, more as a question than a statement.

He was a young man, in his twenties, with a boyish face framed by whiskers, without mustaches. His eyes were his prominent feature; they were like blue-gray glass and had the power to hold your own until you felt powerless to look away. I told him that was not familiar with his reputation, but had been told that he could help me find direction.

"No doubt I can, Mr. Ridley, no doubt I can."

It had been necessary for me to make an appointment through the Seer's manager, the formalities of which were handled by the physician who treated me, hence the Seer also knew me as Mr. Ridley (though, it raised some doubt as to his efficacy as a seer.)

"I am a clairvoyant, have been since a young child. I use my gift to cure physical and mental maladies of those in need, such as yourself, Mr. Ridley. More often, lately, I have spent my time writing and lecturing; preparing the people for the new world that is already upon us. My philosophy has been compared to that of Emanuel Swedenborg— not surprisingly, since, though I have never read any of his works, I have on several occasions been visited by the spirit of that illustrious gentleman. I have also studied the methods of Dr. Mesmer in harnessing animal magnetism and can, at will, induce a state of trance in myself and in others. I was once so deeply entranced that I left the waking world in this very room and when I rejoined it I found myself forty miles away in the Catskill Mountains, at a loss to explain how I had gotten there."

"I have been to the Catskills," I said.

"Yes," he said, "so you understand. We are at the threshold, Mr. Ridley, of a new era. Just this past March I received a spiritual message that a portal had been opened; that communication between our world and that of the spirits will soon be commonplace."

I did not know what to make of the man. Much of what he said made no sense to me, but I could feel the power of his words; just as when Reverend Travis would sermonize on hellfire. But when with the eyes of the Poughkeepsie Seer were locked in gaze with my own, his claim of harnessing animal magnetism seemed like more than idle words.

"I understand that you have been recently wounded, Mr. Ridley and that your life has become shiftless and un-rooted."

I told him the story of Herr Van der Voort and his daughter, and my hasty retreat from Kaaterskill. I had become quite adept at telling the abbreviated version of this story, having already told it to the Saugerties Bard and my Poughkeepsie physician.

The Poughkeepsie Seer closed his eyes as I spoke, sometimes nodding at various points as if comprehending some hidden significance which was lost on me. When I finished, he continued to sit with eyes closed until I feared my story had put him to sleep.

"Do you ever dream, Mr. Ridley?" He said, at last, opening his eyes.

As a rule, my sleep is untroubled by dreams, so I told him my Mott Street dream, of being comforted on the canal by Mirabile, omitting, of course, that it had been induced by opium. I also omitted my rude awakening.

"I believe I can ease your physical pain, Mr. Ridley, and more importantly, I can heal your spiritual pain and set you on your proper path." He said. "I will put us both into trances, and you will join me in a spiritual journey. You will not be able to see what I am seeing, but you will be with me in the spiritual world as we seek the help of the spirits in aiding your recovery."

He moved his chair next to mine and had me turn to face him, our knees nearly touching. The Seer held my palms between his thumbs and fingers and told me to look into his eyes. I did as I was told and gazed into his eyes until I had lost any sense of time. He moved his hands up and down my arms and across my chest as he spoke to me softly, saying I know not what. At once, I was both sitting in the study and completely detached from my body. It was like a deep sleep, yet my eyes were open the whole time. The seer asked me questions, and I responded, but I have no memory of what those questions were or how I answered.

Gradually I came out of the trance, drawn by the Seer's words until I could once again understand their meaning and feel connected to my body and my surroundings. I felt refreshed and invigorated, and, to my surprise, the pain from my wounds had subsided.

"How do you feel, Mr. Ridley?"

"Wonderful," I said.

"We have been on a momentous journey, and I have learned much," he said. "You are a man of great passion, Mr. Ridley, yet often a man of unsound judgment. You must follow your passions unwaveringly; you must take care, always, not to be swayed by worldly temptations. Above all, you must pursue the object of your desire."

"Do you mean Mirabile? Should I travel west?" I asked, thinking of she who had remained the object of my desire through all of my bad judgments and worldly temptations.

"Only you can put a name on it, Mr. Ridley, only you can set the direction. But above all you must follow your passion, Mr. Ridley, you must follow your passion."

I paid the Seer gladly. I was relieved of my physical pain, and his spiritual advice, with the fog of earthly distraction blown away, did mirror my own desire. I was not bound by a damnation predetermined; I was free to seek the object of my passion. I would travel west and find Mirabile.

Yet, I had a lingering skepticism regarding the Poughkeepsie Seer. If he had looked so deeply into my soul and taken me on a spiritual quest, why did he still refer to me as Mr. Ridley? Had none of the spirits thought to inform him that I was actually Jonathan Pratt? This troubled me more on the earthly plane than the spiritual—there were now three people in Poughkeepsie who knew me as George Ridley, and by now the real George Ridley had no doubt reported the theft of his wallet to the police.

The problem with Mr. Ridley's wallet was that it contained too much money. When Jack and I were picking pockets in New York, Dugan had us report a score this big and hand over the wallet to him. This was not so he could keep the money, but so he could return it. A fat wallet meant someone of importance—a banker, or worse, a Tammany politician—someone who could cause us real problems. We did not keep their money. It was better to make many small scores than one big one.

While I had no intention of returning Mr. Ridley's money, I had no desire to be caught impersonating him in Poughkeepsie. I removed several hundred dollars in bank notes from the wallet, then threw the wallet and calling cards into the gutter. The money I hid in my boots.

I thought the fastest way out of town must be by train. I would buy a ticket to Syracuse, heading swiftly toward the object of my desire and away from the scene of my recent crime. I could bid farewell to Mr. Ridley and once again become Jonathan Pratt.

The train depot was a small wooden building between the road and the boarding platform. Inside was a counter for purchasing tickets and rows of benches for waiting. But standing near the counter was a policeman in uniform and at the gate stood another. I had no experience with railroads; maybe those policemen always stood there. But if they were looking for a pickpocket and I were searched and questioned, I would be hard pressed to explain the money in my boots. And there were those in town who could identify me as an imposter.

I stepped on the platform from outside the building, and a policeman approached me.

"Taking a train trip, sonny?"

"No, officer, I just like to look at the engines," I replied.

"Best come back tomorrow to look at the engines," he said, "There may be trouble here today."

That was enough for me. I left for the stagecoach office to see if there were coppers there as well. There were none, so I asked the agent for a ticket on the next coach out of Poughkeepsie.

It was the merest chance that sent me next to Saratoga.

CHAPTER 18

Saratoga Waters; A Camp Meeting; Reunions.

Saratoga was a pleasant surprise. I had expected just another dreary river town filled with hardworking, churchgoing citizens, where I would have to seek out the darker parts of town just to get a drink. But what I found was quite the opposite. It was a resort town and everyone there was bent on having a good time, or at least on feeling better than they did at home.

The town was built around natural springs of mineral water with powerful medicinal qualities. People flocked here from around the world to cure their ills, both real and imagined, by bathing in and dosing themselves with the miraculous waters. I can personally attest to the cathartic properties of the water; after downing two large bumpers of the stuff, I was driven to the outhouse for an extended stay. The baths were less effective. The rough coach ride had broken the spell of the Poughkeepsie Seer, and my wounds began to ache again. A Saratoga doctor recommended cold mineral baths which, though refreshing, did little to quell the pain.

On the major thoroughfares were row after row of grand hotels, each more fashionable than the last. The streets were lined with clothiers offering the latest fashions and restaurants featuring European chefs. Throughout Saratoga could be found every form of public house, from the most genteel tea room to the most vicious gambling hell— and with every shade in between.

The clientele of these establishments were married couples and single men, most of them extremely wealthy and not afraid to let the world know it. They were attracted by the healing waters, but expected all the comforts of home and then some. The rich, in turn, attracted mountebanks, confidence men, fortune tellers, fortune hunters, courtesans, prostitutes and every form of thief known to man.

Most of the visitors, both prey and predators, were from New York City. Present, of course, were the Fifth Avenue types; the women, dressed with conservative elegance, always in the appropriate attire, whether strolling down Church Street or taking tea with their peers; the men, unless the event called for something finer, always dressed for business, as if even at leisure, they were ready to deal. These were the people who were emulated by the confidence men. Broadway was represented as well, by those who closely follow fashion and dress to be seen. The man who sneaks into your hotel room to steal your jewelry while you are taking the waters is likely to be a Broadway swell. And I even saw one of the Bowery B'hoys at Saratoga. The unmistakable uniform—tall hat, long coat, wide cravat, plaid trousers tucked into hobnailed boots—that seemed so natural on the Bowery was hopelessly out of place at the resort. He seemed to turn up all over town; I didn't know what he was up to, but I knew he was not there for the cure.

I had the rhino, since lifting Mr. Ridley's wallet, so I decided to play the part of a man of means. I bought myself a new suit, not too flashy, but one that looked its cost, giving me the air of a man with money in the bank. I took a room at the Grand Union Hotel, the finest in town, and ate at the best restaurants. So successful was I at this ruse that wherever I went, I was winked at by one of the fortune-hunting young women whose sole purpose at Saratoga was to bag a wealthy husband or steal someone else's.

The most telling validation of my perceived wealth was when I was preyed upon by two rather inept confidence men. As I was walking back to the hotel from my spa treatments, a man called out and asked if I had dropped my wallet. He pointed to a wallet on the sidewalk, which of course was not mine. Another man nearby suggested we open it up and, lo and behold; it was filled with cash.

Well, I knew this game; it was the "pigeon drop." Dugan, who had a finger in every rancid criminal pie in New York, employed men who specialized in confidence games of this sort. I knew that if I let the game play out it would proceed something like this: one man would suggest we split the cash three ways after making a cursory attempt to find the owner; other would suggest that, for good faith, we each put up an amount equal to our share, and put it all in the wallet, then meet later to divide the cash. When the money was in the wallet, one of them would pull a switch, and I would be left holding a wallet full of newspaper; the men would be gone forever and so would my money.

The secret to success at this game is to have a good roper to select an easy mark before starting—someone who is not "in the know" and someone not too pious to want a share of the found money. Though I was the former, I pretended to be the latter. I told them we must take the wallet to the police and no matter how hard they tried to persuade me to split the money I would agree to nothing else. The more they pressured me, the more I dug in my heels and said no. Finally, in desperation, they gave it up. They left me with the wallet and hurried away. The wallet, of course, had no money in it but at least they had gotten none of mine.

I notice that someone had been watching the entire proceedings from a restaurant window. His face was now mostly obscured the menu he was reading, but I knew who it was—that ever-present Bowery Boy. I wondered if he had anything to do with the planning of this little performance, then dismissed the thought. Spending much time in a town like Saratoga will have you distrusting everyone you see.

The following day I learned that a camp meeting was to be held outside the city limits. As if the town were not entertaining enough, the great Charles Grandison Finney would be presiding over convocation of the faithful. Their nights would be spent sleeping in tents, their day spent in prayer, with sermons delivered by the most prominent evangelists of the day. Given my ecclesiastical history, it was a show that I did not want to miss.

I joined a group that was heading to the campgrounds by wagon, and when I arrived, I could not believe the size of the gathering. Rows and rows of tents had been pitched, and I saw hundreds of men, women, and children gathered in groups throughout the grounds. There were easily as many seekers of salvation at the camp meeting as there were sinners in Saratoga.

One group was singing hymns, and I joined in on the songs that I knew. When the singing was done, the praying commenced. These were not the quiet, humble prayers I was used to, but load, boisterous pleas, calling upon the Lord to cast the devil from their midst, to help those in need of forgiveness, and to give the faithless the strength they needed to come into the glow of Christ's love. When the prayers were through, I said "Amen" with the rest each time.

As I walked through the grounds, I saw people crying, wailing, struggling with their demons, begging forgiveness for their sins, surrendering their souls to Jesus. Everywhere the glory of God was triumphing over sin, and I was not anxious to stand in any one place for too long.

One of the great ministers was scheduled to speak inside a large tent in the center of the grounds. As I walked toward it, I passed one of the lesser preachers stepping down from his stage and being congratulated by his followers. It was the same scene I had witnessed throughout the grounds, but something about it caught my eye. I turned to look again, and I gasped as I recognized the preacher as Reverend Travis. And there on the stage, laying aside her lap organ, was Mirabile. She was dressed in white, as beautiful and radiant as the day I first saw her. As I walked toward her, she looked up, and I could see that she recognized me as well. She hurried off behind one of the tents, and I followed after her calling her name. When we were both behind the tent and out of eyeshot from the Reverend and his followers she turned toward me.

"Jonathan, how good to see you," Mirabile said. She was smiling, but I sensed her unease.

"It is wonderful to see you, Mirabile," I said.

"You look as though you have done well for yourself, Jonathan."

"You can't imagine, Mirabile," I said, "come with me, let me tell you about it."

She shook her head, "You must leave here, Jonathan. You must go before the Reverend sees you. He hasn't forgiven you for running away."

"Come with me, Mirabile."

"You must leave here, Jonathan."

"Come with me."

She sighed. "Where are you staying Jonathan?"

"Grand Union Hotel."

"I'll meet you there, in the lobby tonight. But you must leave here now."

I could ask for no more. I left the camp meeting elated.

*

The lobby of the Grand Union Hotel was more sumptuous than any room I had ever been in. Comfortable chairs and sofas were placed around the spacious room such that small groups could converse pleasantly and a gentleman alone could enjoy a newspaper without interruption. During the day large windows let in the daylight; at night lamps were lit on every table and overhead a crystal chandelier poured light throughout the room. And it all was reflected from large mirrors on two of the walls. Artwork and tapestries hung from another wall. Exotic potted plants in large pots were positioned around the room; a grandfather clock sonorously chimed the hour, brass trays on marble pedestals caught the ashes of imported cigars sold at a counter nearby. A man could spend time ensconced in a room such as this and believe to his soul that all was right with the world.

Mirabile was to meet me there that night. She did not say when, so after dinner, I went to the lobby and purchased a local newspaper as well as one from New York City. I would read until she arrived. She had been impressed by my new suit. She thought me wealthy now and that, no doubt, was the reason she agreed to meet me. That did not bother me; why would she want anything less? I would continue to play the rich man until my money ran out. There would be time enough for truth later.

I had never seen Mirabile dressed so splendidly. As she entered the lobby, the long, flowing skirt of her pale blue dress accentuated the grace of her movements. Over her bare shoulders, she wore a shawl of white lace and on her head a dainty lace-trimmed bonnet. I rose as she approached me. I longed to pull her close to me, into a tight embrace, then shower her with kisses. Instead, I gently shook her hand.

"You look wonderful, Mirabile," I said as she sat down across from me.

"As do you, Jonathan. I am so impressed by how successful you have become in such a short time. What is your profession now?"

"I am a speculator," I said.

"Is that not akin to a gambler?"

"The difference," I said, "is that speculators never lose."

By way of explanation, I cobbled together a philosophy of "speculation" using the words of Mr. Thayer's occupation while the whole time thinking of Mr. Dugan's. I couched my true profession of thief in the language of business, leaving Mirabile, no doubt perplexed, yet still duly impressed by my achievement.

"And what about you, Mirabile," I asked, "have you and your father reaped the harvest of souls as planned?"

Her expression turned dark at this. "It is the reason I wanted to talk with you, Jonathan," she said softly, "things are not going well."

Mirabile explained that after I left, the Reverend remained committed to the notion of including in the service a demonstration of healing by faith. He cursed me for leaving, but upon arrival at Syracuse, the Reverend found another boy to play the cripple. The new boy was unreliable and not to be trusted around money, but the performance was well-received, and the crowds in attendance continued to grow. The congregations would include actual cripples drawn by Reverend Travis's reputation as a healer, and more often than not, one or more would leave cured or believing himself cured by the Reverend's healing touch. When Reverend Travis realized this was happening, he fired the boy, then tailored his message to those in need of healing. He would put his hand on the afflicted person and invoke the Holy Spirit. If the healing did not occur, he would blame that person's lack of faith.

At first, he would add ringers to the crowd to make sure that at least someone would be healed every time, but he soon came to believe in his own healing power and worked only with those who came voluntarily. So obsessed was the Reverend with his power to heal that he had come to believe himself chosen by God. He put himself above all others, and would not tolerate anyone questioning his divinity.

"He has become insufferable," Mirabile said, "I can no longer stand it."

"Then you must leave," I said.

"And I shall," she said, "but the time is not right. I must return to Rochester first. Seeing you today was an epiphany, Jonathan. I believe that, with your help, I can put that life behind me forever. I have come to ask you if there is any chance of my obtaining that help."

"Of course, Mirabile. I will do whatever you say."

"We leave in the morning for Rochester," she said, "but our route will be circuitous. Can you meet me in Rochester come July?"

"Certainly. How will I find you?"

"I shall find you." She said. Then she rose and put her arms around me and gave me a kiss, this time full on the lips. "I must return now before I am missed. Goodbye until next month, Jonathan."

Mirabile left the hotel, and I watched her through the window as she walked down the street and disappeared into the shadows. So engrossed was I that I did not notice when someone else sat down in the chair that had been occupied by Mirabile.

"Found her at last, didja Pratt?" I turned to see the Bowery Boy who had been at the fringe of every scene since I arrived in Saratoga. And I knew that voice.

"Jack! What are you doing here?"

"I could ask you the same, Pratt, with you dressed like a dandy and staying in a swell hotel. But I first want to thank you for murdering Dugan."

"I didn't murder Dugan." I briefly told Jack the story of the battle in Paradise Park and how, as I was trying to confront Dugan, a Bowery Boy murdered him with a brickbat.

"Well, you stood up to him and distracted him long enough for someone better equipped to do the job. I thank you for that."

"I thought you were in love with Dugan and hated me."

"I did hate you for a time, Pratt," she said, "but I never loved Dugan. I was with Dugan because the nights I spent with him were nights I would not spend whorin'. I found that if I kept him angry enough, I would not have to sleep with him either. It would not have lasted, though. I was about ready to kill him myself, and I thank you for saving me the trouble."

She asked me then how I came to be living such a high life in Saratoga. I told her the whole story of my stay in Kaaterskill, my dalliance with the farmer's daughter and its ignoble ending. Then I told her of the Bard, the doctor and the Seer. And how the fat wallet I had lifted in Poughkeepsie prompted my hasty departure.

"I took the stage to Saratoga, it being the next to leave," I said.

"Still just a will-o'-the-wisp ain't you Pratt?"

"Not anymore," I said, "I'm bound for Rochester to rescue Mirabile."

"You should watch yourself, Pratt, there's something strange about that girl."

"That's rich coming from you," I said, but Jack ignored the jibe.

"As it happens," she said, "I have a mission to Rochester as well."

I asked her to explain, and she said it would make no sense to me unless I heard the whole story of what befell her since Dugan's death. I told her I had no place else to be and would love to hear that story. So she commenced.

"The night of the battle Dugan's red whore came to the room, out of breath, to tell me that he had been killed. She had come to warn me that, without Dugan's protection I was in grave trouble. Bridget was on her way to cut my throat with her razor, and Jimmy, believing that with Dugan gone he was in charge, was coming to take all of Dugan's possessions, including me. My fate depended on which one got there first. Fortunately for me, they were both beaten to Dugan's room by two Bowery Boys coming for the spoils of war.

"It was an awkward scene, as they caught me putting on my canal clothes, hoping to make my escape as a boy. Amused by the novelty of it, and hopeful that I might know some secrets of the Dead Rabbits, they decided to take me to their boss. As they showed no intention to murder me or otherwise misuse me, I went along peacefully.

"Well, no one among the Bowery Boys had any idea what to do with me until I came to the attention of Bill the Butcher. In addition to being an actual butcher, Bill had been a prizefighter and a former member of the Bowery Boys—he's still as big and tough as any of them boys and any of the Dead Rabbits as well. Now he works for the Know-Nothings. Bill and some of the other Know-Nothings thought they might have a use for a girl who could pass for a boy."

"Who are the Know-Nothings?" I asked.

"The Know-Nothings are a group dedicated to the protection of native-born Americans—like me and you, Pratt. They fight against immigrants. They have to stay secret, so if anyone asks about the group, they'll say, 'I know nothing.'"

"Why do they have to stay secret?"

"Not many know this Pratt, but the State of New York is controlled by secret societies in constant warfare with each other."

"You mean like the Dead Rabbits and the Bowery Boys?"

"They're just the armies. The Dead Rabbits work for Tammany Hall, and the Bowery Boys work for the Know-Nothings, but that's just in Manhattan. In the rest of New York, there's the Anti-Rent Party, the Hunkers, the Barnburners, the Patriot Hunters, and the Fenian Brotherhood. And the worst of 'em, the Freemasons; like the Papists, they are trying to control the world. President Polk is a Freemason, but Governor Young is an Anti-mason. The Freemasons murdered William Morgan in Batavia for trying to reveal their secrets, but mostly the war wages constantly, outside of our vision.

"My mission, Pratt, is to carry a secret message from Ned Buntline of the Know-Nothings to Thurlow Weed of the Anti-masons."

"So are you a Know-Nothing yourself Jack?" I asked.
She laughed. "I couldn't tell ya if I was."

CHAPTER 19

Hurry and Wait; Women's Rights; A Long Walk; A Short Voyage.

Jack and I decided to travel together since we were heading to the same place. I was glad to be traveling with her again, and I was glad that she no longer had a grudge against me. I was glad to have the company and, though Jack could be dangerously impetuous, it was still safer than traveling alone.

She continued to dress as a Bowery Boy, and it was a good disguise. People this far north did not know what to make of this swaggering tough, but the notion that it was a girl was the farthest thing from their minds. Jack still carried her rucksack. It was fatter than usual, and I thought she may have had a few more costumes in there. Before we left Saratoga, I bought a simple outfit for traveling and another carpetbag for my good suit. I had no intention of dressing like the Bowery Boy, but I thought it might be too peculiar if he were traveling with a rich man.

We took the Saratoga and Schenectady Railroad. It was my first time on a train; Jack's as well. As a canaller, Jack had a natural dislike of trains, the railroad being the natural competitor to the canal. She spent most of the trip pointing out the flaws in that form of transportation—the soot, the noise, the rocky ride—but she did enjoy watching the scenery rush past, she did enjoy the speed of it. We reached Schenectady, a distance of more than twenty miles, in less than an hour. Though she wasn't fully converted, by the end, she was mightily impressed.

But in Schenectady, we learned the other side of train travel. The next train west was not scheduled for another two hours, and it was running late. All the time we had saved speeding to Schenectady we lost sitting in a waiting room waiting for the next train.

I know, dear reader, that at this point in the story you are less concerned with the merits and drawbacks of train travel than you are with the completeness of my reunion with Jack. By day we were once again a pair of carefree lads seeking adventure, were we also, once more, husband and wife when the sun went down? The answer, I can tell you, unequivocally, was no. I was on a mission now to rescue my sweet Mirabile. I had to stay pure; I thought of no one but her. For Jack, the nights she spent with Dugan had put her off any thoughts of fornication, at least for the time being. She also focused on her mission.

"I have a message from Ned Buntline to Thurlow Weed." She told me again, as we sat in the Schenectady train depot. "It concerns the upcoming elections, both presidential and gubernatorial. With the Democrats in disarray, the Whigs seemed destined to win both. But Buntline and the Know-Nothings want to know if Hamilton Fish can be counted upon to represent our interests, and with no New Yorker in the presidential race, save the washed-up Van Buren, was there a chance to get Millard Fillmore on the ticket?

"Of course this is all just the show," Jack went on, "just as a puppet show; there are many hands unseen that make the puppets dance. Cass and Buchanan and all others offered by the Democrats are controlled by the Freemasons. The question remains, who among the Whigs is sufficiently anti-mason? These questions are answered in secret rooms by men more powerful than politicians. The ebb and flow of power goes on outside of our vision, yet we are controlled nonetheless."

These were not Jacks word. I knew she had been coached, but Jack was a quick study. Secret societies were just her latest hobbyhorse, replacing the apple business. It was best for all concerned to have Jack's efforts concentrated on something, anything, and not flying free.

I tried to listen and pay attention, but each time I heard her explain, it made less sense. Even if it were true, that all the power in the world was a prize for warring societies that I could never join—that democracy was just a show to hide the true contest from the common man— what effect had that on me? I had nothing but the money in my pocket, and even that was not mine, why would I care if it was the Freemasons or the Papists or the Know-Nothings who were really in charge? None of it mattered to me.

It was much like the way I had come to view the Lord's predestination of my soul. I had come to see quite clearly that I was among the damned, predestined for hell, but what of it? It was the Lord's business, not mine. I could not sit back and wait for hell any more than I could rise up and gain heaven by my righteousness. All I could do was live my life and, as flawed as my judgment always was, just try to do what I thought was right.

When the train finally arrived, it was so crowded that we could barely find two seats together. Jack and I sat down across from a couple of women, well dressed and in their middle age, who seemed a bit put off by the prospect of sitting opposite a couple of ruffians for the extent of the train ride. I knew this type; they would come down to Five Points bent on reforming the drunks and whores. They would counsel those who came for shelter to the missions, then hurry back to Fifth Avenue to gossip about it. Jack especially hated them; she would be preached to by neither man nor woman and would rather starve than take a meal at the mission.

As the train departed from the depot, Jack began telling me about the Patriot Hunters, another secret society that was amassing an army to invade Canada. She spoke very softly because these were, after all, secrets. But the women across from us, who apparently were part of a larger group, began talking incessantly, not just to each other but to other members of their party in seats nearby. They all spoke at once which necessitated their speaking ever more loudly. I could not gather what they were saying, but one phrase kept occurring over and over— "women's rights, women's rights, women's rights." I could not fathom what that might mean and why it needed so much discussion. In any case, with Jack speaking so softly and the women speaking so loudly, I followed very little of her tale of the Patriot Hunters and had to keep asking her to repeat.

Jack finally said to the woman across from her, "Would you ladies mind speaking a bit softer? I am having trouble conversing with my friend."

The lady looked down her nose and said, "We shall try."

But they did not try very hard, and soon the chatter was just as loud as it had been before, and I knew Jack's second request would not be as polite as her first.

"Will you please stop running your mouths so I can speak in peace?" Jack shouted, and the ladies all jerked back an inch or so as if an invisible wind had blown them.

I did not know what would come next, but I sought to defuse the situation by changing the subject.

"I overheard you ladies speaking of women's rights a moment ago. I wonder if you might explain the meaning of that." I said with due earnestness to the woman across from Jack.

This had the desired effect, as all were now focused upon me and my edification. They all spoke at once again but soon deferred to the woman across from Jack. As she began to speak, all the other women rose from their seats and gathered around to listen and watch our reactions.

"Women's rights," the lady began, now mounting her high horse, "is the philosophy and belief that a woman should have the same rights as a man. The right to own property, the right to an education, the right to choose her own occupation, these are what we mean by women's rights. We are all on our way to a convention at Seneca Falls where many impassioned women and a few enlightened men will gather to chart the best course for achieving these rights."

Though I had achieved my goal of preventing the imminent conflict between Jack and these women, I was already sorry that I had brought up the matter. These were all issues that Jack had had also confronted, and she had found her own unique solutions. I knew she would have no patience for the women's rights ladies.

"Do you really think yer gonna get your rights by putting on your fine dresses and takin' a train ride half-way 'cross the state to talk about it?" Jack said, "If you want something from a man just stand up and take it from him. They're not as tough as you think."

"I'm afraid it is not that simple, sir." The woman taking a superior tone— always a mistake with Jack. "A married woman is the chattel of her husband, and an unmarried woman has no protection at all. The laws are all in your favor and shall remain so until women have the right to vote."

This was especially ironic because Jack had just finished telling me that voting was just another show to fool the common man into thinking he had power when, in fact, he had none. Jack thought her remark was funny.

"You want to vote? Hell, that's nothin'," said Jack, "I voted three times in the last election: twice for the Know-Nothings and once for Tammany, 'cause they were payin' more."

"Oh, they must think you quite clever down in the Bowery, young man," said our edifier, "but you have no idea of a woman's lot in this country today."

"No idea, you say?" Jack stood up and started to unbutton in her vest.

"Come on, Jack, let's go have a smoke," I said though I knew it was hopeless.

"You think I don't know a woman's lot?" Jack was unbuttoning her shirt now, and the women just stood there gawking, unable to look away.

"No, Jack, don't," I said.

She yanked up her chemise and revealed her breasts to the entire train car. Shaking them back and forth she said, "Here's what I know about a woman's lot: if you want to be treated like a man you can't dress like a lady."

For the smallest of instants, there was absolute calm aboard that train car as the women's rights ladies, eyes wide, took in full horror of the scene. Then all chaos broke loose. The screaming of those women was deafening and would not stop until the conductor came and made Jack button her shirt. He signaled the engineer and the train braked to a complete stop.

And once again Jack and I were prematurely and unceremoniously escorted off of a vehicle of transportation.

*

"Don't say a word, Pratt," Jack said as the train chugged off into woods, trailing billows of black smoke, "I wasn't about to tolerate any nonsense from that woman."

I considered pointing out to Jack that she had a wide array of options available between tolerating nonsense and flashing her breasts in a public train car, but I thought better of it. Instead, I just sighed and said, "It's alright Jack, I've traveled with you before, and I did not expect the trip to be peaceful."

We had no way to determine where we were. From the spot where we left the train, we could see nothing but track to the left and the right and nothing but woods to the front and back. The question at hand was how best to proceed to our destination. If another train came by it would not stop here; we would have to jump on while it was moving. We entertained that idea for a moment then rejected it as too dangerous. Besides, there was no telling when another train was due.

"We should go by canal," said Jack, "We're just about at the Long Level; no locks between here and Syracuse. We can make good time."

"I'm not going back to the canal," I said, "I'm still a wanted man there. You are too."

"That's old news; no one's going to remember us, specially not this far west."

"Won't the canal folks recognize you anyway?" I asked.

"Not if I dress like a woman."

I was still reluctant to return to the canal, but Jack convinced me it was the fastest way west, given our situation. Though slower than the train, canal travel was more reliable and the boats ran much more frequently than the train. But the thought of Jack dressed as a woman convinced me; she would have to behave more demurely to make the costume work, and that alone made me feel safer.

Regardless of what we did next, at the moment we had no choice but to travel on foot to the next town. We set off following the railroad track, the only guarantee we would arrive someplace useful. Fortunately for us, we had been put off the train just a few miles outside of Utica. After about an hour walking the cross ties, we started seeing the buildings of the city. Utica was a factory town boasting huge steam-driven textile mills with loading docks on the track. As we passed, we could see the women inside busily tending their machines.

"Things could be worse, Pratt," said Jack, "We could be them."

We decide that the safest course was to keep following the tracks until we hit the passenger depot. As we approached the depot, one of the workmen attached to the railroad hailed us, and we went over to speak with him.

"You boys been walkin' the track long?" he asked.

"About an hour," I said.

"You didn't happen to see a lunatic in your travels did you?"

"We didn't see anybody."

"There's one out there," he said. "The last train through had to throw one off."

"You don't say," I said.

"A woman dressed as a man."

"You don't say."

"Yes sir, she was raving mad, screaming at the passengers and baring her breasts as brazen as you please."

"Good thing we didn't run into that one," Jack said.

"Don't worry, they'll catch her," said the workman, "Put her in the asylum with the rest of the loonies."

Jack wasn't too concerned that she was now a wanted lunatic at large, but we both agreed that the sooner she dressed as a woman, the better off we would be. There was an alley between the depot and the building next door, and I stood guard at the entrance while Jack went down the alley to change her clothes.

She came out wearing a new turquoise colored dress, a bit wrinkled from the rucksack, but stylish nonetheless. The Know-Nothings had outfitted Jack for just such an occasion as this, where a quick change of identity was necessary. This dress was finer and less flashy than the one I had bought for her. Now she could easily pass for one of the ladies on her way to the women's rights convention.

Then, for good measure, I went down the alley and changed into my good suit. There was a possibility that the authorities had my description as well, so it made sense to change. Besides, we now looked like a distinguished young couple who belonged together.

Finding the canal was easy; these towns are all arranged for the convenience of the canal. We found a ticket agent and booked passage on a packet all the way to Rochester. The agent assured us that we could board the very next boat that arrived. But as we watched that boat pulled towards us, what we saw was more trouble heading our direction. Jack saw it first, but I was the first to say something.

"My God, it's the *Mary Claire*!"

We ducked back into the ticket office to discuss the matter. I insisted that we wait for the next boat, but Jack was anxious to get aboard her old boat and was sure that, dressed as a woman, she could fool Jason and Caleb. I was afraid that my appearance had not changed enough and Jason would instantly recognize me. He would assume that I had been in league with Jack to steal his money and would murder me on the spot. Jack assured me that Jason never paid attention to the male passengers and she was certain that he would not recognize me even if he had met me the day before. So with the gravest of misgivings, I agreed to get on the *Mary Claire*.

I went down the gangplank to board the boat, as I had done several months before and just as then, Captain Jason Horne stopped me. He gave me a quizzical look then said, "Ain't you a preacher?"

I chucked, as if the notion were preposterous, "No sir, I am a speculator from New York."

"You look mighty like a preacher I once had aboard."

"I assure you, sir; I have never before been mistaken for a man of God. "

He tried to catch Jack's eye then. She wore a large bonnet that matched the dress, the sides of which concealed her face unless one looked directly at it. She looked down and away from her brother.

"She's a bit shy," I said, and Jason seemed to accept this. He allowed us to board his boat.

Jack and I stowed our bags in the sleeping areas then went up to sit with the rest of the passengers atop the cabin. It was all so familiar—the smell of the canal water, the sound of Jason's trumpet, the periodic ducking for low bridges. Memories of my first canal voyage came rushing back until I half expected Jack to start tormenting me again. Instead, as the canal boat moved slowly through the lush summer greenery, we began to reminisce about those days. Sure she laughed at how green I was when I first boarded the boat, and how frightened I was at the Scotsman's death, but when we spoke of the day we drank cider by the waterfall, Jack and I both were overcome by waves of nostalgia. Jack leaned over to kiss me, and I did not resist, I kissed her back all the harder.

We were as content as could be riding the canal boat, and I had to agree that canal travel was indeed preferable to train travel (though in all honesty, we had not given the railroad a fair test). But Jack had never ridden a canal boat as a passenger before and had difficulty staying relaxed for very long. She would get up and stroll the deck, viewing the entire boat as if looking for signs of neglect and indications that her brothers were not taking proper care of the boat that she loved.

Jack sat down once more and tried again to relax but soon got up and excused herself to visit the privy. I sat by myself trying to focus on my mission to save Mirabile. It had been aboard this very boat where Mirabile had turned distant towards me, so much so that I believed my hopes for her dashed forever. Was she now truly waiting for me to rescue her? Would that be enough? Would she then be mine forever? If her father had truly gone as mad as she described it would be unconscionable not to help. Whatever the outcome, I thought, I must rescue Mirabile.

Then, from inside the cabin, the peace was shattered by the sound of a violent argument. I could not make out the words, but I knew it was Jack and her brother. I stood up and tried to assess the situation. Then Jack came out of the cabin, and I could hear her quite plainly.

"Goddamn you Jason, you can go straight to hell."

We were not far from the banks of the canal, and I saw Jack make a bounding leap ashore then run toward the woods, her skirts fluttering as she ran. Jason's leap was less graceful, and she had too much head start for him to catch her. I knew I had to move now as well. I ran to the opposite end of the boat and took a flying leap off the top of the cabin. It was a dangerous jump, but I made it safely, though I tripped upon landing and had to scramble to my feet. It gave Jason Horne enough time to change his direction, let his sister go and come see about me. He grabbed me before I fully had my footing and tackled me to the ground.

I thought that I was a dead man; I thought Jason would murder me. Instead, without a word, he tied my hands and pulled me to my feet. He called Caleb to hold the boat and wait for his return; then he led me to the Sheriff of Oneida County.

CHAPTER 20

A Devil's bargain; Perfectionism; Driven Again from Eden.

Jack had stolen another thirty-two dollars from her brothers before fleeing into the woods. Jason took me back to Utica, County Seat of Oneida County to be arrested for that theft as well as for the four hundred dollars she took last April. He sent word back to Caleb to take the boat on to the next town and wait there. If he didn't return the next day Caleb was to continue without him—Jason meant to see this case through to the end.

Fearing the possibility that my true name was already associated with crimes along the canal, I gave my name as George Ridley, the name of the man whose wallet I had lifted in Poughkeepsie. Jason, of course, had no idea what my real name was, but the sheriff looked at me askance when I told him I was George Ridley.

"We'll see about that." He said as he locked me in a jail cell to await the arrival of the Justice of the Peace.

When the Justice arrived I learned why the sheriff had doubted me—my case would be heard by the Honorable George A. Ridley Esq. He was, no doubt, the same George Ridley that I had robbed in Poughkeepsie. In attempting to obscure my true identity I had, unknowingly, greatly multiplied the suspicion against me; I would need to step carefully around this. The Justice, of course, commented immediately.

"George Ridley is your name, sir?" looking over his spectacles and peering down on me from his bench.

"Yes, sir," I said with due humility.

"Are you aware that my name is George Ridley as well?"

"A wondrous coincidence, Your Honor."

"What was your father's name, Mr. Ridley?"

"I never knew my father, sir." I said, "I have been an orphan all my life. George Ridley was the name I was given at the orphanage; where it came from, I know not."

"And where were you orphaned?"

"In the State of Maine, sir."

"And how is it that you are now in the State of New York?"

I told the Justice a long and convoluted story of my life since the Maine orphanage; it was a rich tapestry of fabrication with each lie compounding the previous, but with enough detail from what I had experienced or heard in my travels to make it, I thought, somewhat credible. After escaping from a cruel master at a cooperage where I had been indentured by the orphanage, I traveled to New York City. There, I said, I had made my fortune as a speculator.

"A speculator, you say," said the Justice.

I nodded.

"Have you ever been to Poughkeepsie, Mr. Ridley?"

"Your honor, I can't even pronounce it."

The Justice scowled and said, "Let us go on with the case at hand. Captain Horne says that you came on board his canal boat accompanied by his sister. She had been in disguise, and the two of you were intent on robbing from him. She escaped with thirty-two dollars. He further states that this past April you and she stole four hundred dollars from him under similar circumstances. What have you to say to these charges, Mr. Ridley?"

"First of all, Your Honor, I had no way of knowing that Miss Horne was the sister of the canal boat captain, and I had no way of knowing that she was a thief. As for the second charge, I have never before been on a canal boat and last April I was in New York City practicing my trade."

"That of speculation."

"Yes sir, it left me little time to travel."

"How is it that you were traveling with Miss Horne."

"We had met in Saratoga, and I agreed to accompany her for her protection," anticipating his next question I said, "I was in Saratoga for the therapeutic waters, as I was recovering from a serious accident."

"What kind of accident?" he asked.

"It is rather indelicate, Your Honor. I fell off a speeding horse onto a gravel road and severely wounded my backside." I was prepared to pull down my trousers as proof, but the Justice did not pursue it.

Justice Ridley removed his spectacles and took a moment to contemplate. Then he made his pronouncement.

"As for the theft last April, this court does not have sufficient evidence to prove Mr. Ridley's involvement. However in the recent theft of thirty-two dollars, since Mr. Ridley boarded the boat with Miss Horne, and attempted to flee the scene the same time that she fled with the money, the court has no choice but to find Mr. Ridley guilty."

Then to me, he said, "Young man, whatever your true name is, I feel that you have started down the wrong path at a tender age. I further feel that time in prison, rather than aiding in your reformation, will only destine you to the wrong path for your entire life. So I will give you this choice, you may take a six-month prison sentence at Auburn State Prison, or you can join the society of Shakers and begin a life of purity. "

"What about my money?" said Captain Horne, who had remained silent up to this point.

"Have you thirty-two dollars, young man?" the Justice asked.

"No, sir." I still had some money in my boots but thought it better not to bring it out.

"You appear to be out of luck, Captain, unless you can find your sister."

"Ya call that justice?" Jason shouted.

The Justice scolded Jason for his outburst, then said to me. "Mr. Abernathy of the Shakers will be here this afternoon. Until then you can return to jail and ponder your choices."

When they took me back to jail, I found I was now sharing the cell with another boy about my own age. He introduced himself as Charley. His eye was blackened, and he appeared a bit battered; he told me he had been arrested for fighting. I told him I had been arrested for theft from a canal boat and was given a choice between six months I prison or joining the Shakers.

"Well that's a devil's bargain," said Charley.

I told him that I didn't know anything about the Shakers, but I thought they had to be better than prison.

"They are celibate; that's all you need to know." He told me that the Shaker's lived in an isolated community. They believed that they must stay pure for Christ's second coming, and that meant no that sexual intercourse for anyone. They did nothing but work and pray. "They'll teach you how to make chairs, but you will never be with a woman again."

Charley told me that he was also part of a community that believed in the second coming, and in fact, they believed it had already happened and we were already living in the millennial kingdom. His was called the Oneida Community.

"The difference is," said Charley, "while the Shakers believe in no marriage and no fornication, the Oneida Community believes in complex marriage, where all men are married to all women and fornication is encouraged as long as both parties agree and the mating does not result in pregnancy."

"That sounds like the community for me," I said, "I wonder if the Justice will let me join the Oneida Community instead of the Shakers."

"Our founder, Reverend Noyes, is coming here this afternoon to bail me out," said Charley, "perhaps if he speaks on your behalf, the Justice will let you join our community."

Charley gave me instruction on the beliefs of the Oneida Community—the concept of perfectionism; living free from sin; communalism, shared ownership of possessions; and complex marriage which he had already explained.

"Try to steer clear of complex marriage,' Charley told me, "they don't understand it outside of the community. That is how I ended up here. I told someone I was from the Oneida Community and he said we practiced free-love and all of our women were whores. I could not let that stand, so here I landed."

That afternoon Reverend Noyes came for Charley. He was a very gentle but intense gentleman of about forty years with dark eyes and long chin whiskers. He chastised Charley for fighting instead of turning the other cheek, and Charley apologized profusely. Then Charley told Reverend Noyes about my case, and Noyes took an interest in me. He agreed to stand up for me when I went before the Justice and to do what he could to get me into his community instead of the Shakers.

When I was called back before the Justice of the Peace, I received another great surprise. I was introduced to Mr. Hiram Abernathy of the Shakers, and I could see right away that it was the same Abernathy that we had met in the Adirondacks. It was the Millerite hermit who had been waiting so long for his final judgment and who had given me his money to facilitate his salvation. His beard was shaved and his long ratty locks had been shorn, and he had exchanged his filthy ascension robe for a conservative suit of clothes, but he could do nothing about his eyes. Deep and searching, they were barely of this world; I would recognize them anywhere.

He was now a Shaker—maybe a sensible choice for a disappointed Millerite—and he was there to give me the opportunity to join his stern religion. Also still in court was Captain Jason Horne, hoping somehow to at least get his thirty-two dollars back. And of course, Justice George A. Ridley Esq. was still presiding. All told, the money I had stolen from these three men, either alone or by association with Jack, totaled more than one thousand dollars. I wished to go with Reverend Noyes to the Oneida Community, but all things considered, I felt lucky to be sentenced to only six months in prison. I wished the proceedings to end quickly before any more of my crimes were revealed.

Mr. Abernathy, though eyeing me suspiciously, expressed his willingness to take me to the Shakers, teach me a trade and purify my life. Then, to the surprise of both the Justice, and Mr. Abernathy, Reverend Noyes made a similar offer, stressing the correctness of his doctrine, and proclaiming my natural affinity for it. I offered to explain why I thought Reverend Noyes's religion was true, but the Justice was not interested in hearing. Everyone began speaking at once then, and the Justice pounded his gavel for quiet.

"Reverend Noyes," he said, "I am less familiar with your religion than I am with the Shakers', but in all honesty, I am not fully conversant in either. It is not the role of the criminal court to choose favorites among the various sects. That the convicted man prefers the Oneida Community means nothing to me, and I am half tempted just to send him to Auburn Prison. However, that would do nothing to restore the thirty-two dollars that were stolen from Captain Horne. So I will put the proposition on these terms: whichever of you two gentlemen is willing to pay Captain Horne thirty-two dollars restitution can take custody of my young namesake."

"The Shakers are not in the practice of paying for their converts," said Mr. Abernathy.

"I have thirty-two dollars," said Reverend Noyes, pulling out his wallet.

At that, the Justice of the Peace pounded his gavel and said: "Case closed."

"If the issue is restitution, I might have a complaint against this young man as well," said Abernathy.

But the justice was through with me, and would not listen to anything more.

That evening I rode away in a wagon with Reverend Noyes and Charley to start my new and perfect life as part of the Oneida Community.

*

The Oneida Community was a whole world unto itself. We had a large farm, secluded from society, where we grew our own food, made our own clothing, and manufactured items to sell so we could purchase what we could not produce. We strove for perfection; living a sinless life. Dr. Noyes, by his precise reading of the scriptures, determined that Christ had already returned, in the year 70AD, and his Kingdom was already upon us. It was up to us to institute God's Kingdom on earth. We practiced what Dr. Noyes called "Bible communism" in which all possessions were owned by the Community—as practiced by the primitive Christians. This was not so difficult, really, since there were precious few possessions to own in the Community.

But it was in the area of relations between the sexes the Community's doctrine was most strange and difficult for an outsider to comprehend. Dr.

Noyes believed that love between one man and one woman led to jealousy and selfishness. If a man could not bear to see the woman of his love in the company of other men, then he was not selfless enough for the Kingdom. Thus, as Charley had briefly described to me, the Oneida Community practiced polyandry, or "complex marriage." All of the men were married to all of the women, and sexual intercourse was permitted between any man and woman as long as they both agreed to it.

The way this institution was taught to young people was curious but really quite sensible. In the practice known as "ascending fellowship," each of the virgins, both male and female—and without protest, I allowed myself to be included in this category—was paired up with an older member of the Community who would teach them about sex. Girls were instructed by an older man and boys by an older woman, and the students had a lot more to learn that their counterparts in the outside world.

I was paired with a woman whom I knew only as Mother Sarah. She was a handsome woman, of about forty-five years; kind, patient and quite accomplished in the arts of lovemaking. I spent several wondrous afternoons in Mother Sarah's bedroom. With great detail, she explained the mysteries of a woman's body and taught what a woman likes and what she does not. And she allowed me to practice on her all that I had learned. Though the knowledge that she imparted was, to me, novel and enlightening, I think she could tell that, in practice, I was not a beginner.

The hardest lesson for me was trying to master "male continence." This was a practice similar to what Jack had taught me to avoid pregnancy, but instead of just withdrawing before ejaculating, the man finishes without ejaculating at all. Mother Sarah assured me that it was possible and that the elders of the Community were quite proficient at it. For my part, on the rare occasions when I could accomplish this feat, I had to finish the job myself when alone, lest I explode.

The way that complex marriage worked was this: if a person desired to have sexual relations with another, that person would ask through a third person. If the message returned was "yes" they would meet and fornicate, if not then life went on as if the question had never been asked. In practice it seemed like a needless mechanism that produced the same results as in the outside world; that is, when I desired someone, she did not desire me, yet I seemed to be an object of desire of girls for whom I had no interest. But it was not in my nature to turn anyone down, and many of the girls who were not so pretty in face and form could be quite energetic in bed.

Of course, there was a negative side to our perfect community. Periodically each member would have to endure "mutual criticism" in which members of the Community would point out the flaws in that person's character in front of the whole community. It was not as mutual as I would have liked since the harshest criticism came from the leaders who were, in turn, immune from criticism from someone as low as me. I was chastised for laziness and daydreaming at work and for noticeably coveting girls who would not have me. I had little recourse but to apologize and promise to do better.

All in all, though, it was a peaceful life. We would work all day at our appointed jobs, eat together at the same table, and sing and pray together in the evenings. There was plenty of food and good fellowship, and there was frequent sexual congress with an interesting variety of girls. The Oneida Community was probably as close to perfection as one could expect in this world, and before long, their doctrine was all that I believed, and I earnestly strived to live a sinless life.

I can't say for sure how long I stayed in the Oneida Community. The days, by design, were uneventful and each one flowed seamlessly into the next. The effect was peaceful, eternal and timeless; the movement of the sun across the sky marked nothing more than the time for work and the time for sleep.

Then late one night I was awakened by a rustling outside the window of my little room. I looked out but could see nothing unusual. When I heard it again, I went outside and around to the side of the building to see what was making the noise. There, to my surprise, stood Jack, dressed as a boy again and accompanied by two men carrying rifles.

"Jack!" I whispered loudly, "What are you doing here?"

"I've come to break you out of jail, Pratt."

"This is not a jail."

"Then how come there's a fence all around it." Jack made a sweeping gesture, "We had to walk for miles to find a spot we could climb."

"That's not to keep us in," I said, "it's to keep the world out."

"Tell me, Pratt, didn't the judge send you here for stealin'?"

"Yes."

"Then it's a jail."

"It's not a jail, Jack; it's a perfectionist community."

I tried to explain the difference. I told Jack how we were living a sinless life there; living in peace, loving and sharing the way God intended us to live.

"What about your beloved Mirabile?" was Jack's response.

"It is selfish for one man to possess a woman and keep her from all others."

Jack slapped my face then; she slapped it hard. "Snap out of it, Pratt, you Goddamn idjit.

"I think, Jack," I said, rubbing my smarting cheek, "that you might benefit by some criticism from Dr. Noyes. Why don't you come and join our community?"

"It's worse than I thought; they've stolen your soul!"

"Come join the Kingdom of God, Jack."

"I know you've never forgiven me for taking you from your uncle's sailing ship." Jack was speaking very calmly now. "But this time, Pratt, I know someday you'll thank me." She turned to the riflemen then and said, "OK boys, take care of him."

Her companions then dropped their weapons and pulled me to the ground. They gagged me and bound my arms and legs. Then together, with Jack in the lead, they dragged me out of the Oneida Community.

CHAPTER 21

A Cruel Awakening; A Solemn Oath; Target Practice; A Mighty Storm.

Bound and gagged as I was, in the back of the wagon, I had nothing to do but think. And I had plenty of time for that. It was barely dawn when we left Oneida, and we were still traveling when the sun was high in the sky.

Our course was north and west, was all I could surmise; beyond that, I had no idea where we were. I knew, by now, the way that Jack thought, and I knew she would flee as far away from Oneida and as far away from the canal as she possibly could. The exact destination would probably be determined by Jack's armed guards—whoever they may be. No doubt the wagon belonged to one of them.

The road was bumpy, made all the more discomforting by my inability to cushion myself or hold on to anything sturdy. My first

thought was prayer—I would pray for a short ride on a smooth road; I would pray that, upon arriving at our destination, my captors would do me no more harm. I had, after all, been but recently one of God's perfect Community.

Prayer would be the first thought of anyone at Oneida who found themselves in a similar situation.

But, truth be told, I hadn't the faith to finish a prayer; not even the Lord's Prayer which I knew by heart in two languages. At the Oneida Community, I had attended all the services, followed all the doctrines; was obedient to a fault, surrendering my will to the common good. I had become an exemplary member of the community, and no one would doubt my righteousness. But I had fooled them all, even fooled myself; for I had never been part of God's Kingdom, not really, I had only mouthed the words and aped the actions of the truly righteous. I had been a model follower of Dr. Noyes, but it had not been for the sake of my soul, it had been for worldly rewards. The sexual freedom, of course, was rewarding, but it was the peace, that heavenly peace, the peace that I had not known since leaving Salem, that was the true reward. I would have done most anything they asked to maintain that peace. And now away from the Community, I had no desire to talk to God, even to beg for my sorry hide. I truly was among the damned and deserved all that I had gotten.

That doesn't mean I was not angry when the wagon finally came to a stop that sunny afternoon. Jack came around to the back of the wagon and stood facing me, arms akimbo.

"Can I take the gag off ya now, Pratt or are you gonna start shoutin'?"

I shook my head to indicate that I wouldn't shout. Jack united the gag and removed it from my mouth.

Through clenched teeth, suppressing my desire to scream, I said, "Jack, what the hell are you doing to me?"

"I told you, I broke you out of jail."

"You bring me nothing but hardship, Jack, in ways I never could have imagined."

"You'll thank me someday, Pratt. Now, if I untie your arms and legs will you promise not to fight?"

"When you untie me, Jack, I'll murder you, I'll strangle you."

Jack just nodded. "I have some business to take care of Pratt, so I'm going to leave you here." She said, then raised the gag so I could see it. "Do I need to put this back on ya?"

"Untie me now," I shouted, "so I can cut your Goddamn heart out!"

"So be it." She said and tied the gag back around my mouth.

Jack went away for about three-quarters of an hour, and I cooled down during that time. I had no intention of fighting her and shouting did nothing further my cause. I decided to cooperate when she returned.

She stood at the rear of the wagon once again and said, "We're goin' into this tavern for some food and drink. I'd be pleased if you came along, but it's entirely up to you. Are you going to fight if I untie you?"

I convinced Jack that I would not fight and she untied me. In silence, I followed her inside the tavern. She introduced me to her two companions (their names I no longer remember). I could see now that they were dressed as hunters and had their rifles slung over the backs of their chairs as they sat at the table.

I had no thoughts of fighting, but I did consider running. If I turned and bolted into the woods, I could have gotten far enough away, hidden myself before anyone even turned to follow. And I wasn't even sure that Jack would follow. But where would I go, penniless, in the woods somewhere in the middle of New York State?

Instead, I stayed for dinner. We had beef and potatoes and mugs of ale, and it was wonderful. At Oneida most meals were only vegetables, I thought I would never taste beef again. And of course, we drank no ale there, no intoxicating spirits of any kind. I was soon as happy as I could be. After dinner, we drank whiskey and smoked pipes. And as we drank and smoked we told stories. Jack's hunter friends knew dozens, each one funnier than the last. They were so happy in the telling because they had practiced the stories so many times before and were now delivering them to fresh ears.

We laughed and talked until fatigue overtook us and, try as we might, we could not keep the party going. Jack's friends still had to drive the wagon home. They stood up and faced Jack, each crossing their arms over their chests. Jack stood up and did the same. Then all three dropped their arms at once.

After they had left I asked Jack what that was about and she explained that they were Patriot Hunters, and she was too. That was their sign.

"We are an army, stretched from Vermont to Michigan, ready to take Canada from the British." She told me, "More than that I can't say, but we'll be mustering tomorrow night, and you are welcome to join us."

I told her that if they were all as jolly as the two, I had already met, I would certainly go with her. The tavern had rooms upstairs, and Jack had already taken one. I went upstairs with her, and we both slept well into the next day.

The hunters returned that afternoon and Jack, and I sat in the back of the wagon as they drove us deep into the woods. Jack told me that Ned Buntline had given her the address of one of the Patriot Hunters' leaders in the town of Oswego. She hadn't planned to use it, but after my arrest in Oneida, she went to them for help and ended up joining their army.

"Jail breakin' is the kind of action the Hunters crave," Jack said, "they were more than willing to send their men along with me to break you out of Oneida."

We came at last to a large cabin of logs in a clearing of the forest. I could tell it was occupied by the smoke emanating from a stone chimney. On a pole in front flew a rustic looking flag with a depiction of an eagle in battle with a lion. We went to the door, and one of the men knocked three times.

"Are you a Hunter?" came a voice from inside.

"Yes, on Wednesday." Our man replied. The day being Tuesday, I looked at Jack quizzically.

"Secret code words," Jack whispered.

The door opened, and there was more secret activity. As each of the men entered, he clamped his thumb between his front teeth; the guard at the door nodded and let him pass. Jack made the cross-armed salute I had seen the day before, and she was allowed to pass. I, having no sign to make, was barred from entering.

"He's a candidate for initiation," Jack said.

"No, I'm not," I said.

"Well is he or ain't he?" said the guard.

Jack told me to hush, then nodded to the guard.

"What's his name?"

"Jonathan Pratt." She said. I was not happy that my real name would be used for this.

"Wait here," Said the guard, "We will call Mr. Pratt when we are ready."

"What is going on here Jack?" I said after the guard closed the door, "I don't want to join this army."

"I told you yesterday you were welcome to join, and you thought it was a grand idea."

"I didn't think you meant becoming a member."

"Well, it's too late to turn back now," she said, "Don't worry, you'll like it."

The door opened directly, and two men came out. Without a word, one of them tied a blindfold over my eyes; then I was led into the cabin. After a few steps in we stopped, and a man addressed me with a voice, deep and stern.

"Jonathan Pratt, have you come to join the Society of Hunters, whose purpose is to liberate the Canadian Provinces form British thralldom?"

At this stage what could I say but, "Yes."

He made a short speech then about secrecy and loyalty, and the server penalties for violating either. Then he had me recite an oath.

"Repeat after me, 'I, Jonathan Pratt, solemnly swear in the presence of Almighty God and this lodge of Hunters...'"

I repeated after the voice, each line of an oath that went something like this:

"I, Jonathan Pratt, solemnly swear in the presence of Almighty God and this lodge of Hunters that I will not give the secrets of this degree, or any secret that may come to my knowledge, in the body of this lodge, to any person to whom they do not justly and lawfully belong; that I will not write, print, stain, stamp, hue, scratch, indent, or engrave upon anything whereby the secrets of this degree may be unlawfully obtained.

I pledge my life, my property, and my sacred honor to the Association; I bind myself to its interests, and I promise, until death, that I will attack, combat, and help to destroy, by all means that my superior may think proper, every power, authority, of Royal origin, upon this continent; and especially never to rest till all the tyrants of Britain cease to have any dominion or footing in North America.

I further solemnly swear to obey the orders delivered to me by my superior, and never to disclose any such order, or orders, except to a brother Hunter of the same or higher degree. So help me God."

After I said the words "So help me God," my blindfold was removed.

"Behold the light!" said my master.

Three men stood before me; one held a sword pointed directly at my breast; each of the other two held a pistol pointed at my head. Behind them, another man held a flaming torch.

"As you see the light," he said, "so you also see death, presented to you in the most awful shape and form, from which no earthly power can save you, the moment you attempt to reveal any of the secrets or signs which have, or may be, revealed to you."

I was then a Patriot Hunter. In little more than a day and a half I had gone from studying peace in the Kingdom of God, to studying war in an army bent on invading Canada.

*

Following my initiation, the Hunters opened the curtains, letting the sunshine into the Lodge, and began to socialize and drink from an earthen jug of whiskey. There were about twenty in attendance, most seemed to be men in their forties or older, and the rest were about my own age. I was taken aside by the two who had brought me, to be instructed in the secrets and mysteries of the Patriot Hunters.

There were various degrees of membership in the Hunters; the lowest being Snowshoes, next were Beavers, then Grand Hunters, and the highest degree was Patriot Mason. Jack and I were the only Snowshoes, and everyone was pleased, as it had been some time since new members had been inducted. The younger men were all of the Beaver degree; they were not lacking in enthusiasm but were somehow less focused upon the goal than the older Hunters. The Grand Hunters were the ones who kept hammering the point that we were assembled to drive the British from North America. There were two Patriot Masons, the highest degree, and they were distinguished by the fact that they had participated in the "Great Hunt."

The Great Hunt, like so much of the Hunters' speech, was actually code for something else. It referred to the Battle of the Windmill when land and sea forces of the Patriot Hunters invaded the town of Prescott in Upper Canada.

I had mentioned to one of my instructors that the cabin we were in seemed much larger than necessary for the number of Hunters there. He told me that before the Great Hunt, hundreds of men, from all walks of life, would meet there and prepare for the invasion of Canada. But the battle had been a failure; Commander von Schoultz and ten others were executed by the British. Sixty more were transported to Van Deimen's Land. After that, membership in the Patriot Hunters began to dwindle.

When my training was completed, the meeting proper commenced. The first order of business was the payment of dues. As it was the first muster for Jack and myself, the man in charge said they would waive the obligation, but in subsequent musters, we would be required to pay. Next, he read a tally of Hunters who were in arrears in dues payments—including most of those present—and they were also reminded to settle up next muster.

The next order of business was reading correspondence from other Lodges. At one time, he told us, the reading of correspondence was the most important part of each meeting. This time there were but two letters: one from St. Albans, Vermont, and one from Detroit, Michigan. The letters were written in code, and it was the job of one of the Grand Hunters to translate them. He first read the letter from St. Albans which said, in effect, they were standing strong but had nothing new to report.

"Respond to them thus," said one of the Patriot Masons, "'Oswego stands strong as well, and has garnered new members.'"

The letter from Detroit was rather long, and the translator chose to summarize its content, "Detroit is in disarray and in desperate need of new monies."

"Detroit is always in need of new monies," said one Patriot Mason.

"They are run by a pack of thieves," said the other.

"Tell them we have no funds available at this time," said the first, "but we will think first of Detroit when our fortunes change."

There was no more new business, and as there was still daylight, we all went out behind the lodge for target practice. Each of the Hunters had brought his own weapon for the shooting. There was one old musket on the wall of the Lodge; Jack was allowed to use that. The younger Hunters were the best armed; many had Sharps rifles and Colt revolvers. One of the Beavers, who had recently purchased a Colt, let me use his old flintlock pistol.

Targets were set up some distance away, and we commenced to shooting at them. I had never worked a firearm before, and my pistol missed fire several times before I finally got off a shot. The reloading then took so much time that I resolved, in the unlikely event that I ever invaded Canada, I would find a safe hiding place and only fire my weapon when my foe was upon me with his.

When twilight fell, and the light became insufficient for shooting, we all went back into the lodge for more drinking and storytelling. I handed the pistol back to the Beaver who had loaned it.

"Keep it," he said, "You will need a weapon, and this will do until you get something better. Keep your flint sharp and your powder dry. Keep your gun loaded and primed; you may be called at any hour."

I accepted the piece. To do otherwise would be admitting the truth: that there was no way in hell I was ever joining their invasion of Canada. The Beaver showed me how to carry the pistol in the waist of my trousers and cover the handle with my shirt, keeping it ready at hand but hidden from public view.

I was still carrying it when Jack and I boarded a Lake Ontario steamboat in Oswego—it was my only possession save the clothes on my back. I had spent the last of my money on a steamboat ticket to Rochester. Jack still had money, but she would not say how much.

Everyone we spoke to told us that the fastest route to Rochester was over the lake by steamboat. I was hesitant to get aboard another steam vehicle with Jack, but she promised me she would not even look at a playing card if any were being used on the boat, and she assured me that she would keep her opinions to herself regardless of the conversation we may find ourselves in.

Our boat was called the *Northerner*, and at first glance, it looked as though someone had just added a boiler and a pair of side paddles to an old schooner, but closer examination revealed the boat was specially built for lake travel, with sails to take advantage of the ever-present wind should the engine fail. We were scheduled to leave at 4:00 and would be in Rochester before 9:00; however our departure was contingent upon the arrival in Oswego of the train from Albany. Neither Jack nor I was optimistic, but there was a saloon on board and its operation, apparently, was contingent upon nothing so we took a table there, and remained there when the boat finally departed. The drinks were on Jack.

We had both decided to continue our missions to Rochester, though in each case the fervor was considerably diminished. Jack, who now had membership in two secret societies, found that the whole notion had lost its luster. Secrets revealed had much less appeal than secrets desired. She would meet anyway with Thurlow Weed, send her report back to the Know-Nothings by U.S. Mail and be done with it.

"You should use the Patriot Hunters' code," I said, and Jack laughed to the point that I thought she would fall off her chair.

My hesitancy in fulfilling my mission to rescue Mirabile from her evil and obsessed father stemmed from my own sense of shame. I had not, by any means, remained pure in the period since I had promised to help Mirabile, and while that was an entirely self-imposed vow, it mattered none the less to me. I also feared that I could never live up to Mirabile's purity. Hers was the one soul that had remained righteous throughout, while mine had proven time and again to be damned. I told none of this to Jack, saying instead that there was no point looking for her in Rochester, Mirabile had expected me in July and it was now mid-August.

"That don't matter," Jack said, "I was supposed to go next to the Free-Soil convention in Buffalo, to assess their platform and Van Buren's chances for president. That convention was over last week. We do what we can, but no one can make good on all their promises. The point is, Pratt if this girl is your destiny, what choice do you have?"

As usual, I could not argue with Jack's reasoning.

As we sat so deep in conversation, we had not noticed that the lake had gradually gotten rougher until one huge swell nearly knocked us over. We looked out the windows to see that the sky had turned black as night and dark clouds roiled above us. A bolt of lightning cracked the sky, followed closely by thunder so loud that the sound alone seemed to knock the boat back. Then the rain began; sheets of rain, driving sideways into the boat until I could not tell for sure whether we were even above water.

And still the waves grew wilder, heaving the boat back and forth in the water. Jack and I held on to a railing along the wall of the saloon, and as the boat tipped perilously, we could see the paddlewheel, now fully out of the water, turning helplessly until the wave splashing across the deck doused the fire of the engine.

We had traveled far into the deep water of the lake but had never lost sight of land on our left. We were now being pushed ever closer, back toward the shore, where rocky points waited to rip our vessel to shreds should we manage to stay afloat long enough to reach them. The pilot had lost control of the boat as we rolled in all direction, a plaything of the waves.

Lightning flashed again, filling the room with ghostly illumination. Thunder soon followed, loud as cannon fire, and Jack grabbed me at the sound.

"Jesus Christ," she said, "hold me Pratt, I don't want to die in this water."

I held her as tight as I could and tried not to show fear, but I wished there was someone to hold and comfort me. I was fully convinced that I was but moments away from a watery grave and my soul's arrival in hell.

CHAPTER 22

*Welcome Hospitality; Lingering Fear; Secrets Revealed;
Communicating with the Dead.*

The storm raged throughout the night, waves tossing the boat this way and that, as we waited in abject fear for our imminent collision with the rocky shore. Then with a sudden thud, all movement stopped. Our own momentum threw us to the floor, but the boat was no longer floating free. The deck was now leaning at such an angle that standing upright was impossible. Jack and I leaned against the wall and hoped for no further changes.

It was not until dawn, with the rain stopped and the clouds dissipating, that we saw what happened. In the height of the storm, waves had heaved our boat onto a sandbar with such force that it became stuck in the sand, the hull angled but above the level where waves could further move it. As the storm subsided the boat remained in relative safety, but any further travel on this boat would be impossible. We would wait to be rescued.

Jack and I, concerned with our own safety, had barely been aware of the chaos and confusion which had overtaken the rest of the passengers. Many had not been as lucky as we were when the boat ran aground and had fallen into furniture or into each other in piles of human bodies from which it became virtually impossible to escape. The screaming and wailing of fear and agony that had been drowned out by the wind and rain did not subside when the storm did. The sights and sounds that morning were so horrible that I thought perhaps I had died and gone to hell.

The captain and the crew did what they could to treat the injured and pacify the frightened. The injuries were minor and most of their effort went to getting the passengers upright and organized, preparing for the rescue vessels the captain assured us would be arriving soon.

But rescue has slow in coming. Though it was surely known in Rochester that we were in trouble, the same storm that had disabled us had prevented any attempt at rescue until the morning. The first boats to arrive were rowboats which took away the injured. Soon a small steam ferry came as close as possible to the *Northerner*, and we were able to cross over to it on a wooden gangplank. It had taken two trips to transport all the passengers to Rochester; Jack and I were in the second.

It was nearly evening when our feet finally touched dry land. Newspapermen were waiting on the pier; taking everyone's name and listening to their stories. Normally this was the kind of situation where Jack would take the lead, educating anyone who would listen, informing the world what really happened. But that day she was remarkably quiet, and it had me concerned. I had never seen Jack as frightened as she had been on board that distressed steamboat—and we had been through some frightening times. This time had scared her deeply, and she was not over it yet.

We did not know our way around Rochester, but Jack had gotten a name from the Master Hunters at the Patriot Hunters' Lodge. Mr. Bennet had been a Master himself, in the old days, but they could not vouch for him now except to say that he was not the kind of man to turn a stranger from his door. We asked directions from the men on the pier and they told us it was the best of neighborhoods and we would have no trouble walking there.

It was a fine, two-storied stone house with Greek columns in front. Mr. Bennet, an older man with gray side-whiskers, came to the door himself when we called. He looked bemused to see two such bedraggled ruffians as we had become. Jack gave the cross-armed salute of a Patriot Hunter Snowshoe. I did likewise then, fearing that if I didn't, I might be left outside. He gave us a quizzical look, as if seeing something that he vaguely recognized but could not place then, at once, a smile came to his face.

"Are you a Hunter?" he said.

"On Thursday," Jack said, the day being Wednesday.

"Do come in," he said, barely suppressing a chuckle.

He led us to his study, a dark and serious room with much mahogany and walls lined with books. We sat in comfortably upholstered chairs.

"I did not know that the Patriot Hunters were still extant." He said when we were all seated. "What Lodge are you from?"

We explained that we had come from Oswego and had recently been rescued from a steamboat that had run aground during the storm.

"My goodness, what an ordeal." He said. "You'll want some brandy then."

He poured us each a glass of brandy from a crystal decanter; it was quite fortifying, exactly what was needed. He requested that we tell him all about our voyage. Here, again, I would have expected Jack to take the lead, telling a story filled with adventure, exaggerating when necessary to enhance the drama. But she left it to me and only spoke when I called upon her to verify something I had said.

Mr. Bennet was duly impressed and poured us each another glass of brandy. Then he asked more about the Patriot Hunters. Were they still planning to invade Canada? I told him that they were well armed and made threatening statements, but that invasion was not likely.

"That is well," he said, "The first one was a terrible mistake. There were so many of us then, and it seemed inevitable. If we just lit the fuse, our government would follow, and Upper Canada would become part of the United States. But our government had its hands full in Mexico and did not want to fight another war. After the failed invasion we disbanded in Rochester—came to our senses, really. It had seemed like such a lark until men lost their lives.

"I sense that you boys have more stories to tell," Mr. Bennet said to me, then pointed to Jack who had just nodded off, "but I see that your comrade is quite fatigued. Not surprising considering what you have been through. There will be time for stories in the morning. You are more than welcome to stay here; let me show you to your rooms."

Mr. Bennet showed Jack and me to separate bedrooms on the second floor. The featherbed was clean and soft; I fell into deep slumber immediately upon pulling up the covers.

Some time in the middle of the night I was awakened by the creak of the bedroom door opening. In came Jack, wearing only her shirt. Without a word she climbed into my bed and held me as tightly as she had aboard the floundering steamboat. We made love then—gently, but without hesitation.

"I was so frightened on that boat, Pratt," she said afterward, as we lay side by side, "I have never felt so helpless.

*

We had breakfast the next morning in Mr. Bennet's kitchen. He joined us at the table though he had risen hours before we did. We learned that he was a widower who had owned a grist mill but was now retired. He had a cook—who prepared us a magnificent breakfast—and a live-in housekeeper but otherwise lived alone.

He was anxious to learn more about us, so Jack told him all about the steamboat disaster and our visit to the Patriot Hungers in Oswego. I was happy to hear Jack talking again. If anything, she was more exuberant than usual and had Mr. Bennet laugh a number of times.

"Amazing, truly amazing," Mr. Bennet said when Jack paused to take a bite of eggs. He peered at Jack for a few seconds then said, "I know your secret, you know."

"What secret is that?" Jack said.

"I know you are a girl."

"Yer crazy." She said, but I could see she was blushing.

"I'm a light sleeper," he said, "and I hear everything that goes on in this house. I know the two of you shared a bed last night and, while I have known men who preferred their own sex, I do not take you two to be of that type. Am I wrong or is there a girl inside those clothes."

I had never seen anyone discover that Jack was a girl when she wasn't undressed. I sometimes I forgot myself. She responded like a naughty child trying to plead excuses.

"No, you ain't wrong." She said, "But I can't wear those frills all the time. Besides, it's a man's world; if I dress like a girl, I can't do the things I want."

"It's truly remarkable," he said, "not just the clothes but the way you wear them. It's a perfect disguise."

"It's me bein' me."

"It doesn't hurt that you have a voice like a tin pot full of stones. There is no question but that you would fool most people."

"I fool everyone."

"But when you look close;" Mr. Bennet was still peering at Jack's face, "the eyes, the skin, unmistakably feminine. Now that I know it, I can't see you as anything but a girl."

"Alright, that's enough about me." Jack was starting to get angry. "What about Pratt? Tell me about his secrets."

Mr. Bennet laughed and took his gaze off Jack's face. "I don't think Mr. Pratt has any secrets equal to yours, except perhaps the pistol he keeps hidden under his shirt."

This man was nothing if not observant. I had grown accustomed to carrying the pistol and tended to forget that I had it. While I had no need for a gun away from the Hunter's Lodge, I had no place to leave it. It seemed too valuable to throw away so I thought at some point I would sell it. In the meantime, it stayed tucked into my trousers, covered by my shirt. I would take more care at concealment after Mr. Bennet's observation.

The pistol required explanation if only to reassure Mr. Bennet that he was in no danger of being fired upon or robbed at gunpoint. We told him about target practice with the Hunters, and that led to an explanation of how we had gotten to Oswego, which led in turn to explaining about the Oneida Community. Each story required further explanation and Jack, and I found ourselves recounting our entire journey, first in reverse order, then in no order at all, pulling incidents from one place then another, moving backward and forward in time. We told it all putting ourselves in the best of lights, omitting, for example, that we had ever been thieves or whores. Though we told only a fraction of our story, I don't believe Mr. Bennet believed even half of what we did tell.

"Whither are you bound now?" he asked when we had reached a stopping point in the tale.

"We have some unfinished business in Rochester," Jack said.

Jack told him about the message she had from the Know-Nothings to Thurlow Weed, and how I needed to rescue Mirabile from her faith-healing father.

"I'm afraid I can't help you with Mr. Weed." He said, "I have little use for his brand of politics—the Know-Nothings either, for that matter—but you are free to believe what you will. As far as religion, you have come to the right place. A wider range of ecclesiastical theories than in Rochester today has seldom been seen in the history of mankind. I was caught up in it myself when Finney first came to town, and I took note of the boy who saw visions in his hat and is now a prophet leading his multitudes west. Around the time of the end-of-the-world hysteria I gave up fanaticism and became an occasional Methodist.

"If the preacher you are interested in engages in faith-healing, he is probably long gone. They are seldom in one place for long, as the healed will often relapse, and it is bad for business when they return. In any case, if you go downtown, look at the bills and flyers, talk to the proselytizers, you may learn more than I can tell you."

We thanked Mr. Bennet for his hospitality, and he told us we were welcome to return any time. Jack told him we might be back that evening, depending upon what transpired during the day. Then we went on foot to the heart of Rochester.

Rochester was a remarkable city. It was large and bustling, but unlike New York which was all old, rundown and dirty, Rochester was clean, and everything was new as if it had suddenly popped from the ground like a mushroom after a rainstorm. There were huge grist mills along the Genesee River, with canal boats arriving full of wheat and leaving full of flour. The canal itself went through the city in amazing ways. An aqueduct carried the canal over the river, and canal boats traversed it, a good twenty feet in the air.

As Mr. Bennet had said, there was religion everywhere. In addition to the regular churches, there were bills advertisements all sorts of unusual sects. Some, like the Shakers, the Adventists and the followers of Dr. Noyes, were quite familiar to me. Others were new and exotic. Not just religion, other ideas were being advertised as well, a freed slave named Douglas was scheduled to lecture on abolition, and a women's rights group met regularly.

But the closest I came to finding a faith-healer was an advertisement for a syrup guaranteed to cure consumption, dyspepsia, scrofula, and liver complaints, that was manufactured by a Presbyterian minister named Dunlap.

Jack had no better luck than I had. The information she had been given was hopelessly out of date. Thurlow Weed's Anti-masonic organization no longer existed and she was told by an editor of the *Rochester Republican* that Weed had moved to Albany years ago.

I was just as glad in both cases. The thought of rescuing Mirabile, taking her away—to be what, my wife?—now seemed to me somewhat childish. And I'd had my fill of philosophical organizations and new thinkers, and I was glad that Jack wasn't going to introduce me to another. Now freed from our obligations, maybe Jack and I could just continue to travel together until we found some peaceful place to light. But for several reasons, that was not to be.

While we stood reading a poster advertising some preacher or other, a young woman approached and asked us if we were interested in religion. Jack told her we were looking for a man who practiced faith-healing. The woman said that was all bunk, but there were real miracles afoot —her two little sisters could communicate with the dead. The woman's name was Leah Fox, and she invited us to a séance with her sisters, Maggie and Katie.

This reminded me of what the Poughkeepsie Seer had told me, and I told Jack how he had predicted communication with the dead. This had her intrigued, and Jack wanted to meet these girls. Leah asked us if there were a dead spirit we would like to contact.

"Yes," said Jack, "Eamon Dugan. I want to ask him if he was murdered by Jonathan Pratt."

"I didn't murder Dugan, Jack. I told you that."

"We'll see."

Leah Fox asked us all about ourselves as she led us to their cottage on Troup Street. They required a small donation, then served us tea while we waited for another party to arrive. When everyone was there we went into a small room, and all sat at a round table; Maggie and Katie sat together, with Leah standing behind them. The shades were drawn, and all lights were extinguished, then we all held hands and recited the Lord's Prayer in unison. We sat in silence for a time, and then heard a peculiar tapping sound that seemed to resonate throughout the room.

"Is that you, Mr. Split-foot?"

The response was two taps, meaning "yes."

They asked the spirit a few simple questions, to which he responded with either one or two taps. Then the spirit taped five times in succession, which, we were told, meant that he had a message that would require the alphabet board. This was a board, upon which was printed each letter of the alphabet. Leah would point to each letter in sequence, and when she was pointing the letter, he wanted the spirit would tap. In this way he was able to spell out the message that he was joined by two other spirits who could not stay long— a Mrs. So-and-so (I don't recall the name) who was important to the other group, and Mr. Dugan, who was obviously of interest to us.

Through the same methods, the other group asked questions of Mrs. So-and-so. Yes, she said, she had forgiven whatever trespass concerned them, and she gave her blessing to some enterprise or other. These messages were of grave import to those asking, and the women in the group broke down into tears.

When it was Dugan's turn, Jack asked him "What's it like in hell, Dugan?"

The response he spelled out was "Hot."

"Did Pratt murder you Dugan?"

The response was one tap, "no."

"I told you," I whispered.

"Can they foretell the future?" Jack asked Leah.

"Sometimes," she answered.

"Will, I ever find Thurlow Weed?" Jack asked the spirits.

The response was one tap.

Jack nodded. "Will Pratt find his destiny?"

Two taps.

That was about it. There was some closing ceremony then we all bid each other farewell. I was somewhat skeptical, but the séance left Jack deep in thought.

"You're quiet again," I said.

"They said you'll find your destiny, Pratt. That means you will be off with that woman."

"No, it doesn't. My destiny could be anything. Of course, I'll find it because it's my destiny. But it won't be with Mirabile. I want to stay with you, Jack. I want it to always be like last night."

She put her arm around me as we walked, but just briefly, as she was still mindful that she was dressed as a boy. "I hope it's true, Pratt."

As we turned up the walk to Mr. Bennet's house, a woman standing near the gate called to me.

"Jonathan, I need to talk to you." It was Mirabile. I stopped to see what she wanted.

Jack said not a word but just kept walking.

CHAPTER 23

The Healing Tabernacle; Deadly Betrayal; Trials and Tribulations.

everend Travis had his own little church in an unsavory section of Rochester that Jack and I had not visited. It appeared to be an old dry goods store with the name of the church—The Healing Tabernacle— painted on the front window. The door opened into a room filled with rows of chairs facing a wooden table covered by a purple table cloth, meant to be an altar holding candlesticks and brass plates. Prints depicting biblical scenes were tacked onto the walls, and a wooden cross hung behind the altar. A streetlamp outside threw flickering shadows across the floor, and in the dim light, the room looked profoundly sad to me.

I had reluctantly agreed to follow Mirabile back to the church when we met at Mr. Bennet's gate. After spending the day searching unsuccessfully for any sign of Reverend Travis's ministry, I had finally resolved to give it up and leave Mirabile behind—just a distant memory. But as so often happened, once I decided to go in one direction, circumstances pushed me in another.

"Where have you been, Jonathan? You promised you would be here two months ago." She said, standing at the gate, dressed in the same white dress she was wearing when I first saw her. "My situation has become intolerable."

She told me that the Reverend had become obsessed with the power of divine healing that he believed he possessed. He now had a following who believed as well, and he was able to fill the church on Sunday, and several nights a week as well. But the Reverend no longer cared about money and was spending more on his church than he was bringing in. When Mirabile tried to discuss matters with him, he would beat her.

"I'm not sure how I can help, Mirabile," I said.

"Just stand by my side, Jonathan. Make sure he pauses long enough to hear what I have to say. Make him listen to reason. Please, Jonathan, I have no one else."

Mirabile was in tears, and I had promised I would help her, so I agreed, at last, to go with her and support her as she talked with her father. But, of course, when we got to the church, she revealed that there was more to the story. She led me through the front room of the church and into a small room in the back. In it were just a bed and their trunk and a curtained doorway on the left wall leading into another room. She lit a lamp on the trunk and explained her true intention; she planned to leave him, but could not go without her share of the money they had made. She wanted me to make sure he gave her what she was owed. He always carried the money with him in a leather valise; we would wait until he returned, then confront him.

I knew from experience that this was not the kind of situation that would end peacefully. I had no intention of fighting with Reverend Travis, and I told Mirabile so.

"You said you would help me, Jonathan. You said you would take me away from this life."

"I can't take you away, Mirabile. Not now."

"You said you had feelings for me, Jonathon," she began crying again. "Was it all a lie?"

It wasn't a lie. As hard as I tried to resist it, Mirabile still had a hold over me that I could not fight. I took her in my arms then, and we kissed, long and hard. Our passionate kissing and caressing kept on until at last, Mirabile stepped back, undid her white dress and let it fall to her feet. As she continued to undress, I took off my shirt and pants, carefully placing the pistol atop the trunk. I made no attempt to hide it. When I turned around, she was already in the bed, and I quickly joined her.

Judge me as you will, dear reader, but I had, at long last, attained object of my deepest desire and right or wrong, I could not have acted differently. I was in heaven, but even bringing to bear all the skills I had learned from Mother Sarah, the ecstasy lasted for just the briefest of moments. And nothing could have prepared me for the hell that followed.

A voice bellowed from the doorway, "What's this?"

I rolled over to see Reverend Travis standing there, holding his leather valise. And he was seething with anger.

"Mirabile, what goes on here? And Jonathan, is that you? Have you no shame?"

Mirabile jumped up and stood, stark naked, before him. "I'm leaving you, Isaiah. Give me the bag; I'm taking what's mine."

"In a pig's ass you are," he said and started towards her with violent intent.

Mirabile seized my pistol from the trunk, cocked it and fired just as the Reverend was about to grab her. The sound of the explosion echoed through the building as the ball pierced his chest. With a mournful groan, Reverend Travis fell forward and died on the floor.

"Mirabile, you've murdered your father!"

"He's not my father," she said, "he's my husband. And this has been a long time coming."

She started to dress, then turned to the leather valise, now wedged under the body, straining to pull it loose and finally succeeding. As I started to rise, she opened the bag and withdrew a mean looking dagger.

She stood over me then, wearing just her drawers, teeth bared, blade in hand and said, "Stay where you are Jonathan, or I will stick you like a pig. I've killed one man tonight; I'll not hesitate to kill another."

I stayed in bed and watched for an opportunity that never came.

"I'm sorry it had to be this way, Jonathan," she said, as she rummaged through the bag assessing its contents. Satisfied with the bag, she continued to dress, talking as she did so.

"You may wonder how I came to be married to an old man like that. I was a young girl in Pennsylvania and Travis came through town selling patent medicine. He heard me singing, liked my voice and asked if I wanted to join his traveling show. Unhappy at home, I was quick to say yes.

I was the whole show, singing to draw a crowd, that he then sold medicine. It was just whiskey and red pepper—and opium when we could get it. I didn't cure anybody, but it made them feel better.

Within a month we were married. What I didn't know then, but soon learned, is that to a man like Isaiah Travis, a wife is little more than a slave. He went with other women wherever we went but kept a tight rein on me. When he learned he could make more money in religion with even less work, everything got worse. And, well, you know the rest."

Fully dressed, she brushed herself off, picked up the bag and said, "Thank you, Jonathan, you've been a great help to me, not in the way I expected, but maybe this way is better."

Then she was out the door and gone. I lay there in bed, trying to gather my wits. I was shocked and stunned; wounded as if I were the one who had been shot. But there was yet another shock; someone came into the room, then, through the curtained doorway.

"Jack! What are you doing here?"

She just looked at me and shook her head. "If you know what's good for ya, Pratt, you'll get dressed and get out of here now."

Then she ran out the front door too.

*

There at long last, oh patient reader, is the murder for which I must unjustly pay the price of my earthly life. It was, I know, a long road to travel, but if its ending were to make any sense, it was necessary for me to relate the entire journey—every step contributed to the next, and the outcome was the result of so many bad decisions. If I had just said farewell to Mirabile at the gate walked into Mr. Bennet's house with Jack I would not have been anywhere near Reverend Travis. If I had not joined the Patriot Hunters, I would not have been carrying the pistol used to kill him. Had I stayed in Saratoga instead of traveling with Jack; had I not taken the words of the Poughkeepsie Seer to heart; had I never climbed atop the barrels in Salem to see the beautiful singer that day in April, the gallows would not be my fate.

But it was not only my own decisions that led to this end; had my fortunes not been linked to those of Jack Horne, I would have had any number of safe havens along the way. If she had not engineered my escape from the Oneida Community, I would have remained there, secure and satisfied. Had she not "rescued" me from the *Eastern Star*, I would be happily on my way to Maui. Then again, if she had not pulled me from the canal boat, I would have traveled Rochester with Mirabile and Reverend Travis anyway and perhaps my night in the murder room was inevitable. As I parse the events of my journey ever more thinly, they seem at once to be tightly connected yet utterly random. Was I, in fact, damned at birth and following an inevitable path to execution, or was I, as Jack so often said, just a will-o-the-wisp, blowing whichever way the wind took me?

I had much time to ponder these questions as I sat in the Monroe County Jail awaiting my trial. That night in the backroom of the Healing Tabernacle, I had tried to follow Jack's farewell advice and leave the scene quickly, but I was still profoundly shaken by the night's events and the import of all I had seen and heard. I was slow to rise from the bed and awkward in putting on my clothes. But outside the shot had been heard by the neighbors who raised the alarm, and those who responded were not slow by any means. As I stood holding the pistol, trying to decide if it was better to take it along or leave it behind, two policemen burst into the room. Believing that they had caught me in the act, they arrested me on the spot for murder.

As they took me out of the church, a man on each arm, a crowd began to gather outside. I can't say how popular Reverend Travis's ministry was before his death, but as word spread of his murder, support for his cause became overwhelming. The crowd grew in size and in anger until it reached such a fervor that had any of them chosen to defy the authority of the policemen who held me, a riot would have ensued, and I would have been hanged that night from a Rochester streetlamp.

A coroner's inquest was held the following day. The main points of evidence were the facts that Reverend Travis had died of a gunshot wound and that I was discovered by police standing over the body holding a pistol. Witnesses had seen a woman and a man running from the church after the shot was fired, and although I tried to explain that they had seen the true killer and a witness who could testify to that, it was concluded that the woman was the Reverend's daughter, fleeing for her life, and the man was my accomplice. The congregation knew that Reverend Travis always carried his valuables in a black bag; since that bag was missing, it was, no doubt, in the hands of my accomplice. Robbery was declared the motive, and I was bound for trial.

Public sentiment continued against me. Whatever the citizens of Rochester may have thought of Reverend Travis's peculiar theology just days before, they were now wholeheartedly behind him. The coldblooded murder of a clergyman would not be tolerated in their city.

I had given my true name upon my arrest; there seemed little point now in trying to hide my identity. But when the newspapers learned my name, they began asking questions about my past. Was I the same Jonathan Pratt accused of robbery along the Erie Canal that spring? Was I also the Reverend Jonathan Travis, wanted in Albany for those same crimes, as well as passing counterfeit bank notes? In choosing that alias, had I not shown a connection, if not a blood relation, to the deceased? What was my relation to George Ridley, also accused of canal robbery, who was sent to the Oneida Community to be reformed, but repaid that kindness with escape? The pistol had "Patriot Hunters" carved in the handle; had I been armed, by that now disreputable organization, to assassinate the Reverend?

And it did not stop in Rochester. News of the murder was telegraphed around the country and newspapers everywhere followed it with interest. New York City's papers sent representatives to Rochester, to determine if I was, in fact, the same Jonathan Pratt who allegedly murdered Eamon "Slasher" Dugan, a leader of the Five Points gang, the Dead Rabbits. I had become so notorious I would not have been surprised to hear that the Saugerties Bard had written a song about me.

The one friend I had in Rochester was old Mr. Bennet, and he was a good man to have on my side. He came to visit me in jail and asked me point blank if I was guilty of murder. I told him no.

He looked at me closely for a moment then, with a sigh, said, "I believe you, Jonathan, and I will do what I can to help. "Is Jack the "man" seen leaving the church?"

I told him she was. He said that while we were out that evening, a young woman had come to his house looking for me. She had seen my name in a newspaper story about the steamboat disaster. He told her I would be back later and she waited outside.

"You went with her, Jonathan? I thought Jack was your girl."

"It has always been a complicated relationship."

I had no idea why Jack followed me that night. No doubt she knew that I could not be trusted alone with Mirabile and wanted to catch me in the act. After everything she had seen that night I had no hope over ever seeing Jack again.

"Well, I can't hide my knowledge of you, Jonathan," Mr. Bennet said. "They already know you slept at my house. I won't lie, but I won't volunteer anything that I am not directly asked."

Mr. Bennet also made sure I had representation when I went to court. A Mr. Abrams came to see in jail. He was not interested in whether I was guilty or innocent, but wanted to hear the details of my story. I told the truth, but he learned that I had been in bed with the dead man's wife and that the whole affair had been witnessed by my partner, Jack, who was a girl who dressed as a boy, he told me never to tell it that way again. We would keep it simple. I was there at the request of the dead man's daughter who took my pistol and shot her father. If a man also fled from the church, he was not connected to me.

My trial commenced soon after; the case was heard by the Honorable Judge Buchan of Monroe County. As Mr. Bennet said he would, when he was questioned by District Attorney Bishop, he testified that I had stayed at his home and he knew I was carrying a pistol. Yes, he said, Jack Horne was accompanying me, but he said nothing about Jack being a girl. When the district attorney implied that Jack was the accomplice who fled the church that night, Mr. Abrams objected and was sustained by Judge Buchan.

Mr. Abrams would have many more opportunities to object during that trial. Since Mr. Bennet was the only person in Rochester who knew me or knew anything about the case, the prosecution went far afield to bring in many of the witnesses mentioned in the newspaper. There were Patriot Hunters, Oneida Community members, even some women's rights ladies had something to say. Mr. Abernathy of the Shakers testified that not only was I a canal pirate but I had personally swindled him out of several hundred dollars. In each case, Mr. Abrams would object to the testimony as irrelevant or as hearsay, and more often than not the judge would sustain him, but to my mind, after the words had left their lips, the damage was done. This jury would not disregard anything.

For my own good, Mr. Abrams kept me off the witness stand. He argued that the evidence against me was entirely circumstantial and that those who fled the scene must be found and questioned before a fair judgment can be reached. But in the end, the image of me standing over the murdered man holding a pistol was sufficient to render a verdict. I was found guilty of murder in the first degree and sentenced to hang on September 30.

In the days that followed there was some movement to seek a new trial over some technicality or other, but the Court of Appeals made it quickly and emphatically clear that they had no intention of hearing the case. The verdict would stand.

And so, dear reader, that brings us to the present moment. I have written all night and now, what is left of my candle can be extinguished, as the dawn provides sufficient light for me to finish. The rising of the sun means that my execution is imminent. I have declined both a last meal and a prayer session with a spiritual advisor. The footsteps I hear can only be the sheriff and his men, coming to take me from this cell for the last time and walk me outside to the gallows.

I only hope that justice in the next world is not so cold.

CHAPTER 24

Amen.

It has been some weeks since I put pen to paper, and while that very fact is proof enough that I was not executed on September 30, I did not want to begin again prematurely. Though I was spared on the scheduled date, my life has been in the hands of the State of New York until this very day, and now, once again master of my fate, I feel able and obligated to relate the true ending of my story.

I was taken from my cell, the morning of September 30, and led to the gallows in a procession headed by Monroe County Sheriff Hart. Behind him was my attorney Mr. Abrams. I was next, unrestrained but flanked by two of the sheriff's men should the need arise. Behind me, against my express wishes, followed a Christian minister—Methodist Episcopal, I believe—who prayed for my immortal soul, something I had long since given up for lost. I was determined to die game and walked to the gallows with head high and countenance steeled. I had prepared a brief sentence proclaiming my innocence but would give them no more. Those who had come to witness my cruel death would get no further show of emotion.

But show it was; make no mistake. If I said that ten thousand people came out to watch me die you would think me a liar and begin to doubt the rest of my story. Suffice to say, from my vantage on the platform, I have never seen so many human heads gathered in one place, or would have even believed such as gathering was possible for any event short of Our Savior's return. I must say, the sight of that mass of craven and bloodthirsty humans almost made me anxious to leave this world.

And I very nearly did. The sheriff put the hempen necktie over me and, as the minister led the multitudes in prayer, I mentally rehearsed what I thought would be my last words on earth. All those in the crowd bowed their heads and the silence in that field was broken only by the solemn and dolorous words of the minister's prayer.

Then a voice arose from the fringe of the crowd like a distant shout. The words were incomprehensible, but the voice was unmistakable—it was Jack, dressed as a woman and bellowing like a man, trying to drive a wagon through a crowd unable to part fast enough for her.

"Stop the hanging! Stop the hanging!" shouted Mr. Abrams, who, no doubt, had stood at the ready, waiting for the slightest irregularity to interrupt the proceedings.

The sheriff, none too happy, sent his men out to see about the commotion. They facilitated the parting of the crowd and grabbed the reins to lead the horse forward at a more reasonable pace. The wagon was led to the front, and when it stopped before the platform, Jack stood up and pointed to the back of the wagon.

"There's yer murderer." She said.

There in the wagon, gagged and tied at the hands and feet, was Mirabile Travis.

"It's the missing woman," said Mr. Abrams, "We will surely get a new trial now."

The sheriff took me back to my cell and went to contact the judge to determine what should transpire next. I had no idea what was going on until late that afternoon when Jack came to the cell to see me. She was still dressed as a woman but somewhat ragged and worse for wear.

"Jack! I never thought I would see you again," I said.

"It would serve ya right if ya didn't," she said.

"I never thought you would help me after seeing me with Mirabile."

"I know you pretty well by now, Pratt. I knew if you didn't get that girl out of yer dreams she'd be there forever. But I also knew she meant you no good, so I followed when the two a'ya went to the church to stop the trouble I knew was coming. The gun went off before I could do anything. "

"How did you catch Mirabile?"

I will relate what Jack told me about the capture of Mirabile, but briefly; because it is, after all, her story and not mine. For my part, I think it might be years before I fully understand it.

Jack had gone the church carrying her rucksack and all of her possessions, thinking that, whatever transpired, she would not be staying in Rochester. When she saw Mirabile open the front door of the church, she went around back looking for another way in. She broke in the back door and went into the room behind the curtain, waiting to see what would happen. Of course, Jack saw us making love, and why she didn't burst in then or just leave the place, I still do not know. Instead, she stayed hidden and watched Reverend Travis arrive and then saw Mirabile shoot him.

By then it was too late to come out without starting a bloody battle, so she waited for Mirabile to leave then ran after her. But Mirabile had enough of a head start that she was out of sight when Jack hit the street. Jack assumed Mirabile would take the fasted way out of town, so she hurried to the train station. She found Mirabile there, buying a ticket to Buffalo, so Jack did the same. On the train she changed into a dress, knowing that Mirabile might recognize her as a boy but had never seen her as a girl.

In Buffalo, Jack followed Mirabile to a hotel. Jack checked in too, making sure she kept an eye on Mirabile while she pondered what to do next. She knew that she would somehow need to get Mirabile and the black bag of evidence back to Rochester if she were to save my life.

Through a series of "chance" encounters, Jack befriended Mirabile but gaining her confidence was a long, slow process. Jack learned that Mirabile had a weakness for alcohol and used this knowledge to her advantage. One night in the hotel bar, after too many drinks, Mirabile revealed that she was in trouble and would soon need to leave Buffalo. Jack told her that the only way to guarantee safety was to flee to Canada. Jack told her she could arrange this. They discussed the matter again several times after that night before Mirabile finally agreed that Canada was her safest destination.

Jack obtained a wagon and waited outside the hotel. When Mirabile came out carrying the black bag, jack was ready to put the plan in motion. Mirabile sat in the box with Jack, trusting her to drive the rig to Canada. Jack told her they were heading for the Niagara River ferry at Black Rock, but instead, she drove east. Once they were out of the city, Jack asked Mirabile to climb into the back of the wagon to adjust their luggage. When Mirabile did so, Jack stopped the horse and climbed in back herself. Jack wrestled Mirabile into submission and, using pre-knotted ropes she had planted in the wagon she secured Mirabile's arms and legs and gagged her mouth. Then she drove her captive back to Rochester.

There was much confusion after Jack arrived and interrupted the hanging. Jack claimed that Mirabile murdered Reverend Travis and stole his money. At Mr. Abrams's instance, Mirabile was held in custody and a second inquest was held to determine whether she and not I, should be indicted for the Reverend's murder.

The inquest was somewhat confusing as well, with Jack's assertion that she was both the man who witnessed the murder and the woman who captured the prisoner. She came to court one day dressed as a man, and one dressed as a woman and her point was successfully made. With so much testimony and evidence against her Mirabile began to weaken until finally, under intense questioning, she admitted to murdering her husband, the Reverend Isaiah Travis.

With this revelation, all charges against me were dropped, and I was freed from jail. By rights, we should have stayed to testify again at Mirabile's trial, but I was anxious to leave New York State before they changed their minds again. Though there was no spoken agreement, it was clear that Jack and I would be traveling companions once more. I suggested that we venture to Ohio and see about that cheap land everyone was after.

"Haven't you heard, Pratt?" Jack replied, "They've discovered gold in California. They're pulling big hunks of it right out of the stream. "Why in hell would we go anywhere else?"

Why indeed.

The End.

CHAPTER NOTES

Chapter 1

The accuracy of any personal memoir, such as Jonathan Pratt's confession, is only as good as the memory and honesty of the teller. Recollections, even recent ones, can become distorted; names, dates, places, and events confused or lost altogether. And someone with as much at stake as Jonathan Pratt, on the eve of his execution, cannot be trusted to write with absolute honesty. The purpose of these chapter notes will be to compare Pratt's statements with what is known to be true and attempt to determine to what extent we can trust Jonathan Pratt's memory.

In 1848, Easter Sunday fell on April 23. This will be important going forward, as we follow Pratt's travels and attempt to place events on a timeline.

Pratt's first destination was Mr. Pembroke's cooperage on Water Street in Salem, MA. In 1848 Salem had at least eight cooperage shops, employing more than fifty people. Their owners and locations cannot be easily verified at this point.

Itinerant preachers, traveling evangelists, were common throughout America beginning during the colonial period. There work led directly to the Second Great Awakening in the 1830s and 1840s. Many were circuit riders who helped found the Methodist Episcopal Church in America; others were scoundrels and mountebanks attracted by easy money from a gullible audience. Wise is the man who can tell the difference.

The instrument that Mirabile played was a lap organ or harmonium; a portable pump organ played on the lap. They were manufactured in America beginning around 1830.

Chapter 2

Before the Civil War, the United States government issued no paper currency. All bills in circulation were notes issued by private banks and counterfeiting was rampant. Any transaction involving paper money required the merchant to assess the soundness of the bill itself, the institution it was drawn upon, and the individual attempting to pass it.

Berkshire County is the easternmost county of Massachusetts; Jonathan will soon be in New York.

Chapter 3

In 1845 there were 4,000 cargo and passenger boats on the Erie Canal employing 25,000 men women and children between Albany and Buffalo. Erie Canal packet boats were the preferred means of transportation for those seeking opportunity in the west.

Deacon M. Eaton traveled the Erie Canal for the Bethel Society in the 1840s. His 1845 book Five Years on the Erie Canal recounts numerous cases of reforming hoggees, convincing reluctant clergymen to hold services aboard packets, and bringing passengers— and even the meanest captains – to tears with God's word. It is not unlikely that Deacon Eaton was still on the canal in 1848, but this has not been verified.

Chapter 4

The village of Canajoharie—whose name is derived from the Iroquois word meaning "kettle washing"—is much older than the Erie Canal. It became a favorite stop for Canalers and their passengers because of the well-stocked general store operating there.

In the days when rigidly defined sexual roles extended to extremely gender specific clothing, it was not difficult for an assertive woman to pass as a man by simply dressing and acting the part. It was also the only way for a woman to actively participate in a man's world. On an Erie Canal boat, the only job open to a woman was cook.

There are numerous documented cases of women impersonating men in eighteenth and nineteenth-century America. Deborah Sampson fought in the American Revolution disguised as a man named Robert Shurtleff. The deception was not discovered until she was wounded in battle and examined by a physician. The Civil War also saw many cases on both sides of women fighting dressed as men.

Chapter 5

Though faith healing is rooted in the Bible, modern evangelical faith healing began during the Second Great Awakening with people like Ellen White and Phineas Quimby whose work lives on in the Adventist and Christian Science movements. Of course, from pre-Biblical times to the present faith healing has also been a lucrative field for charlatans.

Chapter 6

Contrary to Jack's belief, their escape from the boat—if it actually happened—was not long remembered. The literature and folklore of the Erie Canal include many stories of men jumping from bridges onto canal boats, but none about leaving a canal boat by climbing upon a bridge.

The Erie Canal brought prosperity to towns throughout New York, but it also brought undesirable elements. The largest concentrations of taverns and brothels grew at the canals extremes: Buffalo in the west, and Watervliet in the East. The town of Watervliet, west of Troy, had a well-earned reputation for drinking, brawling, and debauchery.

Chapter 7

When not pulling the boat, mules slept in a relatively spacious stable in the front of the boad, situated between the galley and the passenger's quarters.

Chapter 8

From Halfmoon, Jonathan and Jack probably traveled northeast and stopped on McDonald's Creek.

The man from the cave was making reference to Exodus 3:12, where, in the King James Version, God says to Moses, "I am that I am."

In 1844, several thousand followers of the Reverend William Miller prepared for the final judgment day which they earnestly believed would occur on March 21, 1843. Miller had calculated the date by a careful study of the dates and prophesies in the Bible. He then traveled throughout New York and New England with an elaborate tent show. He was remarkably successful at selling his idea.

When the world did not end on March 21, 1843, he recalibrated his calculations and predicted the end would be on April 18, 1844. The calculations were revised again after April 18 proved uneventful, and Miller's followers, known as the Millerites, did not lose faith until the world failed to end on October 21, 1844.

Many tales concerning the Millerites have been exaggerated. Not all of them sold their property before the big day. Nor did they all stand on hilltops wearing white ascension robes. But in each case, some did.

Also, contrary to the myth, the lunatic asylums did not fill up after the world failed to end. While some of Miller's followers did go insane, many continued on to form the Seventh Day Adventists who refer to the events of 1844 as "The Great Disappointment." Many others joined the Shakers, another sect that believed the end was at hand but did not put a date on judgment day. Most, though, went back to conventional religion.

Chapter 9

In 1848, Benment's American Hotel on State Street was the finest hotel in Albany, New York; The Temple of Fancy on Broadway was the largest department store.

Just as in Jack's childhood home, many pioneer families traveling west carried only two books: The Bible and The Plays of William Shakespeare. Shakespeare had always been popular in America, among people of every class, and they especially loved to see their native son, Edwin Forest performing in Shakespeare's plays.

In 1848 Edwin Forest was following behind his English rival William Charles Macready who was on tour in America. There is a good chance that they both played Albany that season. When Macready left a city, Forest would open there, performing the same play, inviting comparison. The tours culminated in New York City in May of 1849 when both men were performing Macbeth at the same time. The event sparked a rare alliance of the Irish and nativist gangs of New York, who rioted against the English actor. The Astor Place Riot, as the disturbance was called, left 25 people dead and 120 wounded and had to be quelled by the state militia.

Chapter 10

The game that Jack and Jonathan played on the steamboat was three-card monte, a variation of the much older shell game. Three-card monte was gaining popularity in the 1840s and was played in hotels, mining camps, and steamboats—wherever people with money gathered.

Three-card monte is not really a game since the dealer always wins. For one practiced at manipulating cards, it is an effective way to con an unsuspecting player out of his money. It is often played with teams of two, with the second man serving as a shill to bring players to the dealer. The additional scam of making the player believe that the queen is marked is as old as the game itself.

Rhinebeck is a little town on the east bank of the Hudson River, about sixty miles south of Albany.

The Hudson River is actually a tidal estuary for most of its length, and the influence of tides can be felt as far north as Troy. When the tide is coming in, the Hudson flows north. The boatman is waiting for the tide to go out and facilitate his journey south.

Chapter 11

Jonathan and Jack have landed in the most dangerous section of New York; an area controlled by violent criminal gangs, like the Daybreak Boys, mentioned by the boatman. The Hole-in-the-Wall was a famous dive located in the Fourth Ward, between Five Points—the city's most notorious neighborhood—and the East River. Gallus Maggie did indeed keep order at the Hole-in-the-Wall and was known for biting off the ears of those who would not behave.

It was common practice in the waterfront dives of New York, to drug and shanghai unsuspecting men into service aboard sailing ships. It was not wise to drink alone in these establishments.

Chapter 12

"Moses' Law," as applies to flogging, means forty lashes less one. It was presumed to be an Old Testament law prescribing forty lashes as a death penalty; thus thirty-nine was less severe than a death penalty. In fact, the law was not from the Bible, but part of a more complicated Roman law regarding punishment. Forty lashes were considered sufficient to kill a man, so in order to maintain consistency in punishment, if the man being flogged was still alive after forty lashes, the flogger was killed. The Romans often sentenced a man to thirty-nine lashes for the benefit of the flogger rather than the criminal. Centuries later this tradition was maintained aboard ship as "Moses' Law" for server punishment that did not call for a death penalty.

The Dead Rabbits were the most powerful of several gangs of Irish immigrants controlling lower Manhattan in the 1840s. Their chief rivals were The Bowery Boys, a gang composed of native-born Americans with a hatred for immigrants. Their battles were of epic proportions.

Chapter 13

In the 1840s Five Points was the most notorious slum in America, if not the world. Here is how Charles Dickens described it American Notes, after visiting Five Points in 1842.

"Debauchery has made the very houses prematurely old. See how the rotten beams are tumbling down, and how the patched and broken windows seem to scowl dimly, like eyes that have been hurt in drunken frays. Many of those pigs live here. Do they ever wonder why their masters walk upright in lien of going on all-fours? And why they talk instead of grunting?"

The Tombs was New York City's House of Detention. It housed accused criminals awaiting trial and convicted murderers awaiting execution. Those arrested for the petty crime of stealing apples would probably not be sent to the Tombs, but if the goal was to make an example of the thief, the Tombs was a good place to do it.

The church robbed by Jack was, no doubt, The Transfiguration Roman Catholic Church on Mott Street.

Chapter 14

Picking pockets was a good entry level crime and a skill useful to any thief.

The "badger game" and the "panel game" were two very lucrative con games perpetrated on unwary customers of prostitutes. They were common in New York and other cities throughout the 19th century.

Chapter 15

All sites mentioned were notorious Five Points nightspots, popular with the locals as well as adventurous up-town folks.

1848 was early in the immigration of Chinese to New York; they brought along their fondness for opium. The drug was not illegal at the time and while opium "joints" catered primarily to Chinese, they were open to everyone.

Chapter 16

The peak from which Jonathan views "all creation" was probably Pine Orchard in the Catskill Mountains which is three thousand feet above the Hudson River. From this summit, the mountains of Vermont, Massachusetts and Connecticut can be seen, as well as the valley of the Catskills.

Kaaterskill was the original Dutch spelling of Catskill. The Dutch language was spoken there well into the 19th Century, though communities as exclusively Dutch speaking as the one where Jonathan found himself were probably rare.

Pinkster was a Dutch holiday celebrating the feast of the Pentecost, also known as Whitsunday, falling on the seventh Sunday after Easter. African Americans in the northeast continued the celebration of Pinkster after Dutch influence faded.

In 1848 Pinkster fell on June 11.

Chapter 17

Henry Backus, also known as the Saugerties Bard was a songwriter who traveled through the Hudson Valley from the late 1840s through the 1850s eventually moving to New York City. He wrote topical songs set to familiar melodies of the time—a tradition that would later be practiced by Woody Guthrie and Bob Dylan. The songs, which were self-published, tended to be about sensational events such as murders and disasters. One of his earliest was "The Powder Mill Explosion" published in 1847.

Andrew Jackson Davis, aka "The Poughkeepsie Seer" was a clairvoyant, a spiritual healer and a prolific writer on spiritual matters, who lived and worked in Poughkeepsie, New York beginning in the 1840s. He has been called "the John the Baptist of Modern Spiritualism" because his early writings seemed to predict some events in the rise of Spiritualism in the United States.

While the Hudson River Railroad Line did not officially open until 1849, it is probably safe to assume that sections of track were already operating in the summer of 1848. However, Jonathan would probably not have been able to buy a ticket from Poughkeepsie to Syracuse traveling only by train.

Chapter 18

The healing powers of the waters at Saratoga Springs were known to the Iroquois Indians long before the arrival of white men. The first permanent white settlements were in the 1780s and by the early 1800s hotels were built there— among the oldest was the Grand Union Hotel. As Jonathan describes, the waters have always attracted the rich and famous to Saratoga Springs, and the rich and famous have always attracted grifters. This condition would be amplified in 1863 when America's oldest horseracing track opened there.

Jonathan is probably mistaken that Charles Grandison Finney was preaching in New York in 1848. Though he preached throughout New York State in the 1820s and 1830s and coined the term "Burned-over District" to describe Western New York, in 1848 Finney was a professor at Oberlin

College in Ohio, soon to be its president. It is not impossible that Finney's name was used to promote the camp meeting as that is the type of evangelism that he pioneered.

All of the political organizations mentioned by Jack were to a greater or lesser extent operating in the State of New York in 1848, though not all would be called "secret societies." Also, they were not exactly waging constant warfare, though disputes between Tammany Hall and the Native American Party, or "Know-Nothings" would turn violent—Bill "the Butcher" Poole was murdered by members of Tammany Hall. Also, the Freemasons did kidnap, and probably kill, William Morgan for attempting to reveal their secrets. His abduction led to the formation of the Anti-Masonic Party.

Ned Buntline was the pen name of Edward Judson, a writer, and newspaperman who, in 1848, was also an agitator for the Know-Nothings. He would later travel west and write dime novels that would help create the mythology of the Wild West. Thurlow Weed was a newspaper publisher and political boss in western New York who was active in the Anti-Masonic movement.

Chapter 19

Fear of secret societies in the 1840s was not a small thing in New York State or in the nation at large. Especially vexing were the Freemasons and their connection to the Democratic Party. Thurlow Weed a founder of the Anti-Masonic party and a powerful political boss in New York. His protégé, Hamilton Fish, was elected governor of New York in 1848 as a Whig. Another Weed protégé, Milliard Fillmore from Buffalo, also a Whig, was elected Vice President in 1848. He became president on the death of Zachery Taylor. By 1852 the Whig party was no more, and Fillmore ran for reelection as candidate for the American ("Know-Nothing") Party.

The leading Democratic contenders in 1848 were Freemasons. Lewis Cass was the Masonic Grand Master of the Grand Lodge of Michigan, and James Buchanan was District Deputy Grand Master of the Grand Lodge of Pennsylvania.

In July 1848 the first women's rights convention was held in Seneca Falls, New York. In attendance were Elizabeth Cady Stanton, Lucretia Mott, Amelia Bloomer, and three hundred other women. The Declaration of Sentiments drafted there served as the foundation of the women's rights movement.

Jack was probably not telling the truth about voting three times. Not that it would have been difficult for someone to vote three times in a New York City election, but the Mayoral election was held on April 11, that year, before Jack arrived in the city.

As Jack describes, the "Long Level" is a section of the Erie Canal between Utica and Syracuse which required no locks. It was the first section of the canal to open and its successful operation proved to skeptics that the canal project was feasible.

Utica was a prosperous mill town in the 1840s, but it would be a bad place to be accused of lunacy. Utica was the site of the New York State Lunatic Asylum built in 1843, the first publicly funded institution for treating the mentally ill in New York State.

Chapter 20

The Shakers and the Oneida Community were two utopian societies living apart from the secular world, following Christian values in preparation for the Millennium after the second coming of Christ. While both groups believed in communal ownership of property and possessions, they differed greatly on sexual matters. The Shakers were completely celibate; children were added to their community through adoption or conversion, welcoming orphans and the homeless. The Oneida Community, founded by John Humphrey Noyes, practiced "Complex Marriage" where any man and woman in the community were free to have sex if both were willing.

In 1848 the Shakers had a community near Watervliet, and the Oneida Community had recently been established in Oneida.

It is not unusual that Mr. Abernathy had joined the Shakers. Many former Millerites joined the Shaker movement following the "Great Disappointment."

The Oneida Community was founded in 1848 in Oneida, New York by John Humphrey Noyes. Noyes's teachings began in Putney, Vermont, but he and his followers fled to New York after Noyes was indicted for adultery. The basic tenants of the community's philosophy were: communal ownership of property, equality of the sexes, "Complex Marriage," "Male Continence," and "Mutual Criticism."

There were probably between 80 and 90 members at the time Jonathan was there; by 1878 there were 306. The Oneida Community became famous for the production of animal traps and flatware. Pressure from the outside forced the community to give up complex marriage in 1879. In 1881 they gave up communism and formed a joint-stock company, Oneida Community, Limited. Oneida Ltd. Is still a leading producer of stainless flatware.

Chapter 21

The Patriot Hunters was a secret organization devoted to liberating Canada and driving the British out of North America. They were organized in Hunters Lodges in towns along the Canadian border, from St. Albans, Vermont to Detroit, Michigan. In 1838 the Patriot Hunters invaded Canada at the town of Prescott, across the St. Lawrence River from Ogdensburg, and together with similar groups in Canada, fought the British at "The Battle of the Windmill." The attack failed.

At its height, the Patriot Hunters included attorneys, politicians and newspaper editors, and they had power to sway local elections. Following the failed invasion, their influence dwindled. In 1841, President Tyler issued a proclamation calling the American people to sever their ties with the organization. To the extent that the Patriot Hunters existed at all in 1848, their strength would have been greatly diminished.

From the beginning the Patriot Hunters had been plagued by spies and infiltrators and thus, reminiscent of the Freemasons, they became obsessed with secrecy and security. The oath that Jonathan took was one version of the oath taken by all new recruits.

The Battle of the Windmill did sound the death knell for the Patriot Hunters. Neither the British nor the Americans wished to go to war over the incident. The British treated the invaders as criminals; in 1841 President Tyler issued a proclamation calling on Americans to sever their ties with the Patriot Hunters. Records are sparse (probably deliberately destroyed) but it is safe to assume that some greatly diminished version of the Patriot Hunters was still operating in 1848.

The *Northerner* was a Lake Ontario passenger steamboat in 1848. There is no record of its involvement in a disaster, but Great Lakes navigation has always been unpredictable.

Chapter 22

Rochester, New York, had been the Patriot Hunters' Grand Lodge headquarters in the East (Cleveland, Ohio, was the Grand Lodge headquarters in the West). Like Mr. Bennet, most of the Rochester members had abandoned the lodge by 1848.

Rochester, New York, was America's first boomtown. Driven by the water power of the Genesee River and the transportation opportunities of the Erie Canal it rapidly grew into a major industrial city. Rochester was nicknamed the "Flour City" for the amount of wheat flour it produced. It was also a center of the religious fervor of the Second Great Awakening.

Bennet's mention of "the boy who saw visions in his hat" is a reference to Joseph Smith, who before publishing the Book of Mormon, would stare at a "seer stone" inside his hat as a method of divining the location of hidden treasure. Smith lived in Palmyra, not far from Rochester.

Rochester was also center of reform movements such as abolition of slavery, women's rights, and temperance. In 1848 both Frederick Douglas and Susan B. Anthony lived in Rochester.

Thurlow Weed had been the owner of the Rochester Telegraph and founded the Antimasonic Enquirer in Rochester in the 1820s but moved to Albany in the 1830s. The Fox Sisters, considered the founders of modern

Spiritualism, lived in Rochester and began holding séances in 1848. Kate was 12 years old, and Maggie was 15; their older sister Leah served as their manager. On September 1 of that year, they moved to the cottage on Troup Street. Within a year they were filling large auditoriums and started what became a worldwide religion. In 1888 Maggie revealed that their spirit communication was a hoax; the girls produced the "raps" with their toes.

Chapter 23

Mr. Bennet probably lived in Corn Hill, the most fashionable neighborhood of Rochester in 1848. There is no record of the Healing Tabernacle in Rochester, but it would probably have been located on the other side of the canal.

In 1848, the Monroe County Jail was located on an island near Court Street Bridge in Rochester.

The Honorable Patrick G. Buchan was Judge of the Monroe County Court, and William Bishop was the District Attorney. Mr. James Abrams was a practicing attorney in Rochester.

Chapter 24

The City of Buffalo annexed the town of Black Rock in 1853.

In January 1848, gold was discovered at Sutter's Mill in, beginning the Gold Rush which drew thousands of prospectors to California. At this writing, it is impossible to tell whether Jonathan Pratt and Jack Horne were among them.

ABOUT THE AUTHOR

Robert Wilhelm is the author of three books on historical true crime, *Wicked Victorian Boston*, *The Bloody Century*, and *Murder and Mayhem in Essex County*. He also blogs about murder and other bad behavior in Victorian America at www.MurderByGaslight.com and www.Night-Stick.com. Currently, Robert lives deep in the Adirondack woods and is never sure what century it is.